# THE WHITE COUNTESS

# The White Countess

## Florence Warden

WILDSIDE PRESS

# CHAPTER I

"Oh, Gerard, what a long face! What's the matter? Have you had your pocket picked?"

It was Gerard Angmering's beautiful young wife who put these laughing questions to him, on the threshold of the modest little flat in West Kensington where, like most young couples of moderate means nowadays, they had set up their tent and expected to find peace and joy and all the comforts of home in a jerry-built "mansion" where they paid a hundred a year for the privilege of hearing the conversation of their underneath neighbour up the chimney, and being overheard in like manner by their neighbours overhead and on each side.

Gerard, whose face had instinctively softened at the very first word from his wife, said "Sh—sh," pushed her inside their little drawing-room, and shut the door.

"There's trouble at the bank," said he. "I didn't want to have to tell you. But since you've found me out, why, I suppose I must."

"Oh, Gerard, what do you mean? What trouble?"

"There, there, don't look so frightened, child. It will be all right, all right. At least—I suppose it will, I hope it will. You've heard me speak of Sir Richmond Hornthwaite, the old gentleman who gives us so much trouble—always sending imperative messages for us to go and see him, because he's forgotten something he had to say, or because he wants to have something done for him in a hurry?"

"Yes, oh, yes, the old man who lives at Chislehurst."

"Yes. Well, he's just discovered—or thinks he's discovered, that three cheques have been paid against his account which he never signed, which are, in fact, forgeries."

"Oh, dear! And the bank people are very much upset about it, of course!"

Gerard, who was very pale, nodded. There was a long silence, and Audrey, who was still clinging to her husband, perceived, with a sickening sense of distress and terror, that she had not yet heard the worst.

"Well," she said, quite querulously, "and what else?"

Gerard Angmering turned upon her suddenly eyes in which agony revealed itself unmistakably, appallingly. He tried to speak, but could not. Audrey clung more closely to his arm, put her right hand round his neck, held him close to her, comforting, encouraging, knowing with a loving woman's instinctive knowledge that the worst would be tragically awful to hear.

Not one word did she utter, yet he knew she knew what was coming. So well did he know it that he prefaced his speech, when he got back some remnants of husky, audible voice, by a grave, slow nod of the head.

"Yes," whispered he brokenly, "yes, he accuses me, Audrey. He says—says—I took the cheques from his cheque-book—says I stole them. Good God!"

He staggered to the little sofa, and fell on it, still with those clinging arms tightening round him, with the beautiful appealing eyes of his wife fixed in passionate tenderness and distress upon his face.

But after the first few moments of dumb horror she rebelled at the thought that they could misjudge her Gerard so wickedly. She raised her head quickly, her eyes flashed, she laughed discordantly, angrily, as she looked into his open and still almost boyish face.

"Gerard, Gerard, why do you trouble yourself about it? It's ridiculous, you know! It's farcical! You a thief! *You!* It isn't as if they didn't know you! Why, this old Sir Richmond knows you too! Knows you and likes you! Or why should it always be you he sends for when he wants some one from the bank?"

The young man looked up. Depressed, downcast, overwhelmed as he was, he felt the comfort of this indignation, of this amazement. He turned to her and took her lovely face in his hands, staring down tenderly into the big blue eyes, at the red, parted lips, at the soft waves of golden hair which had got loosened round her forehead.

"Bless your little heart, Audrey, your anger does me good! Upon my word, when they all looked at me as they did, and questioned me as they did, and put it to me that I *must* have been to blame somehow or other in this awful business, I—I—I almost began to think, at last, that I had!"

"Gerard! How can you?"

"Well, it came upon me so suddenly, so unexpectedly, you know, that I felt as if the heavens had fallen, or that I must be somebody else. I could only stare, and stammer, and behave, I suppose, just as a thorough-paced rascal would have done!"

"Oh, Gerard!"

"Well, I couldn't help it. I was struck dumb."

"You should have been indignant. You should have told them what you thought of them!"

"Well, I couldn't. I was too much occupied with what they thought of me!"

"Tell me just what they said."

"Well, they asked me who it was that took Sir Richmond his last cheque-book down. I said it was I. Then they asked me when it was, and if I remembered any of the circumstances of the journey. And after a little help—for I've been down there so often on one errand or another that it was difficult to find the exact date—I found that it was on a Saturday that I took the cheque-book, and that I came back home to have luncheon on my way. Then came a torrent of questions as to the time I stayed in the flat, and as to the people in it, and so on. They wanted to know whether any one was in the flat except you and me. There wasn't, was there?"

Audrey was too much disturbed to remember. But the two set their memories to work, and consulted the servant who formed the whole of their modest staff, and finally they ascertained that, if anybody but themselves had been in the flat on the particular Saturday in question, it was either old Mrs. Webster, a neighbour, or Mr. Candover, a rich friend who had a handsome flat in Victoria Street, and who sometimes brought his motor-car round on Saturdays to take them for a spin into the country.

Both these people being beyond suspicion, the young people, after a few moments of silent dismay and perplexity, turned their thoughts again to what had happened at the office.

"Go on with what they said," said Audrey in a frightened whisper.

"Well, it seems that Sir Richmond, in taking out his cheque-book yesterday, found that a cheque was missing, with the blank counterfoil left in the book. This made him examine the cheque-book, and he found that there were two others missing, in different parts of the book. Then he remembered, or thought he remembered, having noticed, when I gave it to him, that one end of the long envelope it was in was only half gummed. Now he thinks that some one must have opened the envelope—that could be easily done over hot water, of course—and torn out the three cheques."

"But what does that matter? Cheques are numbered, aren't they? Can't they be stopped?"

Gerard shook his head.

"Sir Richmond wired up for his pass-book, and found that the three missing cheques *had* been paid in, without any doubt being roused as to the genuineness of the signature. One was for five hundred and sixty pounds and the other two for more. Altogether he has been robbed of nearly three thousand pounds."

"Oh, Gerard, how dreadful! But still he ought not to be so wicked and unfair as to blame you. How could you help it? Of course it's some one in his own house who has stolen the cheques and forged his name!"

"Well, he denies the possibility of that. He's an old fidget, and his secretary, a woman, is never allowed to touch his keys, so he says, or to go near the safe where he keeps his cheque-books and his money."

"And who were the cheques made out to?"

"The names are all unknown, made up, they think. Not one of the cheques was crossed; they were all paid in, all properly endorsed. But the endorsements are not much of a clue, so they say, because they believe the names to be fictitious."

"And didn't the large sums excite suspicion?" said Audrey.

"Oh, no. Sir Richmond is well known for his charities, and we cash large cheques of his to people we've never heard of often enough. The whole thing is a ghastly mystery, a puzzle from beginning to end."

"Look here, Gerard, I suppose we're alarming ourselves too much. The truth must be found out presently; they'll have clever detectives at work, and I daresay they'll have found out all about it by the time you go to the bank to-morrow morning."

"I hope to Heaven they will!" said the poor fellow, putting his head down in his hands, in an attitude of the deepest dejection.

Audrey passed a loving hand through her young husband's soft curly hair. Light hair it was, though many shades darker than her own pale golden tresses. And his slight figure, which scarcely reached the middle height, his beardless face and grey eyes, made him look younger than his age, which was twenty-five. So that he looked absolutely boyish in his utter despair.

"Listen," whispered Audrey, as she tucked her hand under his arm, and nestled against him, "listen, Gerard, I have an idea. You and I are a pair of great babies, who don't know what to do, or what to say, or how to get out of a difficulty. Let us go and see Mr. Candover, and ask his advice as to what we ought to do."

Gerard sat up.

"By Jove, you're right," said he. "It's—it's a nasty thing to have to go about though," objected he the next minute, as he began to fumble with the door-handle irresolutely.

"Well, you don't suppose *he* will suspect you!" cried she brightly.

"No, I suppose not. Still—I wish we had some one else to go to, some one nearer and——"

"You wouldn't like to go to your uncle, would you?"

"Lord Clanfield! Not likely!"

"Well, then, who *are* we to go to? Who is older and cleverer than we are, I mean!"

Gerard nodded.

"You're right, Audrey, your brains are better than mine. But I tell you, I was so knocked on the head, as it were, by what they said that—that I don't feel as if I should ever be able to think again!"

"Poor boy, poor boy!" she said softly.

She had bravely kept back the tears, but now she had a hard struggle for it, and she dashed out of the room to fetch hat and cloak to avoid breaking down.

Two minutes later they were in a hansom, driving to Victoria Street. Audrey indeed suggested the Underground, for they had been awakened rudely of late to the fact that they were exceeding their income; but Gerard was in no mood for small economies, and indeed every minute was precious, for Mr. Candover was a man of money and of pleasure, and they would be lucky if they caught him at home.

So they drove along fast in the pleasant April evening, not noting the fresh breeze or the soft sunset light, indeed, but each holding the hand of the other furtively, tightly, with a resolute endeavour to keep down ugly doubts and anxieties, and to believe that all would come right.

This Mr. Candover, whom they were going to consult, was their most intimate friend. Meeting him about eight months before, when they were enjoying their honeymoon abroad, they had attracted the older and rather blasé man of the world by their delight in life, by their devotion to each other, by the boyish high spirits of the young husband, the surpassing beauty of the wife.

For Audrey was no ordinary pretty woman. Tall, but not of an unmanageable height, with a good and well-developed figure, she was gifted also with a lovely face, of which the most striking feature was a pair of big blue eyes which made her look a good deal more artless than she was. With hair so fair that all the other women said it was dyed, and a complexion that had no fault save that it was a trifle pale, Audrey had been acclaimed a beauty everywhere, and Mr. Candover was one of the most enthusiastic and open of her admirers.

With the superiority given by his forty-five years, which he only admitted—so he said—because he had two great girls growing up at home who would "give away" any attempts at juvenility on his part, Mr. Candover had taken the young folk under his wing, introduced them to his friends, given luncheons and dinners in their honour, and driven them about in his splendid motor-car, proceedings which the bride and bridegroom found pleasant enough, but which had undoubtedly led them into spending more than they were quite justified in doing at the outset of their married life.

For Gerard had only his salary as clerk at the bank, and a small patrimony of seven thousand pounds, into which matrimony was making great inroads.

Audrey, the orphan daughter of a Lancashire manufacturer who had lost a fortune by unlucky speculation, had indeed two or three thousand pounds of her own, well invested and at her own disposal. But that, Gerard said, was to be looked upon as a nest-egg, not to be touched even when creditors pressed and times grew anxious.

They were lucky in finding Mr. Candover at home. He was dressing for dinner, so they were told by the man in livery who opened the door, and they were shown into the drawing-room, where, even at that anxious moment, Audrey could not forbear casting an admiring glance round at the priceless pictures, the exquisitely harmonious tapestries, the grand piano in its painted case, and the old French furniture which looked, as she said, "as if it had come out of a glorified museum". Mr. Candover's taste was exquisite, and his wealth was enormous, a combination which had produced the best results.

They felt their spirits rise on finding themselves in the neighbourhood of their powerful friend; and when the door was thrown open by the valet, and their host came quickly in, handsome, perfectly dressed, and with a smile of welcome on his face, both felt their hearts beat faster with the certainty that he would be as willing as he would be ready to help them in their trouble by sound advice and counsel.

"This is a delightful surprise," said he, as he took Audrey by the hand, with a certain gentle courtesy of manner which was cosmopolitan rather than British, and met her eyes with chivalrous admiration in his own. "I was going out to dinner. But I shall now stay at home and you must dine with me. I hope it is some pleasant errand that brings you here, as pleasant as the sight of you is to me?"

And he looked from the one to the other with the smile dying away from his face.

His very courtliness, his perfect manner, checked the two blunter, less sophisticated young people on the threshold of their confession. There was something remote from trivial worries, from sordid cares, about this genial, gentle, low-voiced, kindly gentleman, whose trim figure, small fine features, gentle brown eyes and slight dark moustache all seemed to belong rather to a prince who passes his life in cotton-wool than to an ordinary citizen of this work-a-day world.

"Come, what is it? You alarm me!" said he, after a moment's pause, during which the cloud on their usually bright faces had made itself evident.

Gerard broke into his tale without ceremony, baldly, stupidly, incoherently, as he felt. Audrey listened mutely, sitting on a sofa, very upright, clasping her hands.

Mr. Candover, who remained standing as Gerard did, heard the story with deep attention, but without the amazement and distress they had expected. When Gerard paused, Mr. Candover pulled aside a heavy portière, went into the next room, and returned with a spirit decanter and a glass.

"Drink that," he said, as he poured out a wine-glassful of brandy. "You're shaken, upset, not yourself."

Gerard obeyed, swallowed the brandy in gulps, frightened beyond measure at the way in which his story had been received. Audrey tapped her foot impatiently.

"Well, what do you think?" she said.

"I think," said he, "that you have no need to worry yourselves about this. This Sir Richmond is a very old man, and is, as you admit, full of crotchets. My own idea is that the cheques were genuine, and that he has forgotten all about them and who he gave them to. If I'm right, it will only take a few days to find out the truth, and to trace the money to the people to whom he's given it. Secretaries of real charities, or charitable impostors, very likely."

"I never thought of that!" cried Gerard, with sudden relief.

Audrey shook her head.

"The cheques were not all together," said she. "They were torn out of different parts of the book. And he wouldn't forget all three, you know."

Gerard's face fell again. Mr. Candover filled up the glass again; but Audrey, rising quickly from her seat, shook her head and gently checked her husband's hand.

"No," said she. "No more, Gerard. You've had nothing to eat and you want your best brains. Mr. Candover," and she turned to him, with a new dignity and peremptoriness surprising in such a young woman, "you've disappointed me. I thought you would have something better to suggest than—brandy."

Gerard was rather surprised, even alarmed, by his wife's daring.

"I'm afraid, Audrey, it's because there is nothing to be done that Mr. Candover suggests nothing," said he.

Audrey leaned over the little table by which she was standing.

"Can you tell us," she said earnestly, "whether it was on Saturday the third of last month, or Saturday the tenth, that you were with us just after luncheon?"

He looked surprised.

"I don't remember without looking at my diary. But I'll find out if you like," said he.

"Because," she went on, "the bank people are very anxious to know who was at our house that day, when Gerard was carrying the cheque-book down to Sir Richmond. If we could say that you were the only person who was in the flat while Gerard was there, it would help."

"I see." Mr. Candover went over to a writing-table, unlocked a drawer and turned over the leaves of a small diary.

"It was on the third," said he, "that I was with you."

"And it was on the tenth," said she, "that Gerard took the cheque-book down. Well then, it was Mrs. Webster who was with us. And there was nobody else."

"No, I don't think poor old Mrs. Webster would be accused by anybody of stealing blank cheques and forging Sir Richmond's signature," said Mr. Candover, smiling. "And my dear Mrs. Angmering, do calm your fears. Your husband is no more likely to be seriously suspected of such a thing than I or Mrs. Webster. Depend upon it, in the morning, when he gets to the bank, he will find that poor Sir Richmond has wired again to say he's solved the mystery. If not, the bank will set a detective to work, and the crime will be traced to its perpetrator. Do, do be persuaded not to pucker up that lovely face into such sad little frowns. Angmering, comfort your wife; don't let her worry herself. And look here: I've got to go to Paris the first thing to-morrow morning. But if you want any help or advice, wire to me at the Hotel Bristol, or get my secretary, Diggs, to do anything you may want done."

They thanked him, rather dolefully, refused again his entreaties that they would dine with him, and went away, trying to feel comforted, but not succeeding very well.

And after a weary night of fears and doubts, neither husband nor wife was much surprised when a police-officer arrived at the flat, the first thing in the morning, with a warrant for Gerard's arrest.

# CHAPTER II

THE young man himself was resigned, quiet, dignified. Only the trembling of his lip as he turned to speak to his wife betrayed the terrible strain.

Audrey was flushed, bright of eye, strangely composed of manner.

"I'm going," she said in a low voice, "straight to Victoria Street. I've been thinking it all over—all night I was thinking—thinking—of what there was to be done—and I know that you will want some one to—to——"

"I see. To be bail for me?"

"Yes. I'll go to Mr. Candover."

"But he was going to Paris!" objected Gerard, with a frown. He did not like his wife to go on this errand. "He will have started by this time."

"It's early yet," retorted Audrey. "At any rate I must try."

The energy and spirit she displayed put some heart into her husband, and their parting was very quiet, very composed. Within half an hour Audrey was at Mr. Candover's flat, only to find, however, that he was already on his way to Paris. His secretary, Durley Diggs, a little keen-eyed American with green and gold teeth, asked if he could do anything for her.

"Yes," said Audrey promptly. "My husband has been arrested on a charge of fraud. Mr. Candover knows all about it, and told me to come to you if I wanted help. Now I suppose they will want bail, and I want you to find it."

Mr. Diggs was very courteous, very business-like, very anxious to be of use. But Audrey was keen enough to see that he did not want to do this thing. But she insisted so steadily, refused so persistently to listen to his various excuses, that finally he said suddenly: "I'll see if the duchess will do it," and, seizing his hat, was going to rush out, when she insisted upon accompanying him.

"I've got to go out to Epsom. Madame de Vicenza lives at 'The Briars,' a big house out there," objected Diggs, disconcerted by her persistency.

"Well, I'll go with you. I can explain better than you, can't I?"

He was overpowered by her determination, and together they went down to Epsom, drove to "The Briars," which was a large, stately old house standing secluded in its own grounds, where Audrey waited downstairs while Durley Diggs was escorted into the presence of the duchess, as she supposed.

He came down again in the company of a tall, shambling man with round shoulders and a protruding jaw, whom he introduced as Mr. Johnson, the duchess's steward. And this gentleman having stated that he was prepared to give any undertaking on the part of the duchess which might be necessary, to serve any friend of Mr. Candover's, they all three went back to town, and to the Guildhall, where they found, as Audrey had expected, that bail for Gerard was wanted to the amount of two hundred pounds.

Her two companions having satisfied the magistrate, the necessary formalities were entered into, and Gerard and his wife were free to leave the court together.

Audrey was struck by the terrible change which a few hours had made in her husband. That morning he had been anxious indeed, worried, puzzled, distressed beyond measure by the situation in which he found himself. But now she saw at once that his position must be worse than she had supposed.

For in place of anxiety, she saw in his eyes despair, instead of being worried and irritable, he was bowed down by a terrible weight of depression which no tender words, no gentle caresses, no loving looks could remove.

"Gerard, Gerard," whispered she in a passionate outburst of misery and longing to help, when they were in the close cab he insisted on taking, "what is it, dear? What have you heard that makes you so wretched?"

He turned his heavy eyes towards her; he was oppressed, stupefied by the weight of the calamity which had fallen upon him.

"I've found out," said he hoarsely, "that there's something more in all this than we thought. This is no ordinary theft. There's a conspiracy to ruin me—Heaven knows why. A man has sworn that I gave him one of the cheques to get cashed, and that he gave me the money."

Audrey stared incredulously.

"But you can disprove that, can't you?" she said.

"I can deny it; I have denied it, I shall go on denying it. But as for disproving it, there's only my word against his, and the question is which of us will be believed."

"And who is the wretch who says this awful thing?"

"A man whom I've known by sight and to speak to, for a long time I never heard his name or knew who he was till to-day. It appears his name is Gossett, and he's a solicitor's clerk. What it all means or how it has all come about, I don't know. But I feel as if a net had been spread for my feet, that it's tightening, and that there is no escape."

Audrey's brave heart quailed. She, too, had vague suspicions that they must have unseen enemies, to find themselves so suddenly in such a sea of difficulties. But she would not let her fears appear. She affected to laugh at his despair, to feel sure that all that was needed was a good solicitor and a clever counsel to find out the truth and to set everything right. But it was excitement and not hope that kept her spirits so high, and that dried up the tears that it would have done her good to let flow.

The horrible fear was stealing into her heart too that all their efforts might not be enough to save her darling husband from the fate that threatened him.

It was the mystery which hung over every step of the great crime which had been committed which paralysed their brains and stupefied them. Who was the culprit who had stolen the cheques? When had the theft been committed? Was this man Gossett the thief and forger?

Audrey, however, recognised at once that their own brains were not clever enough to solve the puzzle, and she would be content with nothing less than the very best legal advice.

"If it costs every shilling we have in the world, Gerard," said she, "we can afford nothing less than the best brains in England."

She had not exaggerated the difficulties they had to contend with. Not only the eminent firm of solicitors they consulted, but the counsel whom they employed, admitted the amazing nature of the case. Nay, the poor young couple both felt vaguely, though they would scarcely acknowledge it to each other, that the questions Gerard had to answer pointed to the fact that even his own lawyers suspected him of having been concerned in the theft and in the forgery.

Gerard had received a large number of letters from Sir Richmond, so that he was well acquainted with his handwriting and signature. While the most searching inquiries failed to elicit the fact of any person's having had access to the cheque-book with the exception of Gerard and Sir Richmond himself.

Moreover, the man Gossett, who was prepared to swear that Gerard had asked him to take one of the cheques to be cashed, was proved to be a man against whom nothing was known except that he occasionally drank to excess; he lived simply in lodgings off the Tottenham Court Road, and had not been known to indulge in any expense since the date of the cashing of the cheque.

His story was that he had long known Gerard Angmering by sight but not by name, through frequenting the same luncheon-bar. He had often spoken to him, though he had no idea that he belonged to the Bank of the Old Country and Colonies. When the young man had asked him to cash a cheque for him at that bank, Gossett asserted that he agreed to do so, without any thought of harm; that he brought the money in gold and notes to Gerard, who was waiting for him outside Stott's, the luncheon-bar in question. He further alleged that he had received nothing for his trouble, and that he had thought nothing further of it until he was challenged by one of the senior clerks in the bank, who happened to meet him in the street in that neighbourhood, as the man who had cashed the cheque.

That was the whole sum and substance of the information at the disposal of both sides. The cheque had been made payable to Joseph Partridge, "to order," and the amount was seven hundred and sixty-five pounds. This had been paid in gold and notes, but not one of the notes had been traced.

Gerard denied the whole story of the man Gossett as a fabrication from beginning to end. But there was this fact against him, that, whereas there was no sign whatever that Gossett had been spending money freely or that he betted or was addicted to suspicious company, Gerard and his wife, on the other hand, had undoubtedly been living somewhat beyond their means, that they had got into debt, and that they were being harassed by creditors.

While a more condemnatory fact still came out in the fact that the young clerk and his wife had been at the Epsom Spring Meeting with some friends, and that Gerard, while denying that he had had any but trifling bets, admitted that he had lost money there.

Moreover, no such person as "Joseph Partridge" was to be found or heard of; and the other two cheques, details of the cashing of which were not so complete, were both made out in names equally impossible to trace to any actual person.

It was a foregone conclusion that the case would have to go to trial, and when the eve of the fateful day arrived, the depression and certainty of his conviction grew so strongly upon poor Gerard that Audrey, who remained outwardly calm and brave by a great effort, followed him about from room to room, with an appalling fear at her heart that he would never face the ordeal.

At last he turned suddenly to face her, and his haggard eyes, with all the boyish light gone out of them, looked dismally into her anxious, loving face.

"Why do you follow me?" he asked abruptly.

She tried to answer.

"Because—because——"

Then at last she broke down, and for the very first time in all those dreadful days she let herself go in a violent passion of weeping.

Gerard sat down in a low arm-chair, and strained her to him.

"My girl, my own darling," he whispered hoarsely, "I know what is in your mind. But you're wrong, Audrey, you're wrong, my dear. I shall go through with it, and listen, it's all up with me. We don't know how or why, but we're marked, and hunted down, and done for. I shall have to go to prison, and you—Oh, Audrey, that's what breaks my heart—you, *you*! I've got to leave you, and I don't in the least know what I'm leaving you exposed to. For since this awful thing has happened, how can we feel safe

12

for a minute? How can I know what will happen to you, when you haven't got me to take care of you? Oh, Audrey, Audrey, I wish we could both die to-night!"

And he broke down into violent sobs upon his wife's breast.

As he broke down, however, she regained command of herself. The fears which possessed him, indeed, were present to her mind also. The very mystery which surrounded the crime which had been committed against Gerard filled her with dread of what might be in store. But this, after all, was but a small matter compared with that terrible parting which seemed to the young husband and wife, lovers still, like the very wrenching of body and soul asunder.

She laid her hand over his mouth to stop him.

"Don't," she whispered. "It's wicked to say that. We must go through with it, even if the worst comes."

"The worst! Audrey, I'll tell you what the worst is: it's the thought of your being left alone. Will you be true to me? Will you, will you? You're so beautiful that you will be tempted to forget me. Oh, I know! Other men will make love to you, and it will be hard, harder than you think, to stand out."

Audrey made no indignant answer. She only pressed his curly head against her breast and just whispered, "Trust me, dear."

The trial was a short one. Accused of forging Sir Richmond's signature to a cheque, and of fraudulently obtaining the sum of seven hundred and sixty-five pounds, Gerard pleaded "Not guilty" in vain. No evidence of any value could be produced in support of his plea, and in spite of the eloquence of his counsel, who seemed indeed to plead rather for his youth than for his innocence, he was sentenced to a term which was looked upon in the circumstances as a light one, three years' penal servitude.

As the sentence was pronounced a cry, not loud but piercing, rang through the court. And Gerard, recognising the voice of his wife, turned, clutching the rail in front of him, and cast one agonised look around.

He saw Audrey, and his face, which had been deadly pale, grew livid and ghastly, while his eyes seemed to start out of his head with a sudden access of suspicion and rage.

For the half-fainting Audrey was supported by the arms of a handsome, well-dressed man, who hung over her solicitously, tenderly.

And the man was Reginald Candover, Gerard's best friend.

# CHAPTER III

AUDREY was scarcely more than half conscious when she found herself out in the open air, such air as was to be had on a hot, dusty day at the end of May, with a blazing sun pouring down into the busy streets near the Old Bailey, and a keen east wind waiting round the corner, blowing clouds of paper, straw and dust into the faces of the passers-by.

The blinding glare of the sun revived her, however, and made her blink. Looking round, she found herself supported by the arm of a man, listening to a voice she half remembered, and surrounded by a too attentive and too curious, but decidedly sympathetic, crowd.

"Poor thing!" "She's his wife!" "Didn't you see him look at her?" "P'raps he didn't do it, after all!" "Poor thing!"

These and similar comments reached Audrey's ears before they carried any sense to them. But remembrance, full, horrible, came back suddenly, and she drew herself up and struggled to regain her self-command.

"Mr. Candover!"

"Yes, yes. You're all right. I've got my car here; only get through this abominable crowd, and you will be all right."

But Audrey had recovered her wits, and a sudden fierce resentment awoke in her.

This was Gerard's most intimate friend, and he had known all about their distress, yet they had seen nothing of him all through that dreadful time. She tried to draw away the hand which he held fast within his own arm.

"You might have come to us before!" she said, with bitter reproach. "You knew the trouble we were in, and you professed to be so anxious to help us. Yet never once in all that dreadful time have we seen you!"

"I—I told my secretary to do what he could. He did get bail for your husband!" faltered Mr. Candover in a tone of some contrition but still more reproach.

"Because I insisted. I followed him about till he did," retorted Audrey sharply.

"As for myself, I was in Paris. I had to go. I told you so."

"Paris is not at the other end of the world. And you didn't even write to him!"

"Mrs. Angmering, you overwhelm me! Allow me to do the best I can to make amends for what indeed was not my fault. Let me do what poor Angmering would like best, and take care of his wife."

"Thank you. Your kindness comes too late. I can take care of myself."

And Audrey, now that they had come in sight of the smart motor-car which never failed to attract the attention of a crowd when it stopped, refused her companion's entreaties that she would get into it, and dashed across the street to an omnibus.

Mr. Candover was disappointed, but he took his disappointment with philosophy. His good intentions might be resented now, but they would be better appreciated some day.

So he waited nearly a week, and then he called at the flat at West Kensington, and was told that Mrs. Angmering was not at home.

He felt sure that she was, so he lay in wait for her. And when Audrey, very pale, very quiet, wearing a thick veil, came quickly out and down the stairs and out into the street, she was met by her husband's friend, who, raising his hat with a courteous and diffident manner, asked humbly:—

"Won't you speak to me, Mrs. Angmering? Surely, because you're unhappy yourself, you shouldn't make your old friends unhappy!"

Audrey stopped, but she did not hold out her hand. In truth she was at war with all the world. With the judge who had sentenced Gerard, the jury who had tried him, the counsel who had led the case against him, the counsel who had failed to defend him successfully; more than all with the relations who had written her letters full of horror at her husband's supposed misdeeds, accompanied by subdued reminders that, when she left the calm of a Lancashire town for the riot and wickedness of a London life with a London husband, she had only done what she might have expected to lead to misery.

"I don't want to make anybody unhappy," said she in a low voice. "But it's true, Mr. Candover, that just now I don't feel inclined to hold any intercourse with anybody. I want a little—a little time to—to get over it!"

"Indeed, I can quite understand that. But for Gerard's sake you must take care of yourself, you know. You mustn't fret, for one thing. You mustn't let him see, when you meet him again, that you've allowed fretting to mar your beauty."

She frowned impatiently. What did she care for her looks now Gerard could not see her? She felt that, at that moment, she would have liked to pull out her eyelashes and cut off her hair, and efface the charms which she valued for his sake only.

"I'm not going to waste time in fretting. It's of no use," said she.

"Excuse my asking—what are you going to do?"

She hesitated.

"I—I don't quite know—yet."

He looked at his watch.

"Look here. I may take the privilege of an old fogey and an old friend, mayn't I? Let me take you to one of the restaurants—one of the quiet ones," he went on hastily, as she drew herself up, "where we can talk over the situation, and I may be able to help you to decide upon something."

"Thank you very much, but——"

"Come, come, you've dined with me often enough before."

"With Gerard, yes. But not without him."

"Well, do you mean to give up your friends altogether? To live the life of a nun?"

Audrey had recovered her full faculties, and she answered him promptly and steadily:—

"No. I don't mean to lead the life of a nun, but the life of a widow," she said. "While Gerard is in prison I'm going to remain in mourning for him, and when he comes back to me I'm going to—to be alive once more."

"But in the meantime," urged Mr. Candover gently, "even though you don't feel that life is worth living, you must live, you know. And the best way to please Gerard is to keep in good health and in good spirits. I don't mean uproariously high spirits, but the natural ones of youth and beauty. May I ask where you're going now?"

She hesitated.

"I'm going to try to sublet the flat," she answered unwillingly at last.

For she still felt aggrieved at his defection, as she considered it, at the fact that, when a powerful friend like himself might have done much to support Gerard and to create a favourable impression by standing up for him boldly, Mr. Candover, who had professed so much affection for them both, should have remained silent and aloof.

"Won't you let me do the business for you? A man is less likely to be taken advantage of than a woman, you know."

"Thank you, I would rather arrange it all myself. It gives me something to do."

"May I come round to-morrow and bring you some books?"

"Thank you, I have no time for reading now."

"If I were to come, then, should I be told you were out, as I was told just now?" persisted he.

"I—I think so. I leave the same message for all my friends. If they were to persist in seeing me, I should have to go away. Really I should have thought you might understand, Mr. Candover, how very, very retired a life I must live now."

It was very neatly worded, but Mr. Candover understood. Audrey had to be discreet; she was a good and true woman, and the enjoyments which she had loved, the gaieties in which she had taken a foremost and brilliant part with her young husband by her side to share them, were now to be put away, forgotten, to give place to the austerity of the widowhood she professed to have entered.

The man of the world was nonplussed. Give up the chase he would not; but before this inflexible determination he was powerless. At last a bright thought struck him:—

"If I were to bring my two girls up, now, would you see them? They are hardly more than children, and are still at school. But I should like you to know them. And I should like them to know *you*, to have before them the example of a noble woman and a devoted wife."

Audrey was conquered. She could hardly refuse such a request as this.

"I should be very happy to see them," she said gently. "But wait, oh, do please wait a little. To see two happy girls now—would—would——" The tears were so near that she had to collect herself—"would be more than I could bear," she ended in a whisper.

A week later, therefore, Mr. Candover called at the flat one afternoon, bringing with him two shy schoolgirls, still in the awkward stage between childhood and womanhood, though the elder was a tall, well-developed girl whose hair had just been "put up" to celebrate her eighteenth birthday.

She was a bright-faced girl, this Pamela, with irregular features, little twinkling, merry dark eyes, and manners half-shy, half-hoydenish, but rather sweet.

Babs, the younger girl, was rather silent, rather slow. But the pretty features and fair hair promised to develop into great beauty by-and-by.

Both girls had evidently been told enough to interest them in their beautiful hostess, as poor Audrey felt with a pang. And their shy looks and gently subdued voices cut her to the quick, making her feel indeed that she was lonely with a deeper loneliness than that of a widow, for was not Gerard going through worse than death?

Audrey hoped to dispose of her task as hostess within an hour, but as they all stayed on she presently felt compelled to ask them to stay and dine with her, an invitation which was accepted with so much readiness that she perceived at once that this was the end Mr. Candover had had in view.

She felt rather ashamed of her vague mistrust of this amiable and kind friend when, the girls being engaged at the piano in a "brilliant" duet which afforded a perfect cover for conversation, he said to her in a low voice full of feeling:—

"And now, my dear Mrs. Angmering, let me know something of your plans. Both the girls and I hope that you won't give us up altogether, however quiet you mean to be."

Reticence would be out of place, she felt, now that Mr. Candover had so tactfully shown himself in the character of an old friend and a father, instead of the one in which she knew him best, the complimentary, half lover-like man of pleasure and man about town.

"I want," she said, "to do something for myself, to earn money, I mean. I want to have something to show Gerard when I see him again."

Mr. Candover raised his eyebrows.

"Well said, like a brave lady. And what do you propose to do? Perhaps I could help you."

"Well," said Audrey, "I have a taste, perhaps even a talent, for millinery; I have still a little capital; and I thought I might perhaps start a business as lots of women do now. Too many, perhaps," she added thoughtfully.

"Too many do it the wrong way. You must do it the right way," said Mr. Candover with animation. "Now this is a thing I know I can help you in, and you ought to do well. But remember, there must be no half-measures. Don't be modest. That is the golden rule for every sort of business, from that of the company promoter to that of the keeper of a whelk-stall. Blow the trumpet, beat the drum, tell them yours is the greatest show on earth—and they'll believe you."

Audrey laughed nervously.

"Oh, I haven't either impudence or money enough to make a great noise about it," said she.

"Never mind. I'll do that for you. I know of the very woman who would do the hard part of the work; what you have to do is the showy part. You must wear handsome dresses, advertise your own bonnets, and swagger about in a victoria to show them all off."

"Oh, no, no, I'd no idea of doing anything of that sort," said Audrey breathlessly.

"I know you had not. Nevertheless, that's how the thing has to be done. You must take a first floor in the neighbourhood of Bond Street, and you must call yourself by a foreign name, a title for choice."

"Oh, I shouldn't like to do that!"

"You have no choice. Either you must leave the thing undone, or do it well. My dear Mrs. Angmering, I advise you in Gerard's interest as well as your own. Wouldn't you like to be able to meet him, in not so very long a time, with a house of your own, and a turn-out such as you both have admired in the park a hundred times? Of course you would. And the way to get all those nice things, and to hold up your head in the world besides, is to cut a dash with whatever capital you've got, and to begin with a flourish. I'll get you a good little circle of smart clients to make a start with, and if you'll be guided by me, you will make your fortune."

Breathlessly, with many a timid fear, yet with a vague consciousness that there was sound sense in his advice from a worldly point of view, Audrey listened, objected, was talked down and finally conquered.

Within a month, taking step by step, not without caution, but acknowledging the great help of Mr. Candover's judgment, Audrey found herself the responsible tenant of handsomely furnished first-floor showrooms in a good street in the West End, with a staff of assistants, and over them the "valuable woman" of whom Mr. Candover had spoken.

This woman was a sallow, elderly Frenchwoman, who professed to speak no English. She was thin, gaunt, plain of feature, simple of dress. She had keen, hard eyes and a curious look in her face which reminded Audrey of some one she had seen somewhere, but in an elusive way, so that she was unable to fix the resemblance upon any definite person.

This woman's name was Marie Laure, and she had the eye of a lynx and the step of a cat. Audrey was sure that Mademoiselle Laure disliked her, but could not say how she knew it. In the meantime the Frenchwoman was clever, business-like and an excellent manager, so that indeed, as Mr. Candover had said, it was only the showy part of the work that was left to the young nominal head of the business.

Little by little Audrey had discovered that she was sliding into complete confidence in Mr. Candover's advice, so that he was consulted by her in everything, and always with good results.

He fulfilled his promise to bring her customers, and although some of these were not of the type she would have chosen, he laughed at her scarcely expressed scruples, and told her that she did not want to cater for Sunday schools. Then he got her an order for the dresses for a new piece at a theatre, and telling her that she must now advertise herself by the title he had found for her, sent announcements broadcast to the papers that the dresses for the new piece at the Piccadilly Theatre were by that "artistic creator of exquisite motives in millinery and dreams in dresses," the Countess Rocada.

Audrey had already demurred to the assumption of this high-sounding title, but she had given way, feeling herself to be in safe hands with regard to worldly knowledge on such matters, and being moreover glad to hide herself from public curiosity by dropping her own too well-known name.

So she was known to her employees only as Madame Rocada.

And on the very day when this announcement went forth in the press, Audrey found herself overwhelmed by a surprising flow of evidently wealthy customers, both men and women, all well dressed, all curious, all with money to spend, who crowded her rooms from before luncheon-time to within an hour of dinner.

There was a look about these curious customers, an obvious and haughty inquisitiveness about the women, an elaborate courtesy on the part of the men, which Audrey did not like. And she told herself that they had probably found out who she was, and that they had come to stare at her and to gossip about her and "the way she took it".

When they were all gone, the lights turned down, when the assistants had filed out, and the costly dresses and plumed hats had been shrouded in wraps and put away, Audrey, worn out, wounded and miserable, flung herself face downwards on one of the luxurious couches which had been crowded that day with idle visitors, and burst into bitter tears.

A rapid step in the next room, which was another showroom, divided from this only by a handsome portière, the sound of a sharply drawn breath, and then a peal of wild, hysterical laughter, startled her and made her spring to her feet.

# CHAPTER IV

STANDING in the doorway, grasping the portière tightly with her right hand, while her left was pressed against her breast, was a tall, thin woman, dressed from head to foot in white. Seen thus in the dim light of the darkened room, her clinging draperies of some soft, semi-transparent material swathed round her slight form and forming billows of white foam about her feet, her pale face, out of which two great eyes shone like lamps in the darkness, the slow, swaying movement of her body in the opening between the two rooms, all combined to give her an uncanny appearance, to suggest a ghostly vision rather than a woman of flesh and blood.

Even the hoarse laugh she uttered when Audrey sprang up and turned to face her, sounded like the unearthly, weird cry of a lost soul rather than an utterance of living human lips.

Audrey was struck dumb. She saw at once that the strange visitor had come with hostile intent, she read anger, spiteful, bitter anger in her thin face, in the convulsive movements of her gloved fingers.

Was she a madwoman? There was nothing indeed of the disorder of madness about her. From the great white hat, loaded with long white ostrich feathers, which crowned her golden hair, down to the long white gloves which hung in wrinkles on her arms, and the graceful draperies which half-hid, half-revealed, her sinuous and slender figure, the stranger showed every sign of that studied elegance and calculated attractiveness which comes only from taste, care and the long experience of a characteristic but keen feminine intellect.

Audrey, having of late had to study dress as a fine art, acknowledged herself in the presence of a past mistress of it.

No. The lady in the white draperies was not mad, wild as were her eyes, and weirdly alarming as was her mocking laughter.

There was a moment of dead, uncanny silence, when, her laughter having died away on her lips, the stranger, still grasping the dark curtain as if for support, and leaning forward to fix the gaze of her terrible dark eyes on Audrey, stood like a tigress ready to spring, panting, struggling for the breath that came only in painful gasps, preparing herself for an encounter which Audrey felt would be a terrible one.

Audrey looked round her fearfully, wondering whether she could escape the trying ordeal with which she knew herself to be threatened. This woman had, she knew, come to see her, come with some accusation, unguessed at but evidently serious, ready on her lips as it was already burning in her eyes.

There was a door nearly opposite to where Audrey stood by the couch; but it was shut, and there were dress stands and lounges between it and her.

She had a feeling that, if she were to attempt to fly, the tiger-like stranger would spring at her, tear her to pieces with those long, lean, white-gloved hands, that looked claw-like as they moved nervously with every breath she drew.

And Audrey was encumbered with the weight of a magnificent black train, glittering with paillettes and voluminous in its folds, which she put on when she arrived at the showrooms in the morning, and exchanged for a quiet little tailor-made gown to return at night to her two modest rooms on the top floor over a small chemist's shop in a street off Oxford Street.

This handsome black gown increased the effect of a strong contrast between her and her weird visitor. The lady in white was tall, thin; from golden hair and whitened face to sinuous figure, a work of finished art.

Audrey was in the first freshness of her striking natural beauty, easy and graceful of carriage, well developed of figure, with golden hair that lay in natural rings on her forehead, and in a twisted coil, untidy and loose, on the top of her head.

The contrast was between natural and artificial loveliness, and the glaring, panting stranger seemed to appreciate this fact.

Long as the time seemed, it was in truth but a few moments that they both stood silently watching each other, neither ready to utter the first word.

Then, so quickly that it seemed all to take place in the twinkling of an eye, there came a rapid step in the inner room, a hand dragged the white-clad woman roughly away, and at the same time and by the same movement the curtain was drawn across the opening between the rooms, shutting Audrey out into the twilight of the darkened room.

Then she heard the woman's voice, savage, passionate, full of an emotion so strong that it seemed to strangle her, weak and ill as she evidently was.

"Madame Rocada! Madame Rocada!" she cried, gasping out the name in withering tones, hoarse and broken, yet eloquent of rage and scorn. "Let me see her, let me speak to her, let me see what she has to say for herself. Do you think you can stop me, you!"

Audrey, bewildered and alarmed, wondering who it was that had seized the stranger and dragged her away from the door, crept close to the curtain to learn more of this intrusion and the cause.

She had fancied herself alone in the long suite of rooms; for Marie Laure, who slept on the premises in a tiny room at the back, had gone out to do some shopping, and it was in her absence that poor Audrey, broken down and miserable, had indulged in the fit of tears which had been so strangely interrupted.

Whose then was the hand that had seized the stranger? A strong one it must have been, to do so much so quickly!

Surely, thought Audrey, it must be the hand of a man. She crept nearer and nearer to the curtain, making ready to pull it sharply back, and to take the two persons within by surprise.

But even as she advanced, she heard by the fainter sound of the woman's voice that she was being drawn away, and that she was being gagged.

The last words that Audrey caught sounded to her listening ears like the calling of a man by his name:—

"Oh, Eugène, Eugène!"

A chill seized Audrey, and she drew back, frightened, asking herself in a wild impulse of suspicion and dread whether this "Eugène" were some evil genius, the same that had cast his blighting hand upon the fate of Gerard and herself?

Then she heard a door shut, and peering through behind the portière into the inner room, she saw that no one was there.

The building of which this first floor formed a part had been extended at the back, and behind this second large showroom there were two or three smaller rooms, one of which was that of Mademoiselle Laure, and another a private fitting-room. It was this room the door of which Audrey had heard close, and trying it, she now found that it was locked.

She heard voices within, subdued, angry, the whispering voices of a man and a woman, speaking some language which Audrey could not understand.

She knocked, but there was no reply.

Hurriedly withdrawing, therefore, without speaking a word, Audrey went out upon the staircase, and into her own private room, where she kept her walking dress. Changing quickly into this, she had just put on her hat, with the intention of going downstairs to meet Mademoiselle Laure on her return and to consult with her as to what she had better do, when she was startled by the sound of the unlocking of a door, and then by footsteps running rapidly down the stairs.

She flew to the door and looked out; but she was too late to see more than this: that the person who was dashing down the stairs and disappearing by the side door into the street was a man.

Who was it?

And why was not the white-clad lady with him?

Audrey hesitated only one moment, and then, full of fears she could not have defined, ran up to the fitting-room and went in.

The room was quite dark, but she touched the electric button, and at once a flood of soft light filled the apartment.

A cry of horror broke from her lips when, turning her eyes at once towards a big divan which stood under the window, she saw lying at full length upon it the body of the woman in the white dress.

Her white hat was crushed and bent under her poor lifeless head; one hand, still in its long wrinkled white kid glove, was outstretched as if in a last convulsion; one white kid, high-heeled walking shoe lay on the floor. The white ostrich feather boa which had floated round her shoulders when Audrey saw her alive was twisted round her thin throat. The clinging white dress was bound round her motionless limbs.

And over all, dress, gloves, boa, in startling and awful contrast to the white clothes, were marks of blood: blood which had gushed out from her mouth and streamed over everything.

Audrey was aghast. Was this a murdered woman upon whose body she was looking? She could not tell. For the haggard cheeks, the glassy eyes, the laboured breath, the feeble though passionate movements, all of which signs she had noticed in the living woman, the husky voice, the occasional cough, had betrayed unmistakably the fact that the poor woman was in the last stage of consumption, and her death might well have resulted from the bursting of a blood-vessel in a moment of wild excitement.

On the other hand, the sudden disappearance of the man who had met her and dragged her away from the doorway was horribly suggestive. And the feather boa which appeared to be bound round the poor woman's thin and wasted throat might, Audrey thought with horror, have been the means of her death.

One long look she gave before she went to call assistance. And in that look she ascertained that the dead woman must have been of surpassing beauty, for the features were regular and perfectly formed; that she was between forty and fifty years of age appeared equally certain, now that powder and paint could hide the marks of time no longer. And Audrey crept downstairs shuddering, and wondering what fate was upon her, that a second and horrible calamity should happen in her experience within little more than six weeks.

At the foot of the private staircase which led out into the street she was lucky in meeting Mademoiselle Laure, to whom she related, in faltering accents, the terrible experience she had just gone through. By this time, however, poor Audrey, giddy and faint with the scene she had gone through, could scarcely articulate, scarcely make herself intelligible to Mademoiselle Laure, who could or would speak no English.

Audrey, indeed, spoke French well. But excitement either confused her utterance or affected her voice, for it was a long time before the Frenchwoman gathered the gist of her words.

Then Mademoiselle laughed at her.

"You dream, Madame," she answered in her rapid French. "Such things do not happen. The busy day has got on your nerves, and you have imagined horrors which have no existence! Bah! A dead woman—all in white—lying upstairs! No, no. You want your dinner. That is all."

And she laughed, actually laughed, while poor Audrey, stupefied by this unexpected reception of her dreadful news, leaned back against the wall of the narrow passage for a few moments, unable to speak.

At last, seeing that the Frenchwoman remained looking at her in a far from sympathetic manner, she roused herself, and staggering towards the door, said in a whisper:—

"I—I shall go for the police!"

"For what?" echoed Mademoiselle Laure incredulously. "The police! A nice thing for the business that would be, *ma foi*! To have the police here, to hunt and turn the place upside down in their search for the effects of Madame's weak nerves! The police! Oh, no. We will have no police here, be sure of that!"

And the voluble Frenchwoman, with the same expression of mocking incredulity on her thin features, seized Audrey by the arm and held her as she would have gone out.

But the younger woman had a will of her own too.

"Mademoiselle," said she, "you forget that I am the head of this business, the tenant of these premises, and that I have a right to do as I please."

"And I," retorted the Frenchwoman, always using her native language, and speaking fast and with determination, "have a duty to do in protecting you from your own folly. Look here, Madame. I knew when I went out that something would happen to you. You looked as white as a ghost, you were trembling, and on the verge of tears. The worry and fatigue of the busy day, during which you have eaten and drunk nothing, has made you ill. I see the marks of tears upon your face; your hair is in disorder; your hat is not pinned on properly. You are not yourself. I did not like to leave you, and I wish to Heaven I had not done so. You are nervous, unstrung. Come across the road with me, to the confectioner's opposite. You shall drink a glass of wine and swallow a mouthful of food, and then we will come back together."

"Back! Oh, no, no," cried Audrey, shuddering.

The reaction after intense excitement had set in, and she was weak, tremulous and almost hysterical. Still, with all this, she knew what she had to do, what she must do.

"Well," said Mademoiselle Laure, speaking with more kindliness as her companion showed signs of increasing weakness, "will you promise me to stay quietly at the shop while I go for a doctor?"

"A doctor! Oh, yes, yes," said Audrey.

"Come then, quickly. I'm afraid of your fainting on the way."

Audrey shook her head. Supported by her companion's arm, she was now outside, and the fresh air of the evening revived her. They were only just in time, for the shop opposite was closing. They begged permission to enter, and Audrey drank a glass of wine and obediently tried, though she did not succeed in the attempt, to eat a biscuit. For on no other terms would Mademoiselle Laure consent to leave her.

"I will be back, Madame," said the Frenchwoman, with an encouraging smile, as she went quickly to the door, "in five minutes. There is a doctor round the corner. I will fetch him. Wait for me."

Audrey was indeed thankful to have the task of taking the necessary steps transferred to the shoulders of another. At first, in the dazed state which succeeded her first white heat of excitement, she had almost let herself be persuaded by the Frenchwoman into wondering whether she had not been the victim of her own imagination. But before Mademoiselle Laure left her, she had recovered her wits, and recognised that, in fetching a doctor, which was, after all, the most sensible thing that could be done, the woman was acknowledging the fact that there was something in what her employer had said.

The time seemed very long while she waited, but she dared not go back alone to the showrooms, and she now realised that it was not her place to send for the police, but the doctor's.

The woman in charge of the shop grew impatient too, and they both watched the clock until five, ten minutes, a quarter of an hour, twenty minutes had passed.

Then Mademoiselle Laure suddenly appeared at the side-door, on the opposite side of the street, which led to the showrooms. She ran across the road, and beckoned excitedly to Audrey.

She was laughing.

Audrey trembled and could scarcely stand as Mademoiselle Laure took her by the arm and, without a word of explanation, beyond saying that the doctor was there, led the trembling woman back and up the stairs.

"Don't take me in again, don't, don't," whispered Audrey, whose nerve had given way completely under the long and terrible strain.

"But you must come, you must. Don't you want to see the doctor?" said Mademoiselle Laure, whose voice and manner was as derisive as ever.

Audrey let herself be led, reluctant indeed, but submissive as a child, up the stairs and into the first of the two big, handsomely furnished showrooms.

The doctor, an elderly man of strictly professional aspect, who wore gold spectacles and spoke in a quiet and authoritative manner, bowed to her with a keen but kindly look.

At once he offered her a chair, and making a sign to Mademoiselle Laure to draw back the muslin curtain that veiled the nearest of the electric lights, he took Audrey by the wrist.

She drew a breath of amazement. Evidently he looked upon her as a patient.

"Oh, there's—there's nothing the matter with me, doctor," said she breathlessly. "All I want to know is whether the—the poor woman died naturally, or—or was——"

Before she could get any further, she saw the doctor look up and exchange a grave glance with Mademoiselle Laure. Perceiving at once that he appeared to doubt her sanity, angry with the Frenchwoman, and determined to put an end to the misunderstanding, Audrey darted across the room towards the door of the fitting-room. "You have been misinformed, doctor," said she quickly. "It is not to see me that you were called in, but an unhappy woman who——"

She had tried the door of the fitting-room, and it had opened in her hand. Audrey looked in, stopped short, turned giddy, fell back. Then, passing her hand across her eyes, and waiting a moment to recover herself, she went boldly into the room.

For a whole minute she stood staring round her, clenching her hands, trying to understand, to believe the evidence of her eyes.

Not only was the white-clad lady no longer there, but not a sign of her presence, a trace of a tragedy, was to be seen.

"Where—where is she? Where have you put—the body?" hissed she in a hoarse, peremptory whisper.

The doctor shrugged his shoulders, and spoke soothingly.

"Madame," said he, "there has been nobody there. It is the result of an overactive imagination, upon a stomach left too long without food, and an overwrought system. I will write you out a little prescription; you must take a sleeping draught, and I will come and see you in the morning."

And he looked round for paper and a pen.

# CHAPTER V

AUDREY stared at the doctor.

"Thank you," said she, "I don't want either a prescription or a sleeping draught. I'm quite well, quite sane. I can't have been deceived. I saw the woman, I heard her speak, I saw and heard, not so well, but still I did see and hear him—a man who dragged her out of this room and into the next."

The doctor looked puzzled, as well he might. He rose from the chair which he had taken in order to feel her pulse and inquire into her symptoms, and he walked across the room and peered into the empty fitting-room.

Then he looked at her again, and then at Mademoiselle Laure, who was standing motionless, with her arms folded, and her thin lips tightly pressed together, a few paces away from them.

Audrey looked at her too.

"If," said Audrey, "Mademoiselle Laure would speak out, probably she could tell us something."

The Frenchwoman, whether she understood this or not, looked as if she caught only her own name, and she at once said, in French, that she had felt sure Madame must be mistaken when she told her extraordinary story. The doctor bowed his head, but it was evident that his command of colloquial French was not equal to discussion of the matter in any language but his own.

There was a rather awkward pause, and then Audrey said impatiently that she supposed there was nothing more to be done, if Mademoiselle Laure would not speak.

"I shall consult my friends to-morrow, and take legal advice upon this, if necessary," she said. "Dr.——"

"Fendall, my name is Fendall," said he, supplying the name when she paused.

"I am sorry to have disturbed you for nothing, as it appears. But you will be satisfied presently that I was justified in sending for you, and you will be a witness to the fact that I took the proper steps at once."

"Certainly. I hope you will let me persuade you, however, to take a sleeping draught to-night. Or at least to consult your own medical man about your health. You seem, if I may say so, to be in a highly nervous condition, and I feel sure that both rest and careful diet are imperatively necessary for you."

"Thank you," said Audrey shortly. There was his fee to be paid, and she added as he turned with a bow to the door: "Your address, Dr. Fendall, please, and I will write to you in the morning."

He waved his hand.

"Oh, no, no, I have done nothing, and I am only sorry I could not be of use."

The next moment he was gone, and Audrey, after in vain trying to summon courage enough to make another examination of the fitting-room, which would, she felt sure, have revealed some trace of the recent presence of the unhappy woman in the white dress, hastily bade Mademoiselle Laure good-night without further conversation with that reticent and astute-looking person, and went home to her rooms in Earl Street, Oxford Street.

What should she do? Whom should she consult?

Never before had she realised so fully how desperately lonely was her position in the world. Never before had she understood how the unhappy situation of her unfortunate husband had cut her off from every old friend, from the sympathy as well as the support even of her own relations.

From the first the aunt, with whom she had been living at Lytham, had opposed her marriage. It was during a short visit to some friends in London that Audrey had met Gerard, who fell in love with her straightway, followed her on her return to the north, and never rested till he had won her for his wife.

Miss Hester Claughton, Audrey's maiden aunt, had disapproved of him from the first, as frivolous and worldly, and now that this terrible charge had been brought against the young man, and had resulted in the sentence which condemned him in the eyes of the world, Miss Hester did not hesitate to write long letters to her unhappy niece, professedly to express her sympathy, but really containing nothing but variations of the old theme, "I told you so".

Audrey's two brothers were settled, the one in Canada and the other in Hong-Kong, so that rapid communication with them, even if it had been advisable, was out of the question.

The solicitor whom they had employed in the forgery case had earned Audrey's ferocious enmity and disapproval by allowing it to be seen that, while doing his best for his client, he had little doubt as to his guilt.

The only other person whom she could think of whose advice and help might be of assistance was Mr. Candover. And although he was very kind now, Audrey had not yet forgiven him for what she considered his neglect of Gerard during his trial. Besides, carefully courteous and chivalrous as Mr. Candover was, charmingly as he had allayed a certain vague mistrust of hers by introducing his daughters to her, Audrey was clear-sighted enough to understand that it would not do to let this handsome, attractive man of the world become, what he was apparently not unwilling to be, her only adviser and confidant.

What was she then to do? Sure as she felt of her facts as to the occurrences of the previous evening, she hesitated, when she had time to think the matter over, to court publicity of a hideous kind by calling in the police to investigate the matter.

On the other hand, she felt that she could not rest satisfied with the meagre knowledge she had at present. How could she go back to these rooms, with the remembrance of that strange and dreadful scene full in her mind, without one effort to elucidate the mystery?

If Mademoiselle Laure would speak, no doubt something would be learnt. But how to make her open her lips, in the face of her present obstinate determination to know nothing?

Against her will, poor Audrey was at last obliged to acknowledge that there was only one person to whom she could make known her difficulty, with any prospect of advice and help. In desperation she wrote a few lines to Mr. Candover, telling him that something so strange had happened at the showrooms that she did not like even to return to them without consulting some one, and asking if he would meet her at an Oxford Street confectioner's, whose name she gave, at nine o'clock on the following morning.

She sent this note by messenger to Mr. Candover's flat in Victoria Street, and got the answer by the morning's post:—

"DEAR MADAME ROCADA,
"Of course I will be there. I hope it is nothing serious which is troubling you so much.

"Yours always,
"REGINALD CANDOVER."

Audrey frowned when she saw the address. She had taken her rooms in the name of Madame Rocada, "Angmering" being too uncommon a name not to be recognised and commented on. Absolutely sure as she felt of her husband's innocence of the supposed crime for which he was suffering, Audrey preferred not to be the object of the gossip which would certainly have centred round her if her identity had been known.

But she disliked the alias, as she called it, and wished that she had been allowed to take some simpler, less pretentious name than the high-sounding mock-title by which she was now known. Of course, as Mr. Candover said, nobody supposed that the title of "Countess" was anything but a trade fiction, but the whole surroundings of her new calling, combining unlimited show with narrow capital, were distasteful to Audrey.

At nine o'clock punctually Mr. Candover met her, and she at once, having ordered coffee and a roll as an excuse for her presence in the shop, told him the whole story of the events of the previous evening.

He thrust aside as absurd the suggestion of the Frenchwoman and the doctor that Audrey had been misled by her imagination.

"You saw a woman, a stranger, undoubtedly," said he. "People don't imagine such things. And no doubt you saw her dragged away, and saw her lying in the fitting-room. The only thing I doubt is that she can have been dead."

"Don't you think Mademoiselle Laure may have found the dead body and, in her anxiety to hush things up, have removed it?"

"No doubt she could. The old Frenchwoman is artful enough for anything, and clever enough too—but to do such a thing, and to remove all traces of such a tragedy, requires time. Now, by your account, she had no time. You say you were only left alone about twenty minutes or half an hour, and that in that time she had fetched a doctor?"

"Ye-es, but——"

"Well, she might very well have removed the body, but it's impossible, absolutely impossible, that she could have removed all traces, so as to deceive even the doctor!"

"Well, who do you think the woman could have been? She was not English. What could she want with me to be so angry as she was?"

"Impossible to say. Most likely it was not you but old Laure she was angry with—some business rival perhaps, who had wanted the post of forewoman for herself."

"Oh, I never thought of that! But then the man who drew her back, and then locked her in the room, and ran away?"

"Are you *sure* it was a man?"

"Yes. I just saw enough of his figure to be sure of that. And I saw his hand drawing the curtain. Besides, she called him 'Eugène,' pronouncing the name in the French fashion 'Eugène'. Can you find out who this Eugène was?"

"If he was a Frenchman I should hazard the guess that he also was a friend—perhaps a relation, of Marie Laure's. My advice is that you should not worry yourself about this unpleasant incident, should try to forget it in fact——"

"How can I? It's the sort of thing it's impossible to forget!"

"Well, well, don't think about it more than you can help. Keep your thoughts on your business, and on the good beginning you've made. Now all that remains is for you to keep it up, and you'll soon make your fortune. Did you have many people at the rooms yesterday?"

"They were crammed all the afternoon. But oh, I didn't like it! I don't like these 'smart' and would-be smart people at all. The women are loud-voiced, aggressive, horrid. And the men—well, they're worse. City men buying dresses and hats for actresses, not real actresses, you know, but chorus-girls or what they call 'show' girls, who can't even sing in a chorus."

"Hush. You mustn't criticise your clients. All you have to do is to see they pay well for what they buy."

"Ah, but my poor Gerard wouldn't like it. I know how furious he would be if he knew!"

"Gerard would like you to make money, for both your sakes. You needn't tell him any more than you like about these people. You can tell him about the duchesses, and say nothing about the chorus-girls. And by-the-bye, the Duchess de Vicenza is going abroad; that's the woman who stood bail for your husband, you know."

"Who is she? I've never seen her."

"She's a dear, kind creature, and very rich. But she's very old, and doesn't go about at all. She wants to let her place 'The Briars'. Now you want a change, and it would be good for your business to have a place near town where you could invite your more important clients."

"Oh, no, no. I——"

"Listen. If Madame de Vicenza would let this place for a song, as I think she would, you must take my advice, and rent it for the summer. I have an idea that by-and-by you might turn your business into a company—when you've worked it up a bit, you know, and make something out of the sale. You must just let them know, therefore, that you're at 'The Briars,' and I bet you anything you like you'll have a circle of some sort round you in no time, out of which you shall form your company."

But poor Audrey shrank in alarm from these glowing enterprises, which Mr. Candover appeared to evolve so easily, and to realise so quickly.

For a long time it was in vain he talked to her, pointed out how right he had been about her taking the business world by storm with her showrooms, insisted on the duty which devolved upon her of making money for Gerard's sake.

But it was inevitable that, alone as she was but for his help and advice, she should yield at last to his representations; and when he had ascertained for her that the rent she would have to pay for "The Briars" was a mere nominal one, provided she would consent to take on the duchess's servants, Audrey reluctantly consented to take the pretty house at Epsom from the first week in August, when the London season ended and her showrooms were practically shut up, to the first week in October, which was, so Mademoiselle Laure assured her, early enough to begin the autumn fashion campaign.

Young and inexperienced as she was, Audrey could not help thinking, when she found herself in possession at "The Briars," which was a charming house, roomy and tastefully furnished, without any appearance of ostentatious luxury, that she had found everything wonderfully easy so far in her new career.

Mademoiselle Laure was disagreeable, it was true, but she was undoubtedly something of a genius, and she had taken all the real work off her employer's hands. Nothing transpired to clear up the mystery of the lady in white, but not the most minute search on Audrey's part revealed any trace of the tragedy she believed herself to have discovered, nor did anything appear in the daily papers, which she scanned closely for the next week, to throw light upon the affair.

And scarcely was Audrey settled in the house at Epsom, when callers began to arrive in sufficient numbers to justify Mr. Candover's prediction that she would soon have a circle of her own.

Audrey did not care for many of her visitors. Most of them were gentlemen, which she thought strange. But to the pointed inquiries she made to some of them they invariably replied that their wives, daughters and sisters were all away at the seaside or on the continent, which was, she reflected, natural enough in the month of August.

Those ladies who called upon her were of the ultra-smart and aggressive type which Audrey thought more desirable as customers than as friends.

There was Lady Lavering, with the mahogany-coloured hair, whose husband, Sir Richard Lavering, looked old enough to be her great-grandfather. And there was the Hon. Mrs. Lydd, who looked old enough to be her husband's grandmother.

But Audrey, bewildered by her new circumstances, and anxious to profit by the advice given her, was civil to them all, and was such a pathetically attractive figure, in the black she generally wore, with her girlish face and modest manners, that whatever she might think of the style of her new acquaintances, she could not complain of lack of attention, even of enthusiasm, on their part towards her.

She returned the calls of the ladies who lived within calling distance, and within a very short time she had the suggestion made that she should be at home to some of her new acquaintances in the evening. Old Mrs. Lydd and young Lady Lavering both came to the very first of these, and so did Mr. Candover, with his alert young American secretary with the green and gold teeth, and so did quite a dozen gentlemen.

While poor Audrey, not at all pleased to find herself coerced into entertaining against her will, sat with the two ladies in the verandah, enjoying the cool evening air after the hot August day, sounds of the shuffling of tables and the rattling of dice reached her ears, and rising from her chair and peeping into the long drawing-room, she saw that card tables had been produced and opened, and that while poker was being played at the table nearest to where she stood, baccarat was engaging the attention of another group.

She turned, frowning, to her companions.

"I wish they wouldn't play cards," she said. "I have a horror of them."

Instead of expressing agreement or making any comment on her words, Mrs. Lydd and Lady Lavering exchanged a demure look of amusement, which irritated and puzzled her. Presently Lady Lavering indeed joined the baccarat group, and Audrey was left with old Mrs. Lydd, who appeared rather troubled by the enthusiasm which her young husband showed over poker, and vainly tried—being somewhat deaf—to catch the chances of the game from where she sat.

When the old lady got up and went indoors to hear better, Audrey found herself swiftly joined by one of the gentlemen, who paid her such fervent compliments about her beauty, and gazed at her with so much bold admiration that Audrey, with a few chilling words, got up and followed the other ladies into the drawing-room.

By this time the players at the different tables were far too much excited to take any notice of her, and it was with horror that she made the discovery that they were playing for high stakes.

Unable to obtain any attention to her evident displeasure, she looked round for Mr. Candover, whom she found in a corner by himself, an unlighted cigarette between his fingers, pensive and apparently melancholy.

"Mr. Candover," said she, "this is your fault. I think you, who always profess to know so much better than I do what is the right thing, ought to have known better than to expose your friend's wife to this!"

He sprang to his feet, with a look of tender reproach, not wholly unmixed with confusion, in his eyes.

"What—what have I done?" stammered he.

She repeated his words impatiently.

"What have you done? You have brought to my house—or rather you have suggested my bringing there—men whom Gerard would never have allowed me to meet."

"Madame, you astonish me! These men are all of them either very well born or very rich. They are all in the best society, they all belong to the Army and Navy, the Carlton, or——"

"Yes, yes, I daresay. But that's not what I mean. Men without their wives don't count as society at all."

"Sir Richard Lavering and Mr. Lydd, Lord Barre's son, have brought their wives."

Audrey frowned. She did not quite like to say what she thought about either of those ladies.

"It's very difficult to get ladies at all at this time of year."

"Then I don't want their husbands without them," said Audrey sharply.

"You are difficult to please, Madame, to-night. Supposing that the poor fellows are in my own sad plight, and have no wives to bring?"

"Then I should like them to stay away," retorted Audrey. "At any rate I won't have my house used as if it were a gambling club."

"But you used to play poker yourself with Gerard and me and my friends!" objected Mr. Candover rather piteously.

Her face quivered.

"That was very different. Between what I did when Gerard was with me and what I do now, there is, or there ought to be, a wide gulf. I can't understand how a clever man like you can fail to see that."

He looked down at her with an expression of infinite solicitude.

"Perhaps I do see it. Perhaps, seeing it clearly, I yet feel that the course I have proposed to you, the course of conciliating the people who may be of use to you, the making to yourself friends of the Mammon of Unrighteousness in fact, is the best course."

"But I don't like them!" pleaded Audrey. "I don't like the way they behave to me. They think, because I am engaged in business, trade in fact, that they can use my house as they please, and treat me as they please."

"Scarcely that, Madame. You know nobody would dare to treat you in any but the right way in my presence," said Mr. Candover, growing more earnest as he bent to speak low in her ear.

Audrey frowned, finding a difficulty in defining her grievance.

"Of course, they're not openly insulting, I don't mean that. But—there's a subtle difference. Oh, you're a man, why do you pretend not to know between the civility with which a man of this sort treats the women of his own set, and the manner he uses to women whom he looks upon as—as not belonging to his world?"

"Look here, Madame, you must lay aside some of these fine feelings, or you must lay aside the hope of getting on in business. If you like, instead of the men of the Carlton, the Beefsteak and the Jockey Club, I'll bring down next time the members of the Athenæum, including the whole bench of bishops. They won't play cards, they won't pay compliments, but they'll all be too deaf to answer what you say to them, and they won't buy so much as a bonnet," retorted Mr. Candover, impatiently.

"Very well," said Audrey, with spirit, "please bring the bishops next Wednesday."

But when next Wednesday came the bishops did not appear, and the same set as before dropped in one by one. With this difference, that one or two more ladies came.

Audrey, however, liked the members of her own sex still less than she did those of the other who were her guests, and told Mr. Candover so.

But one of the ladies had a beautiful voice, and her husband accompanied her on the piano. Audrey herself played well, and to her great relief the card-tables did not, on this occasion, make their appearance in the drawing-room, where songs from the musical comedies, piquantly rendered, formed the evening's entertainment.

But there was a fine smoking-room with a vaulted ceiling at the other end of the house, where most of the gentlemen spent the evening.

And when, on the following morning, Audrey entered that apartment before the servants did, she found open card-tables, packs of cards and dice, in sufficient numbers to let her know how the majority of her guests had spent, not only the evening, but great part of the night.

# CHAPTER VI

WHAT was she to do? If Mr. Candover had not been her most active if not her only friend, if his manners had not been so tactful, and his delicacy so great that he never came to see her except at her request, she would have left "The Briars," where she felt that she was only nominally mistress of a house which resembled rather a public place of entertainment than a private dwelling, and would have taken refuge in solitary lodgings at the seaside.

But she did not like, she did not dare, to offend such a powerful friend and ally; and besides, painful as in many respects her position was, the truth remained that she had no friends in all the world to whom she could go.

Mrs. Webster, who was in the secret of her troubles about Gerard, was travelling in Scotland, or she would have written to her and suggested that they should stay somewhere together. Her husband's nearest relation, Lord Clanfield, had been offended by the marriage of his nephew with a girl who did not belong to his "set"; and Gerard, who was high-spirited and indignant that his beautiful wife should not be welcomed with the honour she deserved, had retorted by cutting off all communication with his uncle, who, perfectly indifferent to the fact, had never even attempted to make his handsome niece's acquaintance.

In this extremity, feeling the dire need of the companionship of some one to whom she could pour out at least some of the sentiments of her poor little aching heart, Audrey suddenly thought of Mr. Candover's two young daughters, and at once wrote to Pamela, the elder, asking her to request permission to come over to spend an afternoon at "The Briars".

This letter Audrey sent direct to the school at Windsor where the girls were staying.

The next morning came a telegram from Pamela, accepting the invitation jubilantly, in these words:—

"Delighted. Trains awful, will drive from Staines, expect us at one.—PAMELA."

And at one o'clock a fly brought to the gates two smiling, happy girls, overflowing with high spirits, and rejoicing in their holiday.

Audrey felt as if she had come suddenly out of the darkness of a vault into the bright sunshine, so delighted was she, after the distasteful acquaintances and unsympathetic companions of the past few weeks, to find herself once more with these bright, amiable, natural girls, full of the joy of living, and crazily excited over the pleasure of their visit.

"How is it you are able to come so quickly?" asked Audrey, as she led the beaming lassies into the house. "I was afraid it would be a matter of red tape, and that the head of the school would have to write and ask Mr. Candover's permission for you to come, and all that."

Pamela laughed gaily.

"To tell you the truth," she said, "we had a struggle for it. But our lives are so terribly dull, passing not only the terms but the holidays at school as we do, that when we got your invitation, refusal would have led to open revolt. Miss Willett made the usual fuss, of course, and said she 'must ask Mr. Candover'. But when we pointed out that papa had already brought us to see you once already, and when we showed that we were determined to come, she gave way."

"I daresay, Mrs. Angmering," put in Babs, "she wasn't sorry to get rid of us for a few hours, for she can't even go away for a change now, while the holidays are on, because of us."

Audrey looked surprised.

"Why," she said, "I should have thought your father would have been only too glad of the chance of having you with him. He is so fond of you."

"Ye-es, I suppose he is fond of us—when he remembers our existence," said Pamela the ready, with a little shrug.

"Oh, hush, hush, you naughty girl!"

"Well, you must let us be naughty to-day, for we have to be so very, very good all the year round. Oh, what a darling pony!"

She had caught sight, in the paddock beyond the rose-garden, of a little rough-coated animal which Audrey had found in the stables when she took "The Briars". And nothing would satisfy the girls but seizing the pony by the mane, and indulging in impromptu gallops over the field. They were in a state of joyous excitement during luncheon, and afterwards they took Audrey between them, twined their arms round her and walked with her in the pretty shady grounds, bubbling over with happiness at their unexpected holiday, and determined to take advantage of Audrey's offer to have them with her again on the first opportunity.

The delight of the girls at this very simple pleasure was a revelation to Audrey, who had taken it for granted that Mr. Candover, who was so rich and so generous, would have treated his daughters with more consideration for youthful impulses.

Having already made Audrey's acquaintance, the girls now looked upon her as an old friend, and they confided to her the utter loneliness of their lives, and the uncertainty they were in as to their future.

"You know I'm eighteen, and I want to 'come out,'" said Pamela. "And Miss Willett herself thinks it is time I should. But when she writes about it to papa, he doesn't answer, and although he's always kind, he has a way of putting aside any question he doesn't care to answer, so that I've never been able to talk it out with him myself."

"Shall I speak to him for you?" asked Audrey.

"Oh, you darling, I wish you would! It's quite true that I'm dying to leave school now, and to—to—well, I don't exactly know what it is I want to do, except that it isn't lessons!" cried Pamela, whose brilliant beauty and lively manners indeed showed her to be ready to take her first plunge out of the school seclusion into the waters of life.

"And am I to be left all alone?" cried poor Babs plaintively. "It's bad enough with you, Pam, but it will be worse if I'm left with Miss Willett all through the holidays alone, while I know you are enjoying yourself with Mrs. Angmering!"

Audrey caressed her pretty head.

"Supposing," she said, in a voice almost as full of suppressed excitement as that of the girls themselves, "I were to ask Mr. Candover to let you both go away with me somewhere for the Christmas holidays! How would you like that?"

Their answer was such a tumultuous outburst of gratitude and delight that she was, as it were, taken off her feet by it, and the three sat down on a garden seat under a knot of trees, and discussed the idea with noisy and merry comments and peals of laughter which made them all deaf to the sound of approaching footsteps over the gravel paths and the lawn behind them.

They were suddenly startled by the voice of Mr. Candover; and turning quickly with little cries, they were amazed to find themselves face to face, not with the smiling, indulgent father, the chivalrous and kind friend, but with a man whose face was dark with passion, and in whose black eyes there was a look of anger and alarm which struck them dumb, and filled Audrey at least with sudden and strange misgiving.

Mr. Candover looked from her to his daughters, who made no attempt to greet him, so much surprised were they.

"When did I give permission for you to leave your school? What is Miss Willett thinking about to let you come out without it?" asked he sharply.

"Oh, papa," said Pamela, who was the only one who seemed ready to "stand up to" him, "we thought that, in the case of Mrs. Angmering——"

"Hold your tongue. I know nothing of any Mrs. Angmering. You are in the house of Madame Rocada——" Audrey broke into a protest of horror, but he went on, "and you have no business to come out even to see your nearest relations, without my permission. I'm surprised at Miss Willett. Put on your hats, and I will put you in a fly, and you can drive back at once."

Indignant protests on the part of Pamela, tears from Babs, alarm and stupefaction on the face of Audrey, availed nothing.

Within ten minutes the poor girls were driving away, but not before Pamela, with a look of sullen anger and resentment in her lively black eyes, which were so like her father's, had whispered into Audrey's ear:—

"I shall come again, if you'll let me. I'm not a child and I'm not going to be treated as one much longer!"

Poor Audrey did not know what to say, but "Hush, dear, hush!" as she kissed the bright-eyed girl, and waved them both a farewell which was almost tearful.

As soon as they were gone Mr. Candover recovered his usual gentle, kindly manner.

"I hope I didn't hurt your feelings, my dear Madame Rocada, by my bluntness," said he. "But the fact is the girls are both of very difficult character to manage, and it is my particular wish that they should live the quietest of lives, without any dangerous excitements, for a few years longer."

Audrey summoned enough courage for a mild protest.

"Surely it's not a very dangerous excitement to spend the afternoon with me!" she said.

"Of course not. But you forget that you have friends coming——"

Audrey interrupted sharply:—

"Friends! These horrible, noisy, fast men and faster women with their card-playing and their racing jargon are not my friends. Clients, customers, if you like, they may be. But never my friends!"

"Well, they are useful people to know, at least," he persisted, more gently than ever.

Audrey turned away without reply, and the announcement he wished to make to her concerning some of the guests of the evening he had to leave unmade.

It came upon her, therefore, with a shock of surprise when, Mr. Candover having been forced to leave the house, as she gave him no invitation to remain to dine with her, he returned about nine o'clock in the company of half a dozen of the men whom she had had to accept as habitués of the house, and with two young men, both of unmistakably dissipated appearance, who were introduced to her as "Mr. Edgar Angmering" and "Mr. Geoffrey Angmering".

It was with the greatest difficulty that Audrey could keep her countenance. For they were, she knew, the sons of Lord Clanfield, and first cousins of her own husband.

Neither had ever seen her, and she had little difficulty in guessing that they had no idea of the identity of "Madame Rocada".

Whether as a result of the presence of these two noisy young men it is impossible to say, but the evening was an unusually noisy one, and the play was higher than ever.

Moreover, Audrey could not but be aware of the fact that the elder of the two young men had had more champagne than was good for him even before he arrived, and she expressed her indignation and disgust to Mr. Candover in no measured terms.

He was much concerned at her displeasure, and said that they must take care that it did not occur again; this was a rather vague assurance, which had no other result than the reappearance of the two young men a few nights later, in much the same condition as before.

On the following day Audrey wrote an angry letter to Mr. Candover, telling him that she intended to leave "The Briars" without delay, as she would not tolerate any more scenes such as that of the previous night, either in the hope of retaining valuable clients or for any other reason.

She had scarcely finished the letter when a servant came in, and announced: "Lord Clanfield."

Audrey pressed her hand to her heart, which throbbed with frantic excitement. Did he know her? Was he come to make late amends for his neglect of poor Gerard?

She rose from her seat as there entered a dignified man of the middle height, strikingly like Gerard, who indeed resembled him much more closely than did either of his own sons.

Audrey bowed without speaking. She could not, indeed, trust herself to utter a word, even if she had known what to say.

A second glance at his open, honest face showed her that it was with no friendly intention he had come. His first words showed her that it was not to his nephew's wife that his unexpected visit was paid.

"Madame Rocada," said he, in the coldest, sternest of voices, "I have come to request you to do me the favour of forbidding my two sons to enter your house."

A chill seized Audrey. The next moment a sense of resentment rose in her mind and sent a flush to her cheeks.

She looked not only handsome, but stately, as she drew up her tall figure and stood erect in the sunlight, which played upon her golden hair, and sparkled upon the pearl paillettes which studded the dress of cream silk muslin, with a billowy train, which she was wearing.

"Upon what grounds do you make such a singular request, and in such a singular manner?" asked she, subduing her voice to a level and quiet tone.

For one moment he hesitated. Great beauty in a woman compels a sort of respect from any man. And Audrey had never looked lovelier than she did at that moment.

"I regret to have to put it so plainly. I had hoped that you would have spared me the necessity. But since I must be plain, it is because I have just learnt that you, Madame Rocada, are the lady known abroad as the White Countess, the keeper of the Paris gaming-house in which the son of one of my friends, young Hugh Grey, committed suicide two years ago."

# CHAPTER VII

AUDREY was struck dumb.

As if by a flash of lightning, she found her whole mind illuminated, and saw at once the meaning of the visit paid to her showrooms by the lady in white.

The pale, thin woman was, she felt sure, the real Madame Rocada, and it was the discovery that another woman was setting up in business under her name which brought the vengeful stranger on the visit which had turned out so fatally for herself.

The sudden understanding of the strange events in which she had been forced to take so active a part not only paralysed Audrey, but made her feel as if this direct attack were quite a secondary matter.

For there was the question of the disappearance of the White Countess to be met. And though indeed she had heard nothing of the matter since the evening when she had seen the white-clad lady lying, as she believed, dead in the fitting-room, there was suddenly borne in upon her in all its dreadful force the conviction that this was not the end, that she would be forced to hear more about the tragedy by-and-by.

Instead, therefore, of indignantly meeting the charge thus unexpectedly brought against her by the viscount, she drew a long breath, tried to speak, faltered, and seeming to lose her physical strength and her courage at the same time, put out her hand for the support of the writing-table from which she had just risen, and leaned upon it, swaying slightly, and looking, as she felt, the picture of utter distress and dismay.

Absolutely as he believed in her guilt, Lord Clanfield, a chivalrous gentleman, to whom this duty of rescuing his sons from the clutches of the keeper of a gaming-house was utterly distasteful, was extremely distressed by her behaviour.

He was far too simple-minded and unsophisticated, being rather a quiet country gentleman than a man of the world, to have recognised at once, what a shrewder man would have done, the improbability that this fresh-looking young woman could be the same person as the notorious Madame Rocada, whose wiles had brought about the death of the son of his friend.

At the same time, the effect of her extraordinary beauty and of the straightforward dignity of her manner was such that he felt exceedingly uncomfortable, and almost wished that he had not insisted upon taking this matter into his own hands, instead of leaving it to be managed by his solicitors.

After what seemed to both a very long pause, he said, with a change of tone:—

"I regret exceedingly to be forced to this course, Madame Rocada. I have, however, no choice. My sons are, unfortunately, extravagant and difficult to control, and I have therefore thought it best to come straight to you, to ask you to help me in this matter."

Now this speech, uttered in a much less severe tone than his previous words, showed a distinct advance in the direction of friendliness.

Whether or not there was already some doubt in the viscount's mind, he seemed to wish to qualify his blunt accusation.

To Audrey, however, this was a matter of no moment. The statement remained uncontradicted, the awful accusation of her having been a party to, or in some way concerned in, the death of a man.

With this in her mind, she did not appear to hear or understand this second speech, but, as soon as she had recovered herself a little, went straight back to the first.

"What you say of me is wholly untrue," she said in a low, breathless voice. "My name——" Suddenly a flood of blushes suffused her pale face. How could she tell him what her name was? How introduce to the already indignant and reproachful visitor the knowledge that she was the wife of the nephew whom he no doubt believed to be a forger and a swindler? After a short pause she went on, while he waited quietly for her without interruption: "I have nev——"

She stopped again.

"Do you mean to say you have never been to Paris?" asked the viscount, less harshly, but still with evident incredulity.

Audrey raised her head in desperation.

"No. I did not mean that. I have been in Paris. I was there last winter."

Her voice faltered, for she remembered the joy of that merry time. She and Gerard had spent part of their honeymoon there.

After another pause she went on:—

"But I have never kept a gaming-house, I do not keep one now. I have never heard of your friend Grey. I have never had a hand in anybody's death. Your accusation is absurd. As for your sons, I do not want them here. They were brought here, without any invitation from me, by one of my acquaintances. They shall never come here again. And my name is not Madame Rocada. That is merely a trade name, and is not even of my own choosing."

Lord Clanfield looked at her keenly. He was interested, in spite of himself, in this woman, whose manners and appearance were, he felt sure, quite different from those of the ordinary adventuress he had believed her to be. He hesitated, and then said, looking at her with a scrutinising gaze as he spoke:—

"And may I ask what your name really is?"

If there had been even a little kindliness, a little unbending, in his tone and manner, Audrey might perhaps have been tempted to tell him the whole truth as to her identity, and even to plead with him on behalf of that nephew whom she was sure he cruelly misjudged.

But Lord Clanfield, though he was perplexed, was not outwardly softened. If anything, indeed, he was inclined to be indignant that the keeper of a gaming-house, as he believed her to be, should be so amply endowed by nature, so well-bred in manner, as to increase the danger of her acquaintance for susceptible young men.

So Audrey merely said:—

"My name is an honourable one, and I have done nothing to disgrace it."

And as she spoke the thought of poor Gerard, going through the terrible humiliation and hardship of penal servitude, with his heart breaking on her account, suddenly overwhelmed her, and she turned abruptly, and walked away down the long room, afraid of an outburst of tears.

If she had given way to this impulse, if she had broken down into the open and uncontrollable grief which possessed her, it is possible that Lord Clanfield's pity might have been excited, and that a full confession on her part might have followed.

But whether such a confession would have been to the advantage of herself and Gerard is, perhaps, open to question. And it was some inkling of the enormous difficulty of her position in this respect which acted even more powerfully than her sense of dignity in enabling Audrey to control her emotions, and to retire abruptly from the contest.

There was nothing left to Lord Clanfield but to withdraw, with such conventional words of thanks as he could muster for her promise to refuse admittance to his sons. She bowed without a word, and the painful interview came to an abrupt end.

Audrey was left in a state bordering on stupefaction.

Before her on the table lay her letter to Mr. Candover, not yet put into its envelope. She took it up mechanically, read it, and wished she had handed it to Lord Clanfield. At least he would have seen then how anxious she was to get away from this place, how angry she was at the scenes which had taken place there.

But on the other hand, the letter would have been an acknowledgment that there had been scenes of a disagreeable kind; and, though the viscount would have seen that she had influential friends, as Mr. Candover was a man well known in society, Audrey reflected, with a pang of bitterness, that the men friends of an unprotected woman, however influential they may be, are not looked upon as witnesses to character.

And, realising that her complaints to Mr. Candover, however well founded and however passionate, would in all probability be met by him with his usual soothing assurances that she was very well off, and that she ought to take the drawbacks of her position with philosophy, Audrey tore up the letter, and wrote another, not to him, but to the only woman friend who knew of at least one and the greatest of her troubles.

This was Mrs. Webster, a kindly, honest-hearted woman, of mature age, yet not too old as to have lost touch with life and society, and one upon whose goodness of heart she knew that she could rely.

This was what she said:—

"Dear Mrs. Webster,

"I know you are away, so I am sending this letter to your flat to be forwarded, for I want you to come and see me as soon as you are back in town. I have taken this place for two months, one of which has now expired, I am happy to say. You don't know that I've taken a business under the name of 'Madame Rocada,' and though I hate the name and mean to give it up, you had better direct to me by it, as it is the only one I am known by here. I am so terribly lonely, and am in a position of great difficulty for want of some one to advise me, so please, please come and see me as soon as ever you return to town.

"Yours most sincerely,
"Audrey."

She got an answer almost by return of post, to say that Mrs. Webster was already back in town and would come to "The Briars" on the following day.

In the meantime Audrey passed her time in a state of great uncertainty as to what she would do when she left "The Briars," as she had no doubt that Mrs. Webster would advise her to do.

On the one hand she knew that it was hopeless to expect to get, by her own unaided efforts, into another position where she would have a chance of making money, such as she undoubtedly had now.

On the other hand, as she had sunk all the capital she could spare in the flourishing business she had established, there would be very little for her to live upon if she were to throw it up and retire into obscurity in some quiet seaside place, which was the plan she had in her mind.

When Mrs. Webster arrived, as she did just before luncheon-time, Audrey's heart beat high with pleasure and excitement. They had not seen one another since Audrey left her flat, and Mrs. Webster, who was the widow of a barrister, living in modest comfort on a small income which did not allow much margin for dress, was electrified by the magnificence of Audrey's dress and surroundings.

"My dear child," she exclaimed, as she looked at the pretty gown of grey silk muslin trimmed with strips of gorgeous Indian embroidery, "how smart you are! You make me ashamed of my old rags! And how splendidly you're installed here! Good gracious, have you come into a fortune?"

And the good lady looked from Audrey to the beautiful room and the masses of flowers and palms which decorated it, with a slightly dubious uplifting of the eyebrows.

"No, of course not. Sit down, and I'll tell you all about it. I told you I'd gone into business, didn't I? Well, this is part of the stock-in-trade. I've only got this house for another month, but I don't want to keep it even as long as that. Listen."

And she poured into her friend's sympathetic ear the whole history of her start in her new career, of the energetic help given her by Mr. Candover, the prosperous beginning of the business, and then the terrible scene of the coming of the lady in white, of the mystery of her disappearance, and finally she told of her renting "The Briars," and of the card-playing that went on there in spite of her.

Mrs. Webster listened with the keenest interest, but to Audrey's astonishment, she did not share her views as to the impossibility of her retaining her present position.

It was even apparent that she was inclined to share the opinion expressed by Dr. Fendall, that part at least of the extraordinary story she told about the white-robed lady was the result of her imagination.

"If it had all really happened, my dear, I don't see how it is possible to account for your hearing no more of it," she added sagely.

Audrey, though rather discouraged by this attitude on the part of her friend, went on to narrate the circumstances of her coming to "The Briars," of the numerous acquaintances and neighbours who at once visited her, and of the high play in which they indulged under her roof.

Again, to her dismay, Mrs. Webster was more impressed by the rank and position of these visitors than by the gambling in which they indulged.

"Lord Gourock and Sir William Dymchurch!" she exclaimed, with manifest enjoyment of the titles. "Why, they're quite distinguished people, my dear, and I should think you ought to be proud to have them for your friends. As for their playing cards, why, everybody does it nowadays, women as well as men, and particularly people of fashion, such as your visitors are! I cannot understand what you have to complain about."

"Well, they are noisy, some of them," said Audrey, beginning to fear that she had found another opponent in seeking an ally. "And just now I wanted to live so quietly! It seems dreadful to me to have all this going on under what is for the time, at any rate, my roof, when I feel, as I've told you, as if I should like to shut myself up in a convent and never see anybody!"

"That would never do," said Mrs. Webster with decision. "It would be bad for you, and it wouldn't do any good to your poor husband."

"Well, listen to this," said Audrey impatiently, as she went on to narrate her very latest grievance, the visit of Lord Clanfield, and his astounding accusation.

To that Mrs. Webster replied by a question:—

"Well, and what does Mr. Candover say to that?"

"I haven't seen him since, to ask him," she answered. "And to tell you the truth I thought it was better to consult a woman than to have to ask a man about it. I don't want to be dependent for everything upon the advice of Mr. Candover."

"Well, of course it's better to have friends of your own sex too," admitted Mrs. Webster. "But as Mr. Candover was such an intimate friend of your husband's, there can't be much harm in speaking to him, as he knows everything too!" she added in a discreet undertone. "And he's such a very nice man, so handsome, so well-bred, and so nice about his daughters!"

"Ye-es," said Audrey, who knew that a certain vague mistrust in her mind had better not be too openly insisted on as yet. "But what do you think about his having suggested to me this name Rocada? Don't you see that it has put me into a very unpleasant position? Perhaps some others among these people who come think I am the woman who kept a gaming-house in Paris!"

This was certainly not a pleasant suggestion, and Mrs. Webster, after a little reflection, offered to stay at "The Briars" and to be present at one of the evenings which caused Audrey so much distress. The offer was accepted with gratitude, and Mrs. Webster telegraphed to her housekeeper that she would not be home until the following day, and spent not only the day but the night with her unhappy friend.

That very evening the guests arrived in numbers, as they did regularly every Wednesday and Friday. There was the usual preponderance of the male sex, but there were quite enough ladies present to make Mrs. Webster decide that Audrey was too prudish in her strictures.

Mr. Candover, who came early, expressed himself delighted to see Mrs. Webster, and at once opened a long confidential conversation with her, in which he quite won her heart by his earnest solicitude for the poor unprotected young wife, and by the bitter regret he expressed that he had not been in England at the time of poor Gerard's trial, to give him any help which might have been in his power.

He brought tears to the good lady's eyes, and when he told her of the difficulty he experienced in persuading Audrey to do what was best for herself and her husband, and of the obstacles she put in the way of everything that was done for her, Mrs. Webster grew quite indignant at Audrey's stupid obstinacy, and begged him to be patient with her, and to remember the state of over-wrought nerves in which she must be after the terrible excitement and trouble of her husband's trial.

"I do remember that indeed," said he in a low voice. "And I think myself it accounts for some most singular delusions which she has undoubtedly suffered from of late, delusions so strange that they made me quite unhappy as to her mental balance."

"Do you mean the story about the lady in white?" asked Mrs. Webster in a whisper.

Mr. Candover nodded.

"And the visit of Lord Clanfield, and his accusing her of being a woman called the 'White Countess,' who once kept a gaming-house in Paris, do you think that is a delusion too?"

He raised his eyebrows.

"I've heard nothing about that," said he.

"Oh, well then, don't say I said anything about it to you. No doubt she'll tell you about it herself. She seemed very much upset, poor thing!"

In the meantime Audrey, who had a vague consciousness of the existence near her of some perfect organisation which worked out all its ends in an admirable way, recognised the fact that on this particular evening, when she was anxious to prove to Mrs. Webster the difficulty of her position, there was nothing whatever in the demeanour or the actions of her unwelcome visitors to give the slightest colour to her complaints.

One room was, indeed, set apart for cards, but no sounds of undue excitement came thence to the drawing-room, where music and conversation formed the entertainment of the rest of the guests.

Audrey was uneasy, excited, miserable, afraid that the sons of Lord Clanfield might insist upon defying her prohibition to the servants to admit them, and anxious yet nervous about the talk she must have with Mr. Candover.

In the meantime, while he was occupied in conversation with Mrs. Webster, Audrey had a shrewd yet vague suspicion that he was having it all his own way, and persuading the impressionable lady into taking exactly his own views.

Audrey passed through the long drawing-room and glanced into the end room at right angles with it, where the card-playing was going on.

By this time there were certain faces which she knew she might always be sure of seeing on these evenings, and she mentally made a note of them as she looked.

There was Lord Gourock, conspicuous for his perfectly bald head and the heavy white moustache which seemed to have absorbed all his powers of hair-producing. Passive as a statue, with dull yet not unobservant eyes, he sat there, apparently indifferent to whether he gained or lost, as long as he played.

There were two silly-looking youths who put on airs of blasé middle age, and who were, she knew, the sons of men who had made a great deal of money in trade. She knew that both of them always lost heavily, and she wished she could find an opportunity of pointing out to them how silly they were to go on playing in the circumstances. She supposed that they must both be very careless in play or very stupid, for the luck to be so constantly against them.

There was Durley Diggs, Mr. Candover's secretary. He, too, generally complained of having lost, and always got into a state of great elation if he won two or three pounds. He did not care what he played at, poker, baccarat, roulette, it was all the same to him, and he went from table to table, always alert, neat, trim, bright of speech yet quiet in manner, and always perfectly equable of temper even when his fellow-players, as sometimes happened, grew peevish and ill-tempered.

They were not noisy. Except when the young Clanfields, or one or two strangers were of the party, it was remarkable how quiet they all were. Audrey even thought sometimes, when only the habitués were present, that the silence in which they all staked and won or lost was uncanny.

There was another man whom she generally saw in the rooms, the heavy, solemn-looking Jim Johnson, Madame de Vicenza's steward or secretary, Audrey did not exactly know which—who had accompanied her and Durley Diggs to the police court to arrange bail for Gerard.

Audrey noticed how modest this man was, how shy and awkward, how he always avoided the ordeal of greeting her or of bidding her good-bye.

He, too, was generally present, and Audrey thought that he was perhaps instructed by the duchess to frequent the place as much as possible in her absence, to see that no damage was done to the premises while they were sublet.

On this occasion Audrey, glancing round the card-room, saw Johnson's face in profile, and was at once struck by a fact which she was surprised that she had not previously noticed, the extraordinary resemblance between him and the Dr. Fendall whom Mademoiselle Laure had called in on the eventful evening when the white lady appeared at the showrooms and disappeared from them so strangely.

The more she looked, the more certain she felt that the two men must be brothers. There was the same heavy protruding jaw, the same light blue eyes, the same slightly aquiline nose; both were of about the same height, were round-shouldered, and stooped a good deal.

The only noticeable points of difference, indeed, were the fact that while Johnson was clean-shaved, Dr. Fendall wore a greyish moustache, and that whereas the secretary used no glasses, the doctor wore gold-rimmed spectacles.

The longer Audrey looked, the more struck was she by this resemblance, and Johnson himself soon became aware of her curious gaze, grew uneasy under it, glanced at her apprehensively again and again, and finally, at the first opportunity, sprang up from the table at which he was playing and made a dash for the door at the opposite end of the room from that at which Audrey stood.

But she was determined to question him; and retreating hastily through the drawing-room she slipped out quietly into the hall, and came, as she had expected to do, face to face with Johnson, who was in the act of finding his hat from a pile on the hall table.

"Mr. Johnson," said she, "I want to ask you something."

He bowed without speaking, but looked very uncomfortable.

"You are a brother of Dr. Fendall, are you not?"

He burst into an awkward, self-conscious laugh.

"Why, yes, I am," said he. "I am a brother of his. Do—do you know him?"

Audrey looked at him curiously, with a sudden suspicion.

"Then how is it," she asked quickly, "that you haven't the same name?"

# CHAPTER VIII

BEFORE Johnson could answer, Audrey heard Mr. Candover's voice behind her, and turning, she received his answer for the strangely perturbed secretary.

"Mr. Johnson," said he, "is only Dr. Fendall's half-brother; that's why they don't bear the same surname."

"I see."

In that short interruption Johnson had found time to escape, not by the front-door, but back to the card-room, and Mr. Candover, who looked more excited than he usually allowed himself to appear, asked Audrey why she looked so cross.

She was strung up, agitated, eager for the contest with this man whose subtle advice always led her into such difficult places.

"Do I?" she said, putting strong constraint upon herself, and forcing herself to speak calmly, though her eyes blazed and her lips trembled. "Well, I think I am cross. At any rate I'm disgusted, and I'm sure, if you can't guess all the reasons why I am so, you know some of them at least."

"Let us come in here, where we can talk," said he, as he opened the door of the conservatory, near which they were standing. He arranged for her one of the cane-seated lounge chairs which stood about among the flowers, and invited her, with a winning smile, to seat herself in the pile of cushions which he collected from the other seats round him. But she would not sit down. She felt at greater advantage when she could move about, and meet his eyes on the same level as her own.

He was determined to help her in his own way, and he was, she knew, prepared to do battle with her over her fixed resolve to abandon the career he had mapped out for her. And weak though she always felt in the presence of this man with the various arts which he knew so well how to use, the crisis had come, and she felt that she would, she must be strong enough to resist his will.

"Now," said he, leaning back against the glass wall that shut them in, and looking at her with his usual placid and amiable smile, "what is the matter?"

"I'm going away from this place," said Audrey bluntly. "I don't like the people who come here, and I don't like the scenes I am exposed to. And I'm sure you know why."

He had changed his attitude, and his handsome face expressed great astonishment and perplexity.

"But we have talked that out, and I thought you had seen the necessity of taking the rough with the smooth," objected he. "What are you going to do if you give this up?"

"I don't know and I don't care," said Audrey angrily. "But I won't have noisy men like the Angmerings here, and I won't be exposed to the insults of their father any longer."

"Insults! What insults?"

Audrey looked at him askance. She had a very shrewd suspicion that he must have heard all about it already, but she said:—

"Lord Clanfield came here the day before yesterday, and accused me of being a woman called the 'White Countess,' who was concerned in the death of a man. She was the keeper of a Paris gaming-house. But of course you knew. And I want to learn how, knowing her as you must have done, you dared to advise me to call myself by the name of such a woman!"

Horribly frightened by her own boldness, Audrey poured out this tirade at a rapid rate, trying by firmness and clearness of tone to deceive herself into thinking that she was not horribly alarmed.

Mr. Candover took it very quietly, and after a short pause laughed.

"I see, I see. I was afraid those young cubs would frighten you!"

"Lord Clanfield," interrupted Audrey sharply, "requested me not to admit them into my house."

"I should imagine you were not very anxious to admit them," said Mr. Candover. "Nobody else is. As for Lord Clanfield, he's an old crank; won't allow bagatelle on Sundays—if anybody ever wants to play that innocent game on that or any other day! And as for the young cubs, they wouldn't come to much harm here or anywhere else, for there's very little they don't know! I'm very angry that you should have been annoyed by the old fool, but he's an annoyance to everybody. You didn't let him know you were his nephew's wife?"

"No—o—o, though I rather wish I had!" sighed Audrey. "But I told him I was not Madame Rocada, and what I want to know is why you, who must have known all about there being a real woman of that name, the keeper of a gaming-house, should have advised me to call myself by it!"

Her tone was fierce and angry, and Mr. Candover grew earnest as he answered.

"Believe me I never heard of this woman, and I don't believe she ever existed. It was Marie Laure who suggested the name Rocada to me, as being new and striking. And I am sure that this old Clanfield, who is as muddle-headed as one of his own sheep, has got hold of the wrong name. Surely you don't suppose I should have chosen you a name with ugly associations attached to it?"

"I shouldn't have suspected you of such a thing," retorted Audrey, "until I had proof of it."

Mr. Candover protested, growing more and more earnest, reproachful, tender, until they were interrupted by an altercation going on in the hall, and a moment later they saw the two young sons of Lord Clanfield emerging victorious from a sort of polite tussle with the footman, who had informed them clearly and distinctly that Madame Rocada was not at home.

"All right, old chap," said the younger, Geoffrey, a little fellow five feet two inches high, who cultivated the appearance and manners of a stableman so well that even in evening clothes he looked more like his ideal than the son of a man of rank.

The elder brother laughed loudly, but did not join in the discussion. He was very tall and sloping of shoulder, good-looking in a vacuous and brainless fashion, and good-natured to excess.

The two young men evidently looked upon the professed attempt to keep them out as the merest pretence, and when Audrey hurried out of the conservatory and stood in their way, they both bowed to her with the most impudent of half-concealed smiles on their faces.

"I am exceedingly sorry that this should have happened," said she in a low voice, as soon as she had dismissed the footman by a look. "I gave orders that you were to be told, Mr. Angmering, that I was not at home, and gentlemen usually understand what that means."

The elder of the two had the sense to perceive that the lady was in earnest, but the younger, who was as usual in rather an elated condition, laughed as he said:—

"Well, we didn't take it seriously, you know. We looked upon it as a good joke, for we know how hospitable you are, Madame Rocada, and we enjoyed ourselves so awfully the other night——"

"Lord Clanfield," interrupted Audrey icily, "desires that you should not come here, and I desire it also."

Both the young men began to smile.

"Oh, that's it, is it?" said the younger. "I give you my word you needn't worry your head about Lord Clanfield. We certainly shan't tell him we've been here, you know."

The elder of the two young men had by this time seen that they had made some mistake, and he was exceedingly anxious to silence his more obtuse brother. In the meantime he made apologies, sincere and not ungraceful, for their behaviour.

"There's some mistake. We certainly never wished to intrude, Madame," said he. "Of course, if you wish, we'll go away at once."

The younger, however, was indignant at what he considered his brother's stupidity.

"I should have thought, Madame," he said stiffly and aggressively, "that Lord Clanfield's sons were good enough for the rest of your company. I suppose the fact is you've found out that there's a convict in the family, and——"

Audrey, caught unawares, uttered a low but piercing cry. To hear her darling husband thus spoken of, in this brutal and callous manner, was too much for her overwrought nerves. To the consternation of the two young men, who beat a hasty retreat from the house, perplexed and abashed, she staggered and fell back against the door of the conservatory.

She would have fallen backwards, as the door gave way, but for the supporting arm of Mr. Candover, who had been an unseen witness of this scene from his post of observation among the palms and the flowers.

"Audrey, my darling, my darling," whispered he in tones that froze her blood. He was holding her tightly in his arms, his fiery eyes glowing close to her face.

With all her suspicions justified, her doubts, her fears, the unhappy woman struggled, at first weakly, then with sudden vigour, to release herself from the grasp of the man whom she now feared and almost loathed, recognising in him, as she did, in one sudden flash of illumination, her evil genius if not that of her husband also.

"Let me go, Mr. Candover, let me go."

They were within the conservatory doors, which he had contrived to close without releasing her. Still holding her fast, he looked with passionate eyes into her face and whispered:—

"Let you go? Let you go? No, Audrey, no. I've loved you, waited for a kind word from you, patiently, humbly. But one can't be humble and patient for ever. Audrey, you've never been loved before, you don't know what it is to hold a man's heart in your hand, as you hold mine!"

Audrey listened in dumb terror. Loathing the very touch of this man in his new aspect, panting to get free from him, she yet felt the horrible power he possessed, and dreaded its effect upon her.

Waiting for her opportunity, she suddenly tore herself away, and facing him with fierce eyes, cried:—

"You can speak so to me, *you*. The friend of my husband, the man who professed so much for my poor Gerard!"

But Mr. Candover had either forgotten his prudence, or felt that he needed it no longer. Coming closer to her, and trying once more to clasp her in his arms, he cried in a tone of the utmost scorn:—

"Gerard! Gerard! Why do you pretend to care about him? Why keep up the farce of believing him to be what you know he is not? Why not snap your fingers at the memory of the wretch, when you know, and I know, and everybody knows, that his punishment was a just one, that he was a forger and a thief!"

# CHAPTER IX

I<small>F</small> the skies had fallen, poor Audrey could not have been more utterly bewildered, dismayed and shocked than she was by this frank and deliberate statement of Mr. Candover's that he believed Gerard to be guilty of the crime for which he was suffering.

That this chivalrous and kind-hearted gentleman, this devoted friend and helper, should thus suddenly transform himself before her eyes, not only into a traitor to his friend, but into an accuser, a traducer, was so unexpected, so appalling to the young and simple-minded woman and devoted wife that for a few moments she was paralysed, she could neither reproach him nor reply to him.

Mr. Candover, meanwhile, was not at a loss. With his eyes still glowing, his face still flushed, he presently went on, coming nearer to her, and speaking with the same passion as before:—

"Why do you hesitate to admit the truth, that you also know your wretched husband to be unworthy a thought? He didn't even care for you. Lovely as you are, you were never in his eyes the one treasure, the one priceless pearl, that such a woman as you deserved to be. Hateful as the task is, I could prove to you that he never cared for you as he ought to have done, that the money of which he robbed his employers was not spent on you."

By the time he had said these words Audrey had had time to recover from her first stupefaction, and to review her forces mentally.

And to this bewilderment, this horror, there succeeded a mighty fear. Who was this man whom she had believed so good, so kind, such a true friend? What were his motives in uttering these vile words? No passion, however unlawful, however wild, could have prompted an outbreak so violent, so wicked, against the friend he had professed to love and pity.

Did he believe what he said? Was he one of the great army of the outside world, who looked upon Gerard as a criminal well punished? She was frightened, amazed, perplexed rather than passionate or indignant. It was as if the rock on which she had relied had crumbled away, and it was this thought which she expressed when at last she spoke.

Standing by one of the lounge-chairs, and clutching the back tightly, as much for support as to put a barrier between her and the man who had so instantly become in her eyes a sort of demon, she said in a low-pitched, dull voice:—

"And I thought you our friend! I trusted you! And so did he!"

The words were so simple, so free from any trace of affectation or indignation in their unshaken loyalty to her own husband and bewilderment at his friend's change of face, that even Mr. Candover, practised man of the world as he was, was rather thrown off his balance by them, and at a loss what to say.

Since it was evident that his accusations of Gerard had only recoiled on himself, it was useless to go on in the same strain. While to make love again to a woman who stared blankly and apprehensively at him as if at an enraged animal was equally out of the question.

This being the case, Mr. Candover speedily recognised the fact that his attack had been premature, and took refuge in the usual protestations of humility, and of despair at her displeasure.

"And you were right to trust me," he said, after a pause, during which she had continued to look at him with the same steady and scarcely veiled abhorrence. "I think, Madame, you will own I have shown myself worthy of your trust, since it was not until I was driven out of myself by contemplation of your unhappy position that I allowed you even to guess at the feelings which possess me, the passionate longing to protect you with which your lonely position fills me."

"I thank you very much for your kind feelings, but I hope you will not again express them in the same manner," answered Audrey, not indeed with the quiet dignity she would have liked to show, but in an unsteady voice and with little gasps for breath between her words. "And please, first of all, to remember not to call me Madame. I won't be called by that hateful name any longer, whether Lord Clanfield has made a mistake or not about the woman he calls the 'White Countess'. And if you don't tell these people that it's not my name, and that I am not a countess, and have no wish to pretend to be one, why, I shall tell them so myself."

Mr. Candover's eyes were covered at that moment by his downcast eyelids, so that she could not see the look of dismay and rage that shone in them. But she was thankful to see that he had entirely regained his self-command when he looked up and quietly said:—

"And what name do you mean to take? Do you mean to use your own?"

The question was a stab to her. And the shame of her position, the bitterness she felt on account of poor Gerard, cut her so keenly that she could not answer, but stood with her teeth pressed upon her lower lip, and her hands tightly clenched.

She felt that the position in which she found herself was intolerable, and a spirit of fierce resentment took the place of the anguish and fear caused by Mr. Candover's previous behaviour. Disdaining to answer him, and too well aware, indeed, that she would have found a satisfactory reply difficult to make, Audrey, with a gesture which implied that her patience was worn out, swept out of the conservatory without another word.

She saw no more of Mr. Candover that evening, but when she returned to the drawing-room, where her absence had caused Mrs. Webster some uneasiness and surprise, she found two of the gentlemen waiting to take leave of her.

One of these was Durley Diggs, the active little American secretary; the other was a young man in whom Audrey took something of an uneasy interest.

This was a baronet of about two and twenty, a tall, good-looking and good-natured young man who had not long come into the money which he had inherited with his father's estates, and who showed, she thought, most unwise tendencies in the matter of his companions and of his amusements.

Audrey was just in the mood to be reckless of consequences, for she had quite made up her mind not to be the figure-head of this establishment any longer. The scenes which she had gone through with the young Angmerings and with Mr. Candover had left their traces upon her outward demeanour. She was flushed, excited, her mouth was set in a fashion which caused the clever and observant Durley Diggs to note her every movement, her every look, from where he stood behind Sir Harry Archdale.

"I've been most awfully unlucky, Madame Rocada," said the young baronet with the utmost good humour, as he shook hands with her.

"Why do you play then, if you always lose?" she asked, with surprising frankness.

"Well, really, Madame, your house is such a pleasant one, and one enjoys oneself so much here," he answered, after a moment's pause, "that, when one sees other people playing, one must play too."

"I should not, if I found that I always lost," said Audrey, with more and more point, as she noticed that Durley Diggs was moving about uneasily behind Sir Harry. "At least, I should not play in the same house or with the same people, when I found myself always losing."

"By Jove, I believe your plan would be the wisest," answered Sir Harry, after another bewildered pause, during which he had been struck by the fact that the lady was not speaking in jest, as he had at first supposed, but in deadly earnest, with firm lips and grave eyes.

"Who did you play with?" she again asked abruptly.

But at that point Durley Diggs came forward and held out his hand, with the conventional murmurs about "a pleasant evening".

"Have you lost too?" asked Audrey sharply, speaking with more abruptness than she was aware of.

The secretary suddenly changed colour, hesitated a moment, and then answered in so reserved and strange a manner that Audrey, who had put her question in all good faith, had her suspicions roused at once.

"I—I—I lost at first, but—but on the whole evening, I think I came out fairly well," he said, with a curious half-look, veiled and cautious, at the young man by his side.

Sir Harry laughed.

"Well," said he, "if you did as well all round——"

Then he checked himself, as Diggs looked up with an angry eye. "Fortune of war, fortune of war!" laughed Sir Harry, as he again turned to his hostess. "Madame Rocada——"

But Audrey interrupted him sharply.

"Don't call me by that name," said she with decision. "It is not mine; somebody suggested it as a name to use in business, but I hate it and do not mean to be called by it any longer."

"What am I to call you then? Just Madame?" said the young man, rather taken aback by the anger and petulance she showed.

For one moment she hesitated, regretting already that she had said so much. Then recovering herself a little, she answered:—

"Well, there will be no need to call me anything but just 'Madame' during the few days I shall remain here."

"Few days! Oh, I hope you are not going away?"

"I only took this house for two months and the time is nearly over," said Audrey.

"Then I shall come and see you in London, and buy bonnets," laughed Sir Harry. "I'll set up my whole family in headgear, and you shall teach me to have a nice taste in hats."

"I shall not be there either," she answered shortly. "Really, I am nothing but a figure-head there. It is a clever Frenchwoman named Laure who does all the work."

To all this Durley Diggs, who remained near them, listened with attentive ears. The young baronet was not to be put off.

"You won't shake me off so easily as that, Madame," said he, with the daring of youth and good spirits. "Wherever you go I shall find you out, and as long as you will allow me to continue your acquaintance, I shall show myself grateful for the privilege."

She could not help relaxing into a smile at these words, which were uttered in too boyish and withal courteous a manner to be displeasing.

But she did not hold out any hopes, or give him any invitation, and the last glance he gave at her face revealed to him plainly the fact that she was ill at ease.

It was, as usual, very late before all the guests left the house, and Mrs. Webster was too sleepy to talk much that night.

But when she and Audrey met at breakfast on the following morning, she combated most strenuously the decision of the younger lady to give up both her new acquaintances and the business which they supported so royally. On the contrary, everything she had seen and heard on the previous evening convinced Mrs. Webster that there was nothing serious in Audrey's objections to her new mode of life, except that natural disinclination of a woman with a heavy heart to be in a circle where so much gaiety went on.

"Perfectly harmless gaiety, as far as I could see," went on the good lady, who had enjoyed her little talks with barons and baronets, men of note in the great world, and women who, if somehow they were a little less satisfactory than the men whose names they bore, were beautifully dressed and all attractive in one way or another.

Audrey leaned back in her chair.

"I have something else to tell you about," said she in a dull voice, "something which will, I think, make even you change your mind. Mr. Candover presumed last night to—to——"

Mrs. Webster looked at her with apprehension.

"Make love to you?" she suggested with her lips rather than said.

Audrey's reply was a burst of tears.

"Of course I ought to have been prepared," she sobbed, "at least I suppose I ought! Men of that type look upon women who have no one to protect them as fair game. But oh, I had thought he was different! For he has been really kind, and I've been really grateful!"

"There, there, don't fret, dear. It's one of the misfortunes of your good looks to be exposed to that sort of thing. But I didn't think it of Mr. Candover. The way he speaks of you is always quite charming! You must give him the cold shoulder, for a time at least, and I don't suppose you will have anything to complain of again."

Audrey sat up and dried her eyes.

"No, I don't suppose I shall. He seemed very sorry and ashamed of himself," admitted she. "But still it breaks one's heart to have to be always on the defensive with everybody. And he said things—other things, that I can't forgive. So that, while I mean to let him know that I won't have anything to say to him for the future, I can't get over what he did say."

Mrs. Webster looked curious.

"It was something about—about my poor Gerard," said Audrey, so quickly, with such evident reluctance, that her friend guessed at once something of the nature of the offending speech.

"Well, my dear, you have always other friends to come to," the kind-hearted lady said gently. "Remember that. If you have really had to quarrel with Mr. Candover permanently—which I should be sorry for—at least you can always depend upon such help as I can give, and upon my standing by you through thick and thin."

"I know I can," said Audrey, with a grateful but tearful look.

Mrs. Webster did not go back to town till the afternoon, and when Audrey had driven her to the station in the little pony-carriage, and driven back again, she was told that Sir Harry Archdale had called, and that he was in the drawing-room.

Audrey went straight into the long, sunny apartment, where the soft afternoon light came in filtered through tinted curtains and mellowed by the outstretched roof of the wide veranda.

The young man came to meet her with a rather shy and hesitating manner.

"I do hope you won't be very much offended, Madame, by my coming," said he. "I know you don't usually receive except in the evenings. But the fact is——" He paused, and evidently found a difficulty in choosing suitable words. Audrey, however, would not help him. She stood waiting for him to go on, with fear in her great eyes. "Well, you said something to me last night, something very kind, that set me thinking, and that—Really, I'm awfully afraid of what you'll say, but——"

At last she felt bound to help him out. For the poor fellow hesitated, and floundered, and blushed, and stammered, so that it was quite impossible to make any sense of the words he uttered. Audrey, feeling sure that this was a visitor of whom she had no need to be afraid, smiled and sat down, saying:—

"Can I help you? I wanted you not to play cards if you always lost."

"That's it! That's the very thing I meant," cried he in relief. "I wanted to tell you—I've thought over it a great deal, and of course I would never have hinted at such a thing if you had not started the subject yourself. But—there's a man one meets here who is always lucky, extraordinarily lucky, and——"

"Who is it?" asked Audrey sharply.

But Sir Harry hesitated to reply bluntly with the man's name.

"Mind you," he said, "I don't mean for a moment to insinuate that it's anything but a coincidence, but still, I've watched him and it's always the same."

"Who is it?" asked Audrey again.

"One moment, Madame. You might well ask, if I were to say anything not altogether pleasant about one of your guests, why I came to you about it, instead of speaking to some of the men. But one or two fellows to whom I mentioned it laughed at me, and said that if I were to speak to you, I should only get snubbed. I resented that, on your account, knowing how kind and straightforward you were with me last night. And—and I made up my mind to do, what is not really a very nice thing to have to do, to come to you and rely upon your tact to deal with the matter."

"You did just what was right and wise and kind, and I'm very much obliged to you," said Audrey earnestly. "I need not tell you that my position is a very difficult one—I'm not used to entertaining on a large scale, and my position as a business woman puts me at a disadvantage."

"That was exactly what I thought, and why I felt it was a shame you should not know," said the young man eagerly. "Well, the man I mean is Mr. Diggs."

"I thought so," said Audrey. "I won't have him here again. Tell me—I'll keep your confidence—how much he has won from you?"

"Oh, I don't mean to insinuate——"

"Nor I. He is lucky, that's all. But what amount has his luck been worth to him?"

He hesitated, but at last said simply:—

"About four thousand pounds from me, and nearly five thousand from the young Angmerings."

Audrey was overwhelmed.

In stony silence she sat while Sir Harry described the faint suspicions he had from time to time entertained concerning the methods of Mr. Candover's clever secretary, and added simply that he should never have thought of challenging him but for Audrey's own words to him on the previous night.

"Then," went on the young man, "I thought things over, and I remembered his curious manner to you as he said good-night, and I went out of my way to find the young Angmerings this morning, and to put questions to them. The result was that I found this Diggs had used just the same little devices with them as he had done with me, and that they had lost even more than I had to him. Now, you must understand that I don't wish to have any fuss made; I think the Angmerings and I have only paid a proper price for our folly in playing so high. But I made up my mind that, out of gratitude to you for the way you spoke to me last night, I could not do less than come straight here and tell you what I have done."

"I can't thank you enough," said Audrey. "He shall never play in my house again."

Then the young baronet spoke out.

"I knew you would get rid of the fellow when you knew," he said promptly. "The truth is I don't think there's any doubt that he is a sharper, and it must be a paying game!"

The moment Sir Harry had left the house, Audrey sat down to write the following letter:—

"Dear Mr. Candover,

"Will you please convey to your secretary, Mr. Durley Diggs, my refusal to allow him to come here again? It is of no use for him to ask my reasons; he must be satisfied with my decision.

"Yours faithfully,
"Audrey Angmering."

She signed her own name out of bravado, to show Mr. Candover how strong was her determination to drop the title he had chosen for her without delay.

On the following afternoon, when she had suffered considerable trepidation at her own daring, and had watched the post, expecting a letter full of indignation, she was informed that Mr. Candover and Mr. Diggs were in the drawing-room.

Audrey went down to meet them with a bold front but in a state of nervous excitement and apprehension impossible to describe.

Both gentlemen were standing when she entered the room. Mr. Candover was looking grave and dignified; Durley Diggs, though he put his hands in his pockets and tried to assume an air of easy indifference, looked paler than ever.

"I got your letter," said Mr. Candover, "and I thought it only fair to read it to Diggs, who is, as you know, a friend and confidential employee of some years' standing. I think you will acknowledge it to be only right to let him know in what way he has merited such a curt dismissal on your part."

Audrey, with her heart beating very fast, stood firm. She did not ask them to be seated, but remained leaning against a high-backed carved chair, and kept very still.

"What you ask is quite reasonable," she said, looking steadily at Mr. Candover only, "but still I am afraid Mr. Diggs must be satisfied with what I have said. I don't wish him to come here again."

"You will at least tell me who it was that influenced you to come to this rather abrupt decision?"

"No, I refuse to do that."

"And if he should treat this as an injury necessitating the interference of the law?" went on Mr. Candover.

But Audrey, frightened as she was, miserable as she was, knew better than to think Mr. Diggs would take such a step as that. She threw at the secretary a look of disdain and answered steadily:—

"He can do whatever he likes."

Then for the first time Diggs spoke. Darting across the room, and planting himself before her, he thrust his hands deeper into the pockets of his lounge coat and said impudently:—

"Come now, what have I done?"

And Audrey, summoning her spirit, replied at once:—

"You have cheated at cards."

This accusation, evidently unexpected by one at least of her hearers, for a moment struck them both dumb.

It was Mr. Candover who recovered himself the first.

"Cheated at cards!" he repeated incredulously. "Madame, do you know the importance of such an accusation?"

But poor Audrey, now strung up to the sort of reckless defiance which despair and misery sometimes produce even in the feeble, replied boldly:—

"Of course I do. And I would not say such things if I didn't know they were true. Mr. Diggs has won nearly nine thousand pounds from young men in this very house, by methods which were similar in each case, and which I will relate if you like."

"What is more to the point," replied Mr. Candover sternly, "is to know who made these accusations in the first place."

"That I shall not say. It must be enough that I am satisfied that he used unfair means, and that I won't have him in my house again. If it's any question of law or of actions I'm ready to take it upon myself to answer them." And she repeated stubbornly: "I won't have him here again."

For a moment there was dead silence, and Audrey, looking down on the carpet with her heart full of terrors, and clinging tightly to the chair by which she stood, expected an outburst of indignation, or perhaps of something worse.

To her intense surprise, however, when Mr. Candover broke the silence it was to speak to Diggs, and to say, in a solemn voice:—

"Diggs, I hope this is not true. I hope with all my heart that you, who have been my trusted confidant so long, have not done this awful thing of which Madame Rocada accuses you." There was a silence, and glancing at Diggs, Audrey saw that, while he shook his head, he said nothing. Mr. Candover went on: "In any case, I must uphold Madame's decision not to allow you to come here again, for, as she says, the slightest taint of a suspicion of such a kind would be a fatal thing, as you must see for yourself." Diggs nodded, still without speaking or looking up. "And I'm sorry to say I don't care to keep you in my employment unless you can clear yourself of the charge." Still Diggs said nothing. "So, if you please, you will understand that your engagement with me terminates a week from now."

Audrey was listening and watching attentively, and now the thing that struck her the most strongly was that Diggs did not seem surprised at this curt and amazing dismissal. He did not plead that there was no proof against him, he did not show resentment or regret. He simply took his dismissal in all humility, and bowing to them both with a muttered, "Very sorry—Not true—You might know me better," he shuffled nearer and nearer to the door, and then popped out rapidly, quietly and ingloriously.

It was rather a bewildering victory, Audrey thought.

"To tell you the truth, I've had my doubts of the rascal before," said Mr. Candover, when the door had closed on Diggs.

Audrey glanced up and then down, but she said nothing.

"I must go now," said Mr. Candover.

And she made no attempt to detain him.

# CHAPTER X

Now this affair, unpleasant as it was, had been very promptly and satisfactorily settled, and Audrey felt that she ought to feel more contented than she did about it. Mr. Candover had behaved with quite admirable consideration for her, and his dismissal of the secretary whom he had employed and trusted for so long might have been supposed to set Audrey's mind completely at ease.

But suspicions and doubts, once roused, are hard to set at rest, and she had carefully refrained from showing him any effusive gratitude for his action.

After all, how could he have done less without showing himself on the side of the wrongdoer?

For though he might indeed have insisted upon tracing the accusation to its source, there must have followed such an unpleasant exposure, such a scandal, such gossip, that the result might have been to draw disagreeable remarks down upon his own head.

But Audrey was not to be allowed any rest from her troubles. On the following day another difficulty cropped up; for, on returning from her afternoon drive, she heard, with dismay, that one of the Miss Candovers had come and Sir Harry Archdale.

Audrey was bewildered.

"When did they come? How long have they been here?" she asked.

"Miss Candover came soon after you started, Madame, and Sir Harry about ten minutes later. They both said they'd wait till you came back, and they're in the drawing-room."

What would Mr. Candover say to this? Audrey hurried towards the drawing-room, and before she reached it she heard peals of merry laughter, which proved conclusively that the visitors had broken the ice.

On entering the room she found the two young people at the window, playing with her little dogs. Pamela ran towards her, her face beaming, her step as light and her movements as graceful as those of a gazelle.

"Oh, Madame Rocada, don't scold. I see you want to scold. But, indeed, I *had* to come!"

"What will Mr. Candover say?"

The girl's face grew troubled.

"I—I don't know," she said. "But when you know why I've come, you will understand."

Audrey now held out her hand to Sir Harry, who was looking as happy as a schoolboy home for the holidays, and who could scarcely take his eyes off pretty Pamela. He, however, had to explain this second visit.

"I've come," said he in a low voice, "to tell you not to worry yourself about what I said to you the other day. I met Candover last night, and he told me he had dismissed his secretary. Is that your doing?"

"I daresay it is," said Audrey. "But I took care not to mention any names when I spoke to Mr. Candover. I took it upon my own shoulders to say what I thought of Mr. Diggs and his doings."

"That was very good of you, and very effectual," said Sir Harry. "But it's only what one would have expected. No decent man would care to employ a fellow so very shady, if he knew of it."

"Of course not."

"Least of all a man like Mr. Candover."

And Sir Harry cast at Pamela a glance which showed how bright a halo he threw round everything and every one belonging to her.

Pamela, meanwhile, had grown serious and anxious to be able to speak to her hostess. Sir Harry noted this, and said: "Miss Candover wants to speak to you, Madame. Now I hope you won't send me away; I've been manœuvring to get asked to tea. Shall I go out into the garden and feed the rabbits—if there are any rabbits—while she pours out her heart to you?"

Pamela turned to him gratefully. "Would you—would you really?" she said, with pretty gratitude. "I do want to speak to Madame, but I don't want to drive you away."

Audrey, whose spirits rose in the presence of these two bright, good-looking, sympathetic young people, nodded a smiling dismissal to Sir Harry, who promptly took himself off into the garden, and made elaborate pretences of plucking handfuls of grass to feed imaginary animals while the ladies talked.

Pamela seized Audrey by the arm, and made her sit beside her on a couch while she poured into her ear a rather disquieting tale.

"There's been a woman," she said, "a wild-looking, uncanny woman, not quite in her right mind, I think, calling at Miss Willett's, and asking to see us. She says she's our mother, but we know that our mother is dead. We don't quite like to write to my father about it, because he doesn't like to be told annoying things. So I thought I'd run over and see you, and ask you what we'd better do."

Audrey was troubled. There were these vague clouds of distress and mystery in every direction, she thought. How was it? "What does Miss Willett think?" she asked.

"Oh, she's an old maid, and she is simply horror-struck, and can do nothing but hold up her hands and say 'Dear, dear, how dreadful!' and refuse admittance to the woman. But we girls can't be satisfied like that, and so I thought of you. What would you suggest?"

Audrey considered a moment.

"Supposing I were to see her?" she said.

"Oh, would you? That would be sweet of you! We don't dare to see her ourselves, and yet we don't like to take it for granted that—that——"

"Next time she comes—if she does come—give her—let her be given, my address, and refer her to me. Hush, here comes the tea. And we must call our rabbit-lover in."

They went to the window, and made signs to the ostentatiously distant Sir Harry that he might come in, and they had such a merry hour together that it was with difficulty they could make up their minds to break up the party. At last, however, Audrey put Pamela into the pony-carriage and drove her over to Staines, where she could take the train direct to within a short distance of her school, and Sir Harry, very reluctantly, bade them good-bye, with many hints that he should like to come again.

Audrey was quite cheered by the merry young people, who were, after all, of her own generation, though circumstances had combined to make her feel many years older.

But her pleasure was short-lived. There was a card-playing evening in store for her, at which Diggs was, of course, not present. But two days later she received another indignant letter from Lord Clanfield, complaining of her lack of good faith, in that his two sons had been playing cards at her house the whole of the night through.

Audrey was intensely indignant at this letter, and was convinced, since the young Angmerings had certainly not been among the guests on the night he mentioned, that they had themselves deceived their father, and given her address to hide their real whereabouts.

She began a letter to him, at least as indignant as his own, but could not satisfy herself with the wording of it. She tried again and again, and finally made up her mind to give up the attempt and to descend upon the angry father in person, and force him to retract his accusation and to apologise for it.

She was extremely angry about this annoyance, after the strong measures she had taken to insure the exclusion of the young men.

Now Lord Clanfield's place was in Hampshire, and although the actual distance as the crow flies was not so very great between "The Briars" and Angmering Court, the journey was a tedious one, with many changes of train and awkward waits at country stations.

It was not, therefore, until somewhat late in the afternoon that Audrey got out at the nearest station to the viscount's place, and having ascertained that it was only a couple of miles away, went on foot across the fields, according to the direction given her, and reached the gates of the park at about five o'clock.

There was no lodge at the gate, which she opened and passed through, admiring the prospect of hillock and tree, winding road and grassy glade, with an occasional peep at the house, which was a low-built Georgian structure, homely and cosy-looking rather than stately or imposing.

The day had been a glorious one and the sun was still warm and bright. Audrey, who had had little inclination to dwell on the beauty of the place or the delights of the balmy air, was seized with nervousness on finding herself so near the great man of her husband's family, and wondered at her own daring in coming at all.

Along the winding road she went, coming rather suddenly upon a charming flower-garden, divided from the park-land only by a wire fence, and offering to the eye a view of dahlias and gladioli, rich-tinted begonias, feathery pampas grass, and late roses that strewed their sweet petals on the grass.

On the lawn among the flowers there was an umbrella-tent, and under it a wicker lounge-chair. Beside the chair stood a nurse in uniform, and lying full length upon it was a young man, so white, so thin, so haggard of cheek and sunken of eye that he looked more like a dead man than a live one.

Audrey, who was not in the direct line of sight of the nurse and her patient, by reason of a clump of shrubs behind which she had instinctively stopped, clenched her hands, held her breath, and stared with incredulous eyes at the invalid.

Surely, surely she must be dreaming! Surely, surely her misery and her troubles must have turned her brain! And yet she knew, even while she hung forward, gazing in agony at the hollow cheeks and the glassy eye, that she was awake, that she was sane—and that the invalid with the pallid, waxen face, who seemed to have not more than an hour's life left in his wasted, shrunken frame, was Gerard, her husband.

# CHAPTER XI

FOR the first few moments Audrey had no inclination to utter a sound. She was too much taken by surprise, too bewildered, too horror-stricken, even to cry out.

Her tongue, her brain, her limbs seemed paralysed, and she could do nothing but press her face forward between the little branches of the shrubs which concealed her from Gerard's sight, and keep her hungry eyes fixed on his pale face.

Was it really he? Could it be he? His sentence had been one of years, and scarcely four months had passed since he was taken from her.

Surely he would never have been released without her hearing a word about it! Surely, surely in such a few weeks he could not have been transformed from the merry, bright, vigorous young fellow, full of life and high spirits, overwhelmed with melancholy of the most tempestuous sort, into this shadow, this lifeless, colourless framework of a man!

He lay so still in the lounge-chair, without even moving his lips to answer the nurse as she leaned over him and talked to him, that Audrey had a horrible spasm of fear that he was dead, that the feeble remnant of life had passed away even while she watched him with agonised eyes from her place of concealment not thirty yards away.

And she pressed farther forward, straining her eyes, and in so doing disturbed the bushes just sufficiently for the moving branches to catch the eye of the nurse, who was a tall, muscular, grey-haired woman, with a firm, pleasant face.

Gerard himself, on a much lower level than she, neither heard nor saw the movement. The nurse looked apprehensively at the bushes, and descried the woman behind them. Audrey saw that her face changed, and knew that she was alarmed lest her patient should be disturbed by some sudden and startling intrusion.

But she need not have been afraid. Audrey loved her husband too well not to have the right and safe instinct that caution was necessary when dealing with a man who was evidently so ill. She knew that to burst out upon him abruptly, without a word of warning, would be a rash, perhaps a fatal thing. And she held her own emotions in check, even while her heart yearned towards him, and her arms tingled with the longing to take his poor head in her arms and to hug it to her breast.

The nurse, meanwhile, not knowing all that was passing in the mind of the other woman, and guessing only that there was trouble in store, at once took steps to remove her charge out of harm's way.

Audrey could not hear what she said, but knew that she was suggesting that he should go indoors. For a few moments he seemed to pay no heed to her words, but presently, with a petulant frown, as if loth to be disturbed, he allowed her to help him to his feet, and went slowly, leaning on her strong arm, in the direction of the angle of the house, round which they both disappeared.

Audrey, still less than half possessed of her faculties, watched them to the last, and then, stepping back upon the gravel of the drive, tried to take stock of her strange position.

As to Gerard's presence in his uncle's house, the fact was so amazing that her brain reeled under it. Lord Clanfield had never once come forward, since his nephew's marriage, with so much as a kind word to him or his young wife. During all the terrible time of waiting for the trial, not a word had reached his nephew either of reproach, advice or sympathy. Both young husband and young wife had taken it for granted that they were looked upon as effaced, degraded, unworthy of any notice from the august head of the family.

And, proud as well as miserable, they had accepted the situation without a protest.

Now, however, it was clear that Lord Clanfield had interested himself on behalf of his unlucky nephew, and the amazing thing was to find that he had apparently obtained the young man's release so quietly that not a word of it had got into the papers, or to the knowledge of Gerard's own wife!

And then, with startling force, the truth flashed upon Audrey that, even if it had been desired to let her know of her husband's release, there would have been no means of doing so. For, anxious to hide her head from all the world, to sink her identity and be forgotten, she had disappeared from sight as Audrey Angmering, to reappear as Madame Rocada.

And then the full meaning of her position became clear to her. She was coming to see Lord Clanfield in the character by which he knew and suspected her, at the very moment when it was above all things necessary that he should have the best possible opinion of her in the character of his nephew's wife!

What would he say, what would he think when he learned the truth of her double identity? If he had been severe in his judgment before, what would he be now?

Although she could now conclusively prove to him—at least so she believed—that she could not be the White Countess of evil memory, what would he say to her having taken upon herself the invidious name, and still more invidious position, of the apparently too well-known Madame Rocada?

As these thoughts chased each other through her bewildered mind, the unfortunate woman felt a numb despair creeping over her. She dared not meet Lord Clanfield now, she dared not try to see Gerard.

What was there left for her to do?

Go away without making some inquiry, without learning something about her husband and his state of health, and the manner in which he found himself once more under his uncle's roof, well cared for and carefully nursed, she could not and would not.

But how to learn what she wanted to know without making an unseemly and unwise disturbance? How convey to Gerard the fact of her being near him, without either giving him a dangerous shock or running the risk of rousing Lord Clanfield's anger and causing a family scandal?

That was the question which filled Audrey's mind, as she lingered in the drive, looking askance at the house with its old red walls, weather-stained roof and the great green and red masses of ivy and virginia creeper which hung about it picturesquely and made dark fringes over the tall windows.

And while she hesitated, lingered, debated with herself, there came a clattering of hoofs behind her, and stepping out of the road upon the sloping bank, Audrey turned to see Geoffrey Angmering, in a dog-cart, coming at a rapid rate up the drive.

He recognised her at once.

"Madame Rocada! By Jove!" cried he with a grin, as he reined in the horse, jumped down, and told the groom to drive on to the stable. "Well, of all the marvellous meetings—and here! By Jove, it is a surprise!"

Audrey was very pale, very quiet, very dignified. This cub, with the free and easy manners and the impudent stare, could tell her what she wanted to know. But how to get at that knowledge?

To him she was merely Madame Rocada, the woman who kept a house where gambling went on, where he himself and his brother had been "fleeced" at play. Knowing only of her what he did, there was nothing less likely than that he would converse with her about the family secrets or the family scandals. Half-tipsy as he generally was, even the reckless Geoffrey was hardly likely to speak out on such a subject.

She began, therefore, by telling him frankly the object of her visit.

"I am here," she said, "to see Lord Clanfield. He has written accusing me of allowing you and your brother to come to my house to play cards there. Now you know that I have forbidden you to come, and therefore you have been deceiving him, by saying you were at 'The Briars' when you were not there at all."

Geoffrey stared at her with the same impudent look of incredulity and defiance as he had used on the night when she refused admission to her house to him and his brother.

"I think it would have been wiser of you, Madame, to have taken no notice of his letter," he said, with unmistakable mockery in his tone. "He won't believe what you say, if you persist in seeing him, any more than he did before. If I were you, I should go quietly back home again, and if you like I'll drive you to the station in my dog-cart."

The frank impertinence of his manner and of his suggestion almost frightened Audrey. It seemed to betray the fact that he looked upon her as unworthy of much trouble, and as wholly incapable of producing any effect upon his father.

He seemed to say in effect: "If you like to see my father you can, but you may just as well save yourself the trouble."

She hesitated what to reply. To tell the whole truth to him, to say that she was Gerard's wife, was, of course, out of the question. He would certainly receive such a statement with blank incredulity and probably with insult. Luckily, at that moment, when she was uncertain what to do and Geoffrey was growing more and more impertinent in his manner, the elder son of Lord Clanfield, who, if still less endowed with brains, was not quite such an ill-mannered young rascal as his brother, came in sight. He was sauntering out from the house with half a dozen dogs, of various breeds, running and barking round him.

One of these, a bull terrier, spying a stranger in Audrey, rushed at her, and seizing her skirt, began to worry it tearing the light material to ribbons.

"Down, sir, down!" cried Edgar, hastening his steps a little, as he came up to his brother and the lady. "I'm awfully sorry——" he went on, raising his hat as he spoke. When suddenly he recognised her in his turn, and said, in breathless amazement: "Madame Rocada!"

He took her presence in the park in a different way from his brother's, and seemed not only surprised, but rather alarmed by it. "Why, I—what—unexpected——" stammered he, as she bowed gravely and said nothing.

There was a moment's dead silence. Then she, perceiving that this young man was at least much more likely to listen quietly than his brother, said steadily and firmly:—

"My name is not Madame Rocada. It never has been that. I am not a countess, and I have never wished to pretend to be one."

She paused for a moment, and it was Geoffrey who, growing curious at this change in her manner, suddenly put in, half-insolently, half-inquiringly:—

"Well, if you are not Madame Rocada, who are you then?"

Audrey hesitated one moment more only. Then very quietly, very solemnly, fixing her eyes on the face of the elder brother and drawing herself up to her full height, she answered:—

"My name is the same as your own. I am Audrey Angmering, your cousin Gerard's wife."

"The devil you are!" cried Geoffrey, more in amusement than surprise.

But the other saw that there was no pretentiousness, no show of indignation or of self-assertion, in the poor lady's manner, and he silenced his brother by a frown and a curt word half under his breath.

"Do you mean that?" he asked simply.

"Yes. And listen. I know that Gerard is here: I've seen him. And I want to understand all about his coming—about his illness. I—I hadn't even heard of it."

The young man hesitated. Geoffrey was pulling furtively at his sleeve, mutely urging him to have nothing to do with the unhappy woman and her story.

Evidently Edgar did not know what to believe.

"You say you've seen him?" said he.

"Yes. Out in the garden, with a nurse. Surely, surely there can be no harm in telling me just what I want to know. How is it he is there? Why was I not told he was ill?"

As she persisted in her story, it was clear that both the young men were becoming increasingly alarmed and puzzled, and that they were at a loss how to deal with this intricate question.

At last Edgar said quickly:—

"Hadn't you better write about it? Write to Lord Clanfield?"

"No," said Audrey firmly. "I won't write. I must see him. And at once—now—I won't go away till I have seen him. Look, there's no need for you to be afraid. I don't wish to force myself into Gerard's presence until I'm sure I can see him without it's being a shock to him."

"By Jove, it would be!" put in Geoffrey in a tone that brought the angry blood to the poor wife's cheeks.

But Edgar gave him a sort of side kick as a gentle recommendation to be quiet, and after a little hesitation and stammering said:—

"Look here, Madame. I don't think it's of the least use for you to try and see my father or my cousin. I'm almost sure Lord Clanfield wouldn't see you, and that my cousin wouldn't be allowed to see you. You might understand that it wouldn't be wise. But if you like I'll go in and tell him what you've just told me, and I'll bring you word what he says."

Although Audrey was fully resolved that, whether he liked it or not, Lord Clanfield should see her, she thought that compliance with the proposal was the best course to begin with. So she agreed to remain where she was, and not to approach the house for the present, while Edgar returned to it.

Geoffrey, meanwhile, after a muttered exchange of a few words with his brother, retreated into the recesses of the trees of the park, and Audrey guessed that he was, as it were, on guard, set to watch her movements during his brother's absence, and to prevent, if necessary, any attempt on her part to break faith.

In the meantime Edgar fulfilled his mission reluctantly enough. Returning to the house, he went straight to the study, where his father was spending the afternoon with his magazines and books.

"What is the matter? Is Gerard worse?" were the viscount's first words, when his son entered, with a perturbed and uneasy air.

"N-n-no, but—he's likely to be worse if something I've got to tell you is true!" was Edgar's somewhat blundering reply.

"Well!" said Lord Clanfield sharply.

"There's a—a—woman come—she's in the park now, who says—who says she's—his wife."

Lord Clanfield looked more relieved than alarmed. He rose to his feet.

"And don't you think it is his wife? I wish to heaven she would come; for the greatest drawback to his getting better is the terrible depression caused by her disappearance."

Edgar, with whom tact was not a strong point, went on bluntly:—

"Well, he'll be more depressed when he sees her."

"What do you mean?"

"Why, that this woman who says she's his wife, the woman who is in the park now, and who says she will see you or see him before she goes away, is the very woman whose house you've forbidden us to go to, the keeper of a gambling-room—Madame Rocada!"

The shock was so great that Lord Clanfield fell back, scarcely able to speak, breathless, bewildered, horror-struck.

"Are—are you sure?"

"I'm sure that the woman who calls herself Madame Rocada is outside the house at this moment, that she says she came in answer to a letter from you about us——"

"Yes, I did write to her."

"—and that she declares she saw Gerard—you see she knows his name—in a chair in the grounds, with a nurse. And she complains that she had not even heard that he was ill, and she seems as genuinely upset as ever I saw a woman in my life! And I believe she *is* his wife, I do on my honour!"

The viscount made up his mind quickly.

"Get rid of her," said he. "Drive her away at all costs, I don't mean roughly, of course. But you must find some means of getting her outside the grounds before Gerard hears of her being here."

"Not so easy! One can deal with a mad dog more easily than with a determined woman!" retorted Edgar.

"I tell you she must go, must be sent away. Use any argument you like, tell her it would kill him to break the news of her coming too suddenly. That is true, I believe. In the meantime say I undertake to answer her letters if she will write—but it must be to me, not to him. And—and what I shall do is to get my lawyers to see her, to arrange with her—until we know something, find out something."

Edgar, however, still lingered.

"I can never say all that," grumbled he. "Besides, she wouldn't listen. You know she wouldn't."

Remembering what he did of Audrey, poor Lord Clanfield thought this very likely, and his agitation grew stronger and stronger until it found a climax when, perceiving that the window nearest to him had become slightly darkened, he turned, and saw Audrey herself, very white, very quiet, peering in.

"Good Heavens, Madame, you have no right——" began the startled gentleman.

But Audrey leaned with her arms upon the window-ledge, and putting her head forward into the room, said in a low-pitched but determined voice:—

"You must see me. I insist. You must let me in."

And, helpless in these strong if slight fingers, Lord Clanfield gave way. Motioning to his son to open the French window at the other end of the room, he leaned against the old carved white marble mantelpiece and prepared for the worst.

# CHAPTER XII

AUDREY came in trembling, and stood facing Lord Clanfield without a word. She had contrived to give the slip to the not over-vigilant Geoffrey, and had flown like the wind across the flower-garden, peering into the rooms on the ground-floor, in the hope of discovering either Gerard or his uncle.

Now that she had succeeded, her courage failed her, and she was mute and frightened, presenting as great a contrast as possible to any idea the viscount might have formed of a violent and loud-voiced woman forcing her way in with intent to make a disturbance.

"Madame Rocada," he began.

But she stopped him with a rapid gesture.

"Do not call me that. I have already told you that it is not my name, it never was my name. I am your nephew's wife."

Anxious to be out of the way of a scene which promised to be a trying one, Edgar had sidled out of the room as he let the lady in, and the two, distressed woman and scandalised man, were left alone together.

"Am I to believe that?" he stammered after a short pause.

"Bring him face to face with me, and you will be no longer in doubt."

He shook his head.

"I cannot do that. He has been given his liberty on account of the state of his health, which is considered hopeless. In fact, he has been let out to die."

Although she did not utter a word, Lord Clanfield could not help seeing that the grief his words caused her was profound.

"His condition is such that the slightest shock might, I should think, be fatal, and I cannot venture to try experiments."

"Is there no hope, no hope?" asked Audrey in a stifled voice.

"Well, I feared not when I first saw him a couple of days ago. But the fact that he is still alive gives me hopes. If I can get him away to a warmer climate before the winter comes, and rouse him out of his depression, I think we may pull him through."

"What is the matter with him? Is it consumption?"

"That's what we are afraid of. At present we don't know that it is that. He suffers from extreme weakness after pneumonia and the general breakdown which preceded that," went on Lord Clanfield, who could not help answering her questions, they were put so modestly and with such evident warmth of feeling. But he replied with his eyes turned away, reluctantly, as if by an effort. If she was really his nephew's wife, she was certainly not a person to be received otherwise than in the most distant manner, and even then she must understand that such reception was accorded under protest.

"Poor boy, my poor boy! What he must have suffered! And don't you think it would do him good, not harm, to see me, to know I am safe? Oh, I know very well it is on my account, because he doesn't know what has become of me, that he is so miserable. And it's his misery that prevents his getting well! Oh, Lord Clanfield, can't you see that it is?"

The viscount moved nervously.

"I've no doubt," said he stiffly, "that if, when the prison authorities thought of releasing him, they had been able to find his wife, and to give him back to her care, it would have been better for him, much better. But you had disappeared; you had hidden yourself under a fresh name. And—really I'm sorry to have to say it, as I see you are truly sorry for the situation you have brought about, I cannot but think that, if he were to learn the truth about you and about the life you've been leading while he was in prison, it would be the last straw. He would never hold up his head again."

Audrey heard these words with the wildest despair. Well though she knew that Lord Clanfield exaggerated the case, that he looked upon her as a woman who had deliberately chosen to give up her name and her enforced widowhood for a life of pleasure and for companions of the most undesirable type, she knew too that even the truth was bad enough to shock poor Gerard and to wake all sorts of terrible suspicions in his breast.

She was sure that, if she could broach the matter at her own time and in her own way, when the joy of reunion should have soothed his anguish and softened the remembrance of his trials, the sudden and unsympathetic recital of the circumstances of her life, even without exaggeration, would be more than he could bear.

So that these cruel words of the viscount's could not be resented with indignation, his assertions could not even be denied.

She could, however, make an effort to put him right about herself, and, as much for Gerard's sake as her own, she set about doing so with the utmost earnestness.

"Lord Clanfield," she said, in a low, pleading voice, "you do me the most terrible injustice. I've never done anything unworthy of Gerard's wife, indeed. I've done something that neither he nor you would perhaps approve, in starting a millinery business under a high-sounding name, and in allowing myself to be persuaded into receiving all sorts of people in a house I have rented, in the hope of attracting customers for what I sell, and clients for the business. I was advised to do these things, and though it was distasteful, the advice sounded good from the monetary point of view.

78

That's the worst I have done, indeed, indeed it is. Oh, if you don't believe me, I'm sure that Gerard would!"

Lord Clanfield was walking up and down his end of the room, much perturbed and distressed. At last he stopped short and turned to her.

"My dear lady," he said, and the very words indicated a welcome change of temper towards her, she thought, "supposing what you say is true—and I am bound to say I can't quite believe you—what then? Do you really think it is nothing to have brought upon yourself, so lightly as you have done, the suspicions which any reasonable person would naturally entertain of you? Do you think your conduct is such as to be a credit to my family—mine?"

"I've—I've done nothing really wrong," pleaded Audrey humbly.

"Indeed! You are at the head of what is, whatever you may choose to call it, a gaming-house." She uttered an exclamation of dismay, but he went on in spite of her. "You are at the head of another establishment for selling—h'm—bonnets. Now it is perfectly legitimate to sell—h'm—bonnets. But it is not an employment which I can approve of in my nephew's wife."

And the viscount drew himself up with dignity.

"Why didn't you find me out and see what I was doing?" burst out Audrey with sudden spirit. "If you had given it a thought, you would have known that I must do something to live, and it's your fault, after all, that I had to take the advice of such friends as I had, whether it was bad or good."

Lord Clanfield was much displeased by this attack, which was, he considered, unjust and uncalled for. His irritation against her increased.

"Permit me to be the best judge of my own actions," he said icily; "I repeat that I cannot countenance your proceedings, either in regard to my sons or my nephew."

"I was coming to tell you about your sons. If they've told you they come to my house still, they have said what is not true. They do not come. I have forbidden my servants to let them in."

To her annoyance, these words of hers incensed him more than anything else that she had said. She saw plainly that he did not believe her.

"I really think," he said drily, "that there is no need for us to prolong this interview. As for my sons, if they do not desist from courses of which I disapprove, I may—I should regret it, but I may—have to call in the assistance of the police." Audrey uttered a cry, but he went on without taking any notice of her. "As for my nephew, if you force your way into his presence, I cannot answer for the consequences, and I regret that I should in that case feel it my duty to let him know some things which, in his present state, he had better not hear."

"He would not believe you," cried Audrey passionately.

"Possibly not. But in that case, and if he insisted upon taking your part, which would be perfectly natural, I should have to give him up to you entirely, as I decline to receive you here."

Audrey was shaking like a leaf.

"You don't mean that! You couldn't be so cruel! If it were best for him to see me?" pleaded she.

"I deny that it would be best. In any case, I cannot go back from that position. If you leave him here, and suffer him to think, as he now thinks, that you are dead, lost to him, he may get over that shock, in the comfort and relief of finding himself free and tenderly cared for once more. In the meantime, as I cannot but think I have been unjust to him in taking it for granted he was guilty, I will strain every nerve to probe the mystery attending his conviction. But if you insist on taking him away with you—and I daresay he would go, for you are a beautiful and attractive woman and he loves you—then I cast him off, I can do no less, and you must sink or swim together."

"Oh, no, no, I can't think you would be so hard, so cruel, so wicked!" cried poor Audrey, alarmed to see the look of stubborn determination in the viscount's eyes.

But she was wrong. Used all his life to having his own way, except in the matter of the behaviour of his headstrong and not very worthy sons, Lord Clanfield could make up his mind inflexibly, and carry out his plans with the dogged steadfastness of a not unjust or unkindly, but narrow mind.

He believed that he might have been unjust to Gerard, that there was a possibility that the young man's reiterated asseverations of his innocence might have something in them, after all.

But the more inclined he was to believe this, the less likely was he to believe in the complete innocence and guilelessness of Gerard's wife. It even occurred to him as possible that this beautiful woman, who had shown herself so frivolous if not worse, might have connived in some diabolical plot to get her husband out of the way.

"I hope I am not wicked," he said coldly. "And, indeed, I did not expect to hear that word applied to me. I have done my best, I am still doing my best, for my nephew, and I shall continue to do it if I am suffered to do it in the way I think right. However, the matter is in your hands, madam, and it is for you to decide what course we are both to pursue."

Audrey, who had refused all Lord Clanfield's perfunctory invitations to be seated, was standing, just as she had been ever since her entrance, forlorn and desolate, in the middle of the floor. Her hands were tightly clenched, her eyes showed the terrible conflict which was going on within her.

Must she give him up? Could she? Ought she? Would it really be best for him, as Lord Clanfield said?

On the one hand were the care, the luxury, the atmosphere of a beautiful English home, the protection, the very powerful protection of an eminent name, the energetic endeavours of his relations to have the taint removed from his name.

On the other hand, there was nothing but her own love, and such efforts as she, poor, weak, helpless woman that she was, could make on his behalf.

And, while it was true that she felt certain he must be suffering deeply from her disappearance, and the suspense he must be in as to what had become of her, yet she did not disguise from herself the fact that the knowledge of the position in which she had so strangely got placed might give him even more pain and more anxiety than the suspense from which he was now suffering on her account.

In the silence which followed the viscount's words, a dead silence in which the slightest sound was audible to them both, there came a halting step outside the door of the room, and then a knock.

Recognising the step, or guessing whose it was, Audrey raised her head, and uttered, in a hoarse whisper, the one word: "Gerard!"

Lord Clanfield looked angrily, uneasily at the door, the window and at Audrey. Then, crossing the floor quickly towards the French window, he pushed it wide open, inviting her by a gesture to go out.

She threw at him one imploring look, saw that he was unyielding, and summoning all her self-control, made one tottering step towards the open window.

But her docility came too late. Before she had reached the window the door opened, and Gerard, leaning on a stick, appeared in the doorway.

"Uncle, may I come in?"

But the words had scarcely passed his lips when he saw who it was that was cowering between him and the viscount, and throwing down his stick, he crossed the intervening space at one bound, and flinging himself into his wife's arms, clung to her, his face, his voice full of a passionate joy.

"Audrey! Audrey! And I thought you were dead! Oh, thank God, thank God!"

For a few moments there was not a word more spoken. Audrey did indeed try to articulate, but the words stuck in her throat; she could utter nothing more coherent than low moans indicative of emotions which indeed were deeper and more painful than she could well express.

In the meantime Lord Clanfield stood motionless beside the open French window, and the first thing that Audrey said was to him.

"Lord Clanfield," she cried, when she had suddenly caught a glimpse of his face, and read that there was no softening there, "I—I want to speak to you. I want you to hear what I have to tell Gerard. You know that it's true, and he wouldn't believe me if you were not here to support what I'm going to say."

Gerard, whose flushed face looked human once more, the death-like pallor and dull eyes having become transformed, looked at his wife with amazement mingled with his joy.

"What is this wonderful thing that I'm to hear and not to believe?" he asked, looking with a joyous smile from his wife to his uncle, and now dimly conscious that something was not quite right between these two.

Audrey had withdrawn herself from his embrace, and was supporting him on her strong young arm, facing the viscount the while.

"I have to tell you, Gerard, something you won't like to hear. While you were away, I made up my mind to try to make some money, and I've gone—into well, business, trade. I've had, of course, to sink my own name, and that is why you could not find me. Now Lord Clanfield very naturally disapproves of any connection of his family being engaged in this way, and I am conscious that he is within his rights in objecting. I think you might perhaps object too."

"Well, it is rather astonishing!" gasped Gerard, to whom the constrained tone in which the information was conveyed was rather disturbing. "But, of course, you can give it up, can't you?"

She threw one imploring look at Lord Clanfield, to ascertain whether he would accept that as sufficient propitiation. But one glance was enough to show her that he would not.

"Unfortunately," she answered, with a trembling voice, "I can't—and I won't—at present. Unless Lord Clanfield wishes it."

"My wishes have nothing to do with it," said Lord Clanfield coldly.

Then she understood that the decision lay with her still.

"I won't give it up," she said quietly, "and I won't let you, Gerard, have anything to do with it. You are ill; you need care, more care than I could give you. And I am strong and eager to make money. Will you, Lord Clanfield, take care of him, so that I can go quietly on with my work without any one's knowing who I am, or what my name is?"

Lord Clanfield, although this was the very decision at which he had wished her to arrive, was taken aback when it was reached.

"Do—do you mean it? Will you consent to leave him with me?" he said incredulously.

"And am I to have nothing to say in the matter?" asked Gerard, with not unnatural irritation.

Audrey, having made up her mind what she ought to do, turned to him with a laugh which indeed was forced, but which she carried through cleverly and well.

"Nothing whatever," she said. "At present, at any rate. Stay here where you are well cared for, and rest assured I am well off too, working hard, and making money. Oh, lots of money! And don't look so worried. You ought to be as happy in knowing that I am well, as I am in knowing that you are free and—and in good hands. Good-bye, my dear, dear boy. Thank God for letting me see you, know that——"

A catch in her voice stopped her, and she threw her arms round him and pressed her lips to his, while Lord Clanfield, stiff, upright, and unbending, stood at the window with his back towards them.

Gerard stared into her face with haggard, disappointed eyes.

"Do you mean you're going? That I'm to lose you already? What does it mean, Audrey, what does it mean?"

"It means," answered she readily, "that we're doing the best for us both. For us both."

"When will you come again?"

"I'll—I'll let you know."

She tore herself away from him and fled through the window with one swift glance at Lord Clanfield, and the whispered words:—

"I've done my part. Do yours!"

# CHAPTER XIII

MORE dead than alive, Audrey, when she had left Lord Clanfield's house, hurried through the flower-garden, where she passed Geoffrey, indignant at her having given him the slip but not ready with a coherent protest, and came to a sudden standstill under the spreading branches of an old beech-tree, against the trunk of which she leaned for support.

Panting and breathless, too deeply agitated for connected thought, she cast longing eyes back at the old red-brick house, and felt the first pang of the parting with her husband.

She had left him so abruptly, not daring to stay, not daring to speak clearly to him, that she asked herself, in dismay, whether the bewilderment in which he must be would not more than counterbalance the joy he had felt in seeing her again.

Perhaps, after all, Lord Clanfield was right, and the meeting, unavoidable as it had been, might have done the invalid more harm than good.

In a state of fresh suspense, she asked herself whether she would not do better to go back again, to make inquiries about him, to make one more attempt to soften the viscount's heart towards her.

But she knew, even while she thus debated with herself, that she would find no melting in the obstinate and autocratic old gentleman, whose prejudices as well as principles she had offended, and whose pride she had wounded by her counter-attacks.

No. She must refrain at all hazards from irritating him further, and she could trust him to fulfil his promise to be kind to Gerard if he were allowed to work in his own way.

In the meantime, how would he satisfy his nephew's demands to know more about her? Would Lord Clanfield tell him all he knew, and worse, all he suspected about her? Would he tell of the splendid house where she was surrounded by luxury, visited by troops of acquaintances, all belonging to a set more noted for its enjoyment of life than for its austerity?

Surely, surely he would never do such a cruel thing as to try to oust her from his nephew's heart by means which would inevitably do more harm to Gerard than to her!

And then in the midst of her trouble and distress there came into Audrey's heart a comforting thought: Gerard would never believe her other than true to him in word and deed without such overwhelming proof to the contrary as even malignity could not bring!

Struggling to regain her self-command, and drying the tears which would flow, she recovered enough composure to resume her walk towards the park gates.

But as she went, she cast many a look behind, perhaps with the secret hope that she might be called back, that she might even see Gerard himself in pursuit of her.

And on one of these occasions she caught sight, not indeed of any member of the viscount's household, but of a figure which seemed familiar. This was her first impression when she perceived, a long way behind her, a man going in the same direction as herself. The second impression was less pleasant: the man stopped short when she turned, and Audrey suddenly wondered whether he was following her.

On this assumption she waited, looking at him. He seemed disconcerted by her action, and, after turning away so that she could not see his face, he walked until he reached the shelter of an intervening clump of ornamental firs, after which she saw no more of him for the time.

At first she thought she would go back and try to find out who the man was. But on second thoughts she decided that, if he was really dogging her footsteps, her best plan would be to go on to the station without looking back, trusting to chance for some convenient season for identifying him.

This was a sensible decision, and, as she had supposed, she found the desired opportunity before reaching the little country railway station.

Coming to a knoll of rising ground, she passed it and waited on the other side. In a few minutes the man she had descried in the park came into full view.

And she recognised one of the footmen in the service of the Duchess de Vicenza, a man with a clever face and watchful, cunning eyes, whose duty it was to open the door for arriving guests.

"Barnard!" ejaculated she, under her breath.

It was evident to her that the man had been following her, and she guessed that he must have been in pursuit from the time she left "The Briars" in the morning. He pretended not to see her, but from the slight change of countenance which she noticed, she was convinced, not only that he was fulfilling an allotted duty, but that he was infinitely vexed at being seen, and that he guessed that he was found out.

She let him go past, and he was much too astute, now that he had once been caught, to betray himself further by looking round. He disappeared from sight before she moved from the spot where she had taken up her stand, and she saw no more of him till she reached "The Briars"; but she had shrewd suspicions that, though unseen, he was not far away.

This incident filled her with fresh misgivings to add to the vexations and griefs from which she was already suffering.

She was sure that the man would never have set out to follow her on his own responsibility; he must be fulfilling orders which had been given him.

By whom, then, were those orders given?

Surely not by the old duchess, whose only care was understood to be that her house and grounds should be kept in proper order.

Who, then, was it that had set him to play the spy upon her?

And once more, as had happened to her so often previously, a sudden uncomfortable sensation, as of being a puppet in unseen hands, a tool in the employ of some powerful organisation, seized her and made her shudder.

If only she could break away from the strange, invisible but strong ties that seemed to bind her to a position she loathed, to hold her in a course which was, she felt, suicidal to her self-respect, and to her hopes of restored happiness with her husband!

And then the poor creature realised, as she had never done before, that to break these ties abruptly would bring her no nearer to Gerard, no nearer to his uncle's regard, while it would bring upon her the blame of her one woman friend, Mrs. Webster, and certainly the disapproval and resentment of the one man who had done the most to help her—Mr. Candover.

It seemed to her fortunate that, when she reached "The Briars," only just in time for a late and hurried dinner, she found Mr. Candover himself there to see her.

He had come, he said, to submit to her certain notions of Mademoiselle Laure's concerning the winter campaign. The Frenchwoman was still in Paris, but she had made extensive purchases of models, and wanted the approval of her nominal chief for certain others.

Audrey, however, was tired, impatient, petulant.

"Why does she send you to me?" she asked. "Surely she knows more about these things than I do, and I gave her *carte blanche* to buy what she thought proper. Besides——"

"Well," interrupted Mr. Candover quickly, "I think you ought to be consulted. You have excellent taste, and——"

"Oh, no, I know nothing and care nothing about these things! I wear the dresses she tells me to wear, I recommend those she advises me to recommend. I am a mere puppet, without a will of my own or a word to say on my own account!"

Mr. Candover took her petulance sublimely. He was as patient as a lamb.

"Oh, don't say that. You won't when you have rested a little, and had something to eat. Don't let me detain you. I can wait here, if I may, while you dine."

Audrey bit her lip.

"You have dined, yourself?" she asked perfunctorily.

For some reason, perhaps it was on account of Lord Clanfield's disapproval of her friends, she did not feel kindly disposed to Mr. Candover at that moment. She had, even while he consulted her on this question of fashions, an uneasy, dim, vague sense that he was connected with her misfortunes; connected wilfully, and not by unhappy chance. At another time she might have been ashamed of this vague feeling, but at this moment of irritation, disappointment and despair, she could not be just, she was at the mercy of—instincts.

And her instincts, at this moment of depression, were all in arms against him.

"Yes, thanks. I dined early, before leaving town. You will see me to settle this matter, won't you?"

He was winning, persuasive, gentle. Wounded, irritable, full of misgivings as she was, she could not help finding his deference, his almost humble courtesy, both welcome and soothing.

She left him, and dining hurriedly, dressed herself with care, as a woman does when she is conscious that there is an ordeal of some sort in prospect.

And when she came down to the drawing-room she was at least outwardly calm, radiant and beautiful, even if her mind was torn with perplexing questions.

She had intentionally said no word as yet to Mr. Candover of the momentous news of Gerard's release. Not a word, either, of her visit to Lord Clanfield's. These pieces of information would, she knew, open up such a wide field for discussion that they could not be approached except with full leisure. That leisure, had, however now come, and she knew, as she swept into the drawing-room, in her dress of cream silk muslin with huge rosettes of palest turquoise velvet, that there was a struggle in store.

She wanted to withdraw from the wretched position in which she found herself, cut off from husband and relations. He would want her to snap her fingers at prejudices and principles alike, and to continue at her post.

Thus much she knew, but what she did not know, until she began to approach the subject, was that Mr. Candover was already in possession of the greater part of her news.

"I have something to tell you," she began, not taking the chair she generally used, low and easy, but a higher, more stiff-backed one in which she could assume more dignity; "something that will, I think, surprise you very much."

"Well!"

"Gerard is released—is at his uncle's, Lord Clanfield's."

"So I heard—yesterday. And you are going to join him there?"

87

Did he, could he, know, the cruelty of this question? It broke down all poor Audrey's defences, her pride, her self-command; and turning her head away to hide the tears that sprang to her eyes, she bit her trembling lip and tried in vain to recover her coolness.

Meanwhile, however, Mr. Candover quickly perceived his mistake.

"Oh, what have I done? Believe me, I had no intention of—of—Tell me. I don't understand yet; what is the position?"

After a brief struggle, Audrey regained enough composure to answer, not in a firm, even tone, but in short, broken sentences:—

"They disapprove—Lord Clanfield disapproves strongly, utterly, of what I have done, what I am doing. He dislikes the notion of my being in business, on the one hand, of my receiving guests who gamble on the other. I feel he is justified."

"Well, but surely Gerard doesn't disapprove! Knowing you were left insufficiently provided for, surely he applauds your spirit in striking out a line for yourself! He wouldn't be a man if he didn't!"

"He can say nothing. He is ill, very ill. So ill that his best chance is to stay where he is so well cared for, even if—it means——"

"Means what?"

"Even if it involves a temporary separation."

Mr. Candover leapt to his feet.

"Surely," he cried with passionate excitement, "no man worthy of the name would submit to such a state of things for a moment! He would say: 'My wife, my poor wife whom I was forced to leave alone and unprotected, is my first care. I will not stay at my ease with the relatives who have snubbed and neglected her, and left her to the kindness and care of people who are not connected with her or with me by any ties but those of friendship!' Surely, surely, Madame——Audrey, you would never cling so tenderly to a husband who could let you go and keep safe and snug himself in the house of a man who had no respect and regard for his true wife!"

Audrey was trembling and again on the verge of tears. She saw that this was a possible view to take of the situation of affairs, even though it was not the right one. She interposed earnestly:—

"You don't understand. It was I who took upon myself to arrange matters with Lord Clanfield. Knowing that even to Gerard, my engaging in business—not to speak of other things—would be a great shock, I hurried everything through so quickly that we had scarcely met and rejoiced in meeting, when I ran away again. I left him no time to speak, no chance to object. I took advantage of the fact that he couldn't run after me, to run away!"

Mr. Candover was standing near her, bending his eyes upon her with such a look of passionate devotion as she could not and would not meet. He appeared, indeed, to have almost lost his self-possession in anger at this treatment of her.

"As long as he had a leg to stand on," he persisted emphatically, "he should have run. Why, I would have crawled on my hands and knees sooner than let you go away from me in such a case! Audrey, it is hard, terrible, to see you used like this, to know that you are not appreciated as you ought to be by the man who has the blessing and honour of being your husband. No, I won't stop, I won't be shut up! I tell you it makes my blood boil to think of your being exposed to the insolence of those men, who think, because they are well-born, they have a right to trample under foot all decency, all duty, in dealing with the rest of mankind. Oh, Audrey Audrey," and as he spoke he came nearer to her, his eyes ablaze with passion, "forgive me if I say too much, but it's because I feel, I feel as if my own heart would burst to think of it!"

Although he spoke with intense passion, with torrential excitement, he took care not to wound her susceptibilities by so much as a too near approach. Keeping near her, indeed, but clenching his fists as if to keep away from her the hands that longed to touch hers, hovering over her rather than assuming any airs of authority or insolence, Mr. Candover succeeded in rousing in her a spark of the gratitude he was so anxious to excite. Seeing his opportunity in a certain softening of her features, a relaxing of her attitude, he was drawing stealthily nearer when, suddenly realising her danger, her weakness, she raised her head, and went on with her exculpation of Gerard.

"He cannot choose, he is in the hands of others," she said. "For not only is he so ill that there's a doubt whether we can save him, but his uncle has undertaken to sift the evidence against him, the false evidence that got his conviction. So that on Lord Clanfield may be said to depend not only his life, but his honour."

Mr. Candover seemed struck by this fact. So strongly impressed was he by it indeed that he at once changed his attitude, and from the passionate, enthusiastic friend became the cool-headed, cautious, sceptical man of the world.

"They had better leave things alone," said he drily, after a pause. "To prove him innocent would be—excuse my saying so—extremely difficult. Indeed, it's not at all likely that, with all his social influence, Lord Clanfield will be able to get the case reopened. It is all done, ended, and well-nigh forgotten by this time. Gerard had better let sleeping dogs lie."

There was a deep note of warning, almost of menace in his tone, which could not fail to impress Audrey, even while it roused her indignation.

"I know you believe him guilty. You have said so," she said, with fire. "But I *know* that he is innocent. And if Lord Clanfield were to heap up insults upon me, and were to refuse ever to speak to me again, I would forgive him everything if—if only—he would save my darling Gerard's life, and prove his innocence to the world!"

"*Your* innocence does you credit, Madame," sneered Mr. Candover as Audrey rose and walked away.

# CHAPTER XIV

I⊤ was one of the terrible evenings which Audrey had begun to hate, pleasant though every one tried to make them to her. The guests were lively and bright, always complimentary and sympathetic to herself, and observant of the rules of decorum in her presence, however high the play might be in the next room. They even broke up earlier now than they had done at first, and before one o'clock they were all gone.

Audrey, however, was restless, ill at ease, full of vain longings for another sight of her husband's face, and unable to sleep for the dreams in which she saw again, as she had seen that afternoon, the pitiful, white, drawn features, the sad, sunken eyes, or else the transformed, flushed countenance and brilliant, almost feverish eyes which had looked into hers and told her more plainly than he could with his lips that he had loved her and longed for her as she had for him.

She walked up and down her room, in soft-soled slippers that made no noise, wrapping her dressing-gown tightly round her—for she felt chilly and the night air was cold—hoping to tire herself out, to be able to forget her misery and her anxiety for a time in sound sleep.

And as she walked, she fancied that she heard, very faintly and as if muffled by distance, the sound of an altercation of some sort. She stopped, went closer to her locked door, and listened. She was sure, quite sure that she heard men's voices, angry, excited, violently vociferous.

She gently turned the key, then the handle, and peeped out.

She was shocked to see that one of the men-servants, the very Barnard whom she had caught following her that day, was quietly sitting on the wide ledge, which made a fairly good seat, of the window at the extreme north end of the corridor.

This corridor ran the whole length of the main building of the house, with bedrooms on one side, and a row of tall, deep-set windows on the other. These windows overlooked the courtyard, and the billiard-room, an annexe to the main building and at right angles with it, which was kept shut up by the Duchess de Vicenza's order.

In consequence of the ugliness of the outlook the lower part of all these windows was filled in with painted glass, and any eyes less sharp than those of Audrey might have failed to descry the servant in the corner, leaning back as he was against the darkened panes.

Perhaps even Audrey might have failed to see him if she had not had her attention attracted by a deep-drawn breath, almost a snore, which announced that the watcher was asleep.

Waking suddenly to the fact that this man, who had been a spy by day, was a spy by night also, Audrey left her door ajar, in order to make as little noise as possible, and gliding along the corridor in the direction of the front staircase, ran quickly down into the hall, and listened again.

She heard the sound of angry voices intermittently as she went; and divining that they proceeded from the side of the house nearest to the road, which was shut out by a high wall, she drew back the bolts of the front-door, and slipped out into the covered passage which led thence to the outer door in the wall.

In this outer door there was a little grating with a sliding panel, and hearing voices and footsteps, some of which she recognised in the road outside, Audrey slid back the panel and looked out.

She could see but little, for it was only four o'clock, and the morning was dark. She, however, could distinguish the figure of Johnson, the duchess's secretary, and that of one of the young Angmerings.

By what she heard in the confused talk of half a dozen men, all of whose voices she had heard before and who were, therefore, as she knew, habitués of the house, she gathered that there had been a quarrel, a dispute something indeed very much of the nature of a "row," that Johnson was the person who had been accused of unfair practices, and that his accuser was Edgar Angmering.

Where did they all come from?

They passed from right to left, quickly, not talking loudly, though they were all much excited, alike in accusation and in denial.

In a very few moments they had all passed out of hearing, and Audrey, cold, shivering more with horror than from the chill morning air, crept softly upstairs, saw that the man Barnard had disappeared, and, locking herself in her own room, understood fully for the first time for what sort of organisation she had been entrapped into playing hostess.

Durley Diggs accused, and now Johnson. Whether or not this latest disturbance were only the result of some gambler's quarrel in which Johnson himself was not more to blame than the rest, Audrey could not help being struck by the coincidence that the accusation should be brought against the representative of the duchess.

Who was this duchess? Was she a lady of rank? Or was she only the bearer of a fancy title, such as that which had been forced upon Audrey herself?

Was she, in short, the proprietor of a gaming-house, of which the management had ostensibly passed out of her hands and into those of Audrey herself?

The poor young wife was overwhelmed by these suspicions, which involved so many others that she scarcely dared to face any one of them.

After a short and uneasy sleep towards morning, she rose to find herself called upon to take some decisive action, and began by making an exhaustive tour of the premises, which ended in her feeling sure that the room which was used by the gamblers, probably night after night, and certainly till the early hours of the morning, must be that which was called the billiard-room.

This was a long and wide apartment, built out between the house itself and the outer wall, and having, as she now noted for the first time, a door leading straight into the road.

Audrey tried the inner door, found it locked, as usual, and demanded the key of the housekeeper.

She was, of course, met by a point-blank refusal. At this Audrey's tone changed. The housekeeper, a thin, dry-eyed woman, was not insolent; she only stated that she had been forbidden to open this room for anybody, by the duchess's express desire. Audrey looked her straight in the eyes.

"Well," she said, "I can't force you to give me the key. But, as I have reason to know that some persons got into that room during the night, I shall, if you persist in refusing, call in the police and have the lock forced."

The woman's face grew grey with alarm.

"You would not do that, Madame, without consulting—Mr.—Mr.—Mr. Johnson, surely?" she stammered.

"Without consulting anybody," replied Audrey calmly.

Only for a moment did the woman hesitate; then she handed the key with a shrug of desperation to Audrey, who at once opened the door, and found herself, as she had expected, face to face with abundant evidences of the fact that it was there that the card-playing had been going on. Stray coins, soiled and torn cards, overturned chairs, a broken candlestick which looked as if it had been used as a missile, proved conclusively the uses to which the room had been put, while the billiard-table, which gave the name to it, was only a small one, six feet in length, which stood across one end of the apartment, and looked as if it had been but little used.

Audrey was quite sure, to begin with, that it had not been used during her tenancy of the house, as the click of the balls is unmistakable, and could not have failed to reach her ears through the skylights with which the room was furnished instead of windows.

Now she understood why Lord Clanfield had not believed her assertion that his sons had been refused the house. She could not doubt—nay, she had the evidence of her own ears to prove—that they had only gone out by the front-door, to come in again by that which led direct into this room. And with a heightened colour and a fast-beating heart she returned to the morning-room, after having returned the keys to the housekeeper in significant silence, and wrote this letter:—

"MY LORD,

"I regret very much to have to admit that, in telling you as I did that your sons were not allowed to enter this house, I unintentionally said what was not true. I had prevented their entering by the front-door of the house; but I have discovered, during the past few hours, that advantage has been taken of my ignorance of the full extent of these premises, and that a room, which I had never been allowed to see, and which I was assured was unused, has been devoted—probably night after night—to the purpose of gambling. I recognised the voice of one of your sons among several persons who came out of that room at about four o'clock this morning, and I insisted upon being allowed to enter and examine it.

"As I have some reason to suspect that my movements are watched here—by whose order I have yet to discover—I shall put this letter into the town post-box with my own hands.

"I am going to venture to enclose a few lines for Gerard in this letter to you, and I shall be deeply grateful if you will allow him to have this enclosure. I am going to put it into an unsealed envelope, so that you may be convinced that I am keeping faith, and that I will not hold any communication with him but such as you may allow. I venture to think you will agree with me in thinking that a few words of vague encouragement, such as I am sending him, can do no harm whatever, and may help to make him resigned to a separation which, whatever you may think, I am sure he feels no less keenly than I do.

"Yours with gratitude for your kindness to my husband,
                                                "AUDREY ANGMERING."

She posted this letter herself with the enclosure, but she could not be sure that she was not followed and observed, and although she knew the letter would be delivered intact, she guessed that the billiard-room would not be used that night.

Her surmise was a shrewd one. Not only was Barnard, the spy, absent from the corridor, where she did not doubt he had always been posted to give the alarm in case of need, but certain dimly seen figures whom she descried in the shrubbery on the opposite side of the road, and guessed to be watchers sent by Lord Clanfield, neither saw nor heard anything to intimate that "The Briars" was other than what it pretended to be, a quiet and most decorous country house the inhabitants of which passed their long nights in innocent sleep, as decent folk should.

Poor Audrey was disappointed not to have received any acknowledgment of her letter. She had hoped that such a clear proof that she had been misled would have extorted some sort of reply from the viscount. He might at least have objected to her writing to Gerard, or have said that he had handed him her little, loving, harmless letter.

When the next morning came, and the post still brought no news from Lord Clanfield, her spirits, which had risen with a little flicker of hope, fell again.

Would he come that day? If only he would condescend to pay her another visit, she felt that what she would be able to show him might perhaps move even him to see that she was, in her way, scarcely less an object of pity than her husband, scarcely less in need of help and advice than he.

And the tears blinded her so much, when she saw that there was only one letter for her, and that one in Pamela's big, sprawling, would-be-masculine but very girlish handwriting, that for some minutes she could not see to open the letter.

When she did so, however, the interest if not the consternation she felt dried her tears.

"Dear Mrs. A——" the letter began; for it was thus that Pamela compromised between the real name her father had forbidden her to use, and the sham title which Audrey had refused to allow:—

"I am now going to beg you to do what you so sweetly promised you would, and to see the woman who persists that she is our mother. I have not been allowed to see her myself, nor, of course, has Babs. But Miss Willett has spoken to her, and says she is sure she is quite mad, and that if she even understands what she says, it isn't true. Do, do see her, and tell us what you think. I managed to send out this message to her by one of the servants, that you were a great friend of ours, and that you would see her and tell her anything she wanted to know. I thought I might say all that, and I do hope you won't be angry. I don't think you will. I sent her your address too, and as this was to-day, I daresay you will see something of her soon after you get this. That is, if there is anything that is worth hearing in what she says. Although of course I can't believe that what she says is true, yet, never having known our mother, you may guess how sad and how strange it has made both us girls feel. Do, do let me hear at once, if you see her, what you think.

"Ever yours,<br>"Pamela."

Audrey, miserable and lonely herself, was touched by the misery and loneliness of these two bright, sweet young girls, as expressed so ingenuously in this letter. Though she felt rather nervous as to the possible visit of the woman, she was interested, too, and anxious if she could to clear up the mystery for the young creatures.

On many accounts, however, she dreaded as much as she wished for the visit which she felt sure would soon follow.

And before the morning was over her expectation was realised. A servant announced that "some one" wished to see "Madame Rocada".

Audrey, with an impatient frown, such as now always crossed her face at the mention of the name, told the man to show the visitor into the morning-room.

Audrey, who was only waiting to get this visit over, before going up to town to see Mrs. Webster, and to ask to be put up for the night at her flat, went at once to the room in question, where she found, standing in the middle of the floor, a woman whom she at once set down, in her own mind, as mad.

Very tall, very thin, with good if somewhat large features, and white cheeks so sunken as to be filled with black shadow, the nameless visitor stared at her intently out of two large, deep-set black eyes that seemed to pierce like a knife. Her black hair, which was streaked with grey, was arranged in an old-fashioned way in a long curtain on each side of her haggard face, and her dress, which was almost as old-fashioned as the coiffure, was rusty black also.

A small black bonnet, almost as plain as that of a nurse, tied with black ribbons under the chin, added to her gaunt and funereal appearance.

She spoke at once, and her voice sounded hollow and unnatural, corresponding in all respects to her appearance. Staring intently at Audrey, she said solemnly, almost as if it had been an accusation:—

"Madame Rocada, I believe."

In spite of the oddity of her appearance and dress, there was something in the woman's deportment which convinced Audrey that she was a lady by birth and breeding, wreck though she had become. She could not have defined her reasons for believing this, nevertheless the consciousness of the fact was strong upon her, and helped to give her a sympathetic interest in her strange visitor.

To the first words, however, Audrey replied sharply:—

"No. That is not my name. It is Angmering, Mrs. Angmering."

The visitor frowned.

"But you are the lady the girls—my daughters—sent me to see?"

"Yes, oh, yes. I had a letter from one of them, and I've been expecting you."

As she spoke, she held out the letter, without, however, intending to give it up.

Rather to her dismay, the woman snatched it out of her hand.

"From my girl, my own girl! One of my own daughters, whom I'm not allowed to see! Who don't believe in my existence! Oh, it's more than I can bear!"

She broke down suddenly into a sort of hysterical sobbing without tears, and Audrey watched her with mingled sympathy and dismay.

Suddenly as she had broken out, she recovered, and, still with the same wild, intent look in her eyes, stared round the room until her gaze had taken in every object within her view. Then she turned abruptly to Audrey, who was getting alarmed by her behaviour.

Taking a great stride towards her, the woman in black put her face close to that of the younger woman, and said in a dictatorial tone:—

"You are very beautiful, too beautiful to be good! Who are you?"

Amazed at this address, Audrey could only stammer out an incoherent reply which her visitor did not heed. Staring once more round the room, and then bringing her eyes quickly to bear once again upon her victim, she asked as suddenly as before:—

"Now answer me truly. Is *he* here?"

"He! Who?" stammered Audrey.

The woman shook her head, as if dismissing the question as childish.

"Because," she went on, "if he were to know I have come, if he were to know I've tried to see my girls, he would murder me, yes, murder me, with as little compunction as if I were the cat!"

"Who do you mean? Who would do this?" cried Audrey, with sudden shrillness.

The woman fixed the great black eyes in another lugubrious stare upon her face:—

"Who? Why, my husband—Eugène."

Eugène! It was the name by which the White Countess had called out to her assailant on the terrible evening at the showrooms!

Audrey held her breath; she knew that the key to more than one mystery would, in another moment, be in her hands.

# CHAPTER XV

"EUGÈNE!" repeated Audrey, with faltering lips.

The strange woman looked at her intently.

"Ah! You don't know him by that name perhaps!"

Audrey, trembling, returned the woman's keen look with one as penetrating.

"What makes you think he is here?" she asked sharply.

The visitor, thus recalled to the object of her visit, hesitated for the first time.

"Since you know the girls," she said, "I presume you know their father too."

"Yes."

"And as I find you are a very beautiful woman, my suspicion is confirmed. You are one of his victims, or his tools, as all the pretty women whom he meets become."

Audrey, with fears which she could not express tightening round her heart, signed to the weird woman to sit down. Drawing a chair close to that which her visitor took, she sat down by her, and lowering her voice, said:—

"Tell me everything, everything. I am in a maze; I am in a position in which I can't move hand or foot without coming to some corner from which I can't escape. If you can tell me anything to help me, I shall be grateful, more grateful than I can express. Now who is the man you mean? What is his other name? If you are his wife and those girls are your children and his, you can trust me. I am a wife myself——"

"Whose?" said the woman shortly.

"My husband's name is Gerard Angmering, and he is the nephew of Lord Clanfield," she answered simply.

"Why isn't he here with you? Why are you alone? Where is he?"

She poured out the questions one after the other, so quickly that it was impossible to answer any of them until she stopped speaking.

Audrey bit her lip.

"Never mind that," she said. "Let it be enough for you that he is all the world to me, and that, if you find me here alone, it is neither by his wish nor by mine."

The strange woman was peering into her face with a penetration which was uncanny. When she had finished her inspection and Audrey, irritated and perplexed, paused, the visitor laughed harshly.

"I see, I see. You *are* one of the victims! Now tell me, what are you doing here? What goes on here? Is it gambling, or——"

With the blood rushing to her cheeks Audrey rose up with a cry.

"Oh, how did you know?" she cried breathlessly.

The visitor said nothing for a moment, but stared at her in the same piercing way. Then she got up, went softly across the room to the door, opened it quickly, and looked out.

"What are you doing?" said Audrey.

"Eugène uses spies," replied the visitor briefly, as she walked slowly round the room, apparently examining the furniture, the very walls, to see whether there was any possibility of their being overheard by unseen ears. Having satisfied herself, she came back to her seat. "And so," she said bluntly, "this is a gambling-house, and you are the decoy?"

"How dare you call me that?" panted Audrey, more angry than she could express.

But the woman went steadily on: "You, with your pretty face and figure, your well-bred air and your handsome dresses, are the nominal head of this house, I suppose?"

"What do you mean?"

"Oh, don't be offended. Why should you be, when what I say is true? Listen. I was his wife, you know. He was a rich man when I married him, and I brought him money myself. All went well while the money lasted, and we could live well and ostentatiously, keep horses and carriages—there were no motor-cars in those days—and a yacht and every luxury. Then the money ran short—the times changed, difficulties grew. Things grew worse and worse and presently they began to mend again, mend mysteriously. It was some time before I knew that there was anything wrong about the new prosperity, but when the knowledge did come, when I understood that I was expected to share in the vile work—to help in ugly schemes—cheating at cards—forgery—fraud—he was clever at them all—I stood firm, I refused."

She paused, and the remembrance of the far-away time she referred to seemed to increase the intense melancholy of her worn face, to render her deep voice more hollow. When she went on speaking, there came again over her face that wild look which had made the servants at Miss Willett's, and Audrey herself, take her for a madwoman.

"When he found he could do nothing with me, he changed his plans. Since I would not help him, I must go. By every cruel device, every wicked stratagem he tried to drive me out of my mind; he sent my two children away from me, he worked upon my nerves until I became hysterical, used threats which nobody would believe, threats of abandoning my little children, of murdering me."

"Why didn't you tell some one?" said Audrey.

"Because nobody would have believed me. He was gentle, handsome, with a caressing voice and charming manner. I was hysterical, irritable, proud, perhaps overbearing and too unhappy to be liked. Everybody took his part, and said how hard it was for genial, charming Eugène Reynolds to be tied to such an unamiable wife."

"Why didn't you run away from him?"

"I tried, but he was too clever for me. He knew that I would have moved heaven and earth to find my children, that I would have exposed, denounced him, once safely away from his diabolical influence, once free to breathe and to act for myself. For, though I hated him, I feared him too, and dared scarcely move without his permission. I don't know how I managed to keep firm in refusing to help him. I think now it was his fear that I should break down and blunder that saved me. For I used to feel that, if he had gone on insisting, I should have yielded at last. As it was, I was of no use to him, so he hated me, and again and again I thought he would kill me. And I told his friends so, and that was my undoing. He, with his sweet voice and caressing ways, to attempt to kill me, a tall, strong, powerful woman! The thing was absurd. And then the way was smooth for what he did. He got two doctors to certify that I was insane—one of them believed it, I'm sure, and the other was the sort of flabby man who can be led to believe anything—and I was shut up in a lunatic asylum."

There was a pause, and then she said in a hollow whisper:—

"I've been there fourteen years!"

"What!" cried Audrey, aghast, incredulous, horror-struck.

"Fourteen years," repeated the woman, "ever since my elder child, Pamela, was four years old. I knew they were told—both of them—that I was dead, and that was all I was allowed to know. Can you wonder that there was no difficulty in believing me insane? But I never was insane, no, not for an hour. Always, always I had the idea in my mind that I must get out, I must find them, I must save them from such a father. But the years went by, and I could never get away. It was in the west country, close to the Welsh border, that I was shut up, and I was out of the world, out of touch with everything. I never got a chance of escape till six months ago, when they thought I had worn out my old longings to be free, and then I came straight to London, and hunted, and hunted, till I found out where Eugène had hidden himself, and the new name by which he was known."

"And what is that?" asked Audrey.

"Reginald Candover," replied the woman quickly.

Although she had been prepared for this, Audrey could not hear it without a fresh shudder.

"How can I believe all this?" she asked suddenly, turning pale as certain possibilities connected with this terrible discovery occurred to her. "I can't, I won't believe it!"

The visitor shrugged her shoulders.

"Why should you believe it? It is no affair of mine whether you do or not," she said simply. "All I came here for was to learn something of my children. Pamela sent me your name and address as a friend of theirs, and all I ask of you is to tell me all you can about them. What are they going to do? They are nearly grown up, and want a mother's care. Who is going to give it them?"

Audrey listened with blanching cheeks. This insistence on the one point, the girls, always the two girls, was to her mind more convincing than anything else of the truth of the woman's story.

"I don't know anything about that," said Audrey. "They are getting impatient at being left at school, and are always importuning to be taken away. Pamela wants to come to me. But I don't want her here, and to do him justice, their father seems just as unwilling to bring them away from school as they are anxious to come."

A look of relief came over the poor woman's face.

"You really believe that?" she said eagerly.

"I do indeed. I've had proof of it. Remember, even bad men are generally good to their own children!"

The stranger sighed.

"Some are, I know. But if you have received as much ill treatment from a man as I have from my husband, you find it difficult to believe any good of him. Besides——" A new thought seemed to fill her with new horror, and again she looked cautiously round, and lowered her voice still further. "There's his sister. Even if he were to wish to keep his daughters from harm, his sister is such a wicked woman that, if he were to put them into her care, they would be worse off than ever."

"His sister! Has he a sister?"

"A half-sister. A woman without heart or conscience, and with no passion but for money, and no affection for any one but her half-brother. She hated me because I was English, and so were all my ways and all my tastes."

"Wasn't she English then?"

"No, nor he either. They are both of mixed nationality, and speak three or four languages equally well. And each is as clever and as wicked as the other. Do you mean to say you have never met her?"

And again both her look and tone grew incredulous.

"Never to my knowledge," said Audrey. "Perhaps she is dead."

The stranger heaved a sigh which Audrey could not but think was one of hope. She gazed long and earnestly at the younger woman.

"I'm sorry I said what I did—about your being too beautiful to be good," she said suddenly. "I think you are good; I think I could trust you! Will you keep an eye on my girls?"

Audrey's face puckered with distress.

"There's nothing I would do more willingly," said she, "but how am I to do it? He is their father; I can't interfere with his wishes; it would even do more harm than good for me to tell them the truth about you. The advice I strongly give you is to refrain from trying to see them, since their knowing the whole truth, or even a part of it, could only lead to dissensions, and might perhaps change their father's feelings towards them, which seem at present to be right and natural ones, to anger and bitterness."

The poor woman's face grew dark with distress.

"I know quite well you're right," said she. "But it's so hard, so very hard." She paused and appeared to reflect deeply for some moments. Then she went on abruptly: "If I do as you suggest, if I go back, away, without trying to see them again, will you write to me and let me know what they are doing, and how they are?"

Her tone was so humble, so imploring, that, absorbed as she was in her own anxieties, suggested by her visitor's revelations, Audrey felt the tears rising to her eyes.

"I will do what I can," she said earnestly. "But it is so little! For now that I know so much, I shall at once break off acquaintance with him."

The other laughed mockingly.

"You may think you will, but you will not," she said, with confidence. "Once in his net, no one gets away so easily. You will try and you will think you have succeeded; but you will feel the meshes about your feet, and you will be brought back, brought safely back into the net—every time!"

The words filled Audrey with unspeakable horror. For even while she would have contradicted, have protested, have scouted the idea presented to her, there rose up in her mind the terrible fear that it was a true one! Had she not tried already more than once to escape from the net, and had she not always been brought back, surely yet so gently that she was hardly aware of the compelling force at all?

She burst out into violence, clenching her teeth.

"I will escape," she said. "I will not continue my acquaintance with a man whom I know to be wicked!"

The stranger laughed again.

"You have only my word for it, you know, the word of a woman who has been declared mad! Better forget what I have said, or disregard it, and go on as if nothing had happened to open your eyes even the least bit. You can do no good by protesting, and may do yourself harm. You little guess how strong the forces are which you would have to fight against."

But there she was wrong. Gradually Audrey's instincts had been telling her what her visitor now openly confirmed, and the knowledge of the strength of the organisation she would have to contend against was growing every moment more profound.

"Where shall you go," she asked abruptly, "when you leave here? You want me to write to you. Where shall I write to? And how shall I address you?"

The visitor replied after a moment's hesitation; perhaps some lingering doubts of Audrey still had to be overcome or some suspicion as to whether Eugène's influence might not be strong enough to extract from this beautiful, gentle-mannered woman the information he might want about his hated wife.

At last, however, she made up her mind suddenly, and answered:—

"I am living in Hertfordshire with a maiden sister, and openly under the name in which Eugène married me—Mrs. Reynolds. I've lived there nearly six months now, ever since I got away from the asylum. Probably the asylum people haven't told him of my escape, and are still taking the money for my maintenance. At any rate I've been so cautious in my inquiries to find out him and my daughters, that I don't think he knows where I am. Now he will find out of course. I've no doubt there are spies in this house who will inform him of my visit. But," she added with confidence, "as I've been living in freedom for so long, it would take some formalities to get me back again, and—well, I can afford to risk it. I've learnt something about my girls, and I have, I hope, found that they've got a friend."

Quite suddenly she turned upon Audrey such an imploring, piteous look that the younger woman was deeply moved.

"I have need of friends myself," said she, in a broken voice, "and I have no power, no influence with anybody. But if I could do anything for them, believe me I would, oh, I would!"

The stranger rose, held out her long, slim hand, and grasped that of Audrey.

"I thank you, and I trust you," she said simply under her breath. Then she turned to the door, but paused to say: "No. I won't go out like that. Better not. These people will let him know who has been here. For both our sakes we must play them a trick. Ring the bell, and let them find you cowering in a corner of the room, as if you were frightened. Tell the servants I'm a madwoman who has been raving incoherently, and that you can't make out who I am."

"But," said Audrey, "might that not help him to get you back to the asylum again?"

The visitor laughed shrewdly.

"He won't trouble about putting me in if he thinks I really am mad," she replied quietly.

There was strong sense in this view, and Audrey carried out her suggestion to the letter, rang the bell, then withdrew into a corner of the room, behind an armchair, while the visitor stood, gaunt and forbidding, in the middle of the floor.

When Barnard appeared in answer to her summons, Audrey told him, with an appearance of alarm, to show the lady out, and made gestures to him to intimate that she was mad. The gaunt visitor went with a wild laugh, muttering to herself, and carried out her part of the stratagem so well that Barnard himself closed the door very quickly behind her, under the impression that he was indeed shutting out a dangerous lunatic.

Then Audrey, suffering from the reaction after the intense excitement caused by the interview with her visitor, went shuddering and shivering up the stairs, locked herself into her room, and at once began to pack up for immediate departure.

Whether she were brought back into the net or not, she would at any rate make a valiant attempt to get clear of it!

# CHAPTER XVI

As she went on with her packing, Audrey reviewed the situation, and came to a decision upon certain vital points.

In the first place, she would not be browbeaten by Mr. Candover into silence about the gambling that was carried on, or the cheating which accompanied it.

In the second place, she would no longer allow herself to be used as a decoy by this man, who, if half what her late visitor had said should prove to be true, was no better than a swindler.

She would therefore at once give up, not only the dubious title chosen for her by him or by Mademoiselle Laure, but the business run under that name. She thought, since she had put her own money into the venture, and had therefore a right to get some at least of it back, that she would see Mademoiselle Laure, and find out whether that astute Frenchwoman were willing to buy her out, giving Audrey a small sum for her interest.

Unfortunately, Mr. Candover had conducted the negotiations with the help of his own solicitor, and the contracts and papers connected with the sale were in his hands.

And Audrey suddenly asked herself, as she sat back on the floor in the midst of her work, whether she might not find, on investigation, that there had been trickery on his part in this matter, as there appeared to be in everything with which he had to do.

And she rose to her feet with a low cry, as the thought flashed into her mind that perhaps this rich, disinterested Mr. Candover, whom she and Gerard had both liked and trusted so much, was connected with her husband's misfortunes as well as with her own.

But this thought she would not have dared to put into words. Once in her mind, however, it stayed there with terrible persistency, till Audrey's brain reeled, and she asked herself whether her best course would not be to go to the solicitor, the very solicitor who had offended her so much by believing Gerard guilty.

And then, as she came to what she was sure was a sensible decision, that she would go to him, and put up with his dry manner and his penetrating questions, it flashed upon her that, instead of taking her part against Mr. Candover and expressing a readiness to investigate his conduct, the solicitor might perhaps be more inclined to investigate hers!

For she, poor child, in her friendless and lonely condition after Gerard's going away, had let herself drift entirely into the ways suggested by Mr. Candover, had gone with him to his solicitor instead of consulting her husband's, to arrange the lease of the showrooms, had, indeed, put herself as completely into his hands, in her ignorance and desolation, as if she had been a child and he her natural guardian.

And would the stern lawyer whom she had dreaded and disliked for his curt interrogation of Gerard be more likely to look upon her with a kind eye than he had been before? He had plainly shown his belief that the young couple had got into debt through the extravagance of the beautiful wife; and this being so, he would naturally put the worst construction upon her motives in taking to the business on the one hand and in renting "The Briars" on the other.

What should she do? To whom should she turn? It was with a feeling of despair at her heart that she went downstairs, after nearly three hours' hard work in packing and preparing for her departure.

Her luncheon had been waiting more than an hour when she came down ready dressed for her journey; and she uttered a cry of surprise and dismay when she came face to face, in the hall outside the dining-room, with Mr. Candover.

"Hallo!" said he, "I see I'm only just in time to catch you. Going out?"

"Going away," replied Audrey curtly, as he opened the door for her.

"May I come in and speak to you? It's important. And tell the man not to wait. I want to say something for your ears alone."

This was said in a whisper, and Audrey complied with his request, and, at the urgent instance of Mr. Candover, sat down at the table, where, however, she tried in vain to eat.

To find herself so suddenly in the presence of this man, whom she now dreaded as much as she had once trusted him, was an ordeal she had not expected to have to undergo so soon. She could not, she would not pretend that nothing had happened to disturb her; on the contrary, every word, every look was constrained and cold. Mr. Candover, gentle and patient as ever, broke the ice himself as soon as they were alone.

"What's this I hear," he began, "about your having been frightened by a madwoman this morning? Barnard tells me he found you cowering behind a chair, and the woman muttering at you in a threatening manner."

He looked at her fixedly, and she blushed deeply as she answered:—

"I was rather frightened, but I don't think she really meant to do any harm. She muttered and talked wildly, and told an extraordinary story in a rambling manner. I got to the bell, when she had been talking for some time, and rang, and Barnard showed her out."

He looked at her keenly, and seemed undecided whether to ask her more questions, but finally refrained, and said:—

"There's another thing I want to talk about, and it is what brought me down here. The housekeeper says you insisted yesterday upon having the keys of the billiard-room given to you, and she is afraid of what Madame de Vicenza will say if it comes to her ears."

Audrey, who was looking down at her plate, answered quietly:—

"Something else will have to come to Madame de Vicenza's ears, Mr. Candover. For the second time since I have been staying in this house a man has been caught—or suspected of—cheating at cards."

"Impossible!" Mr. Candover was evidently surprised at this intelligence, or, as Audrey shrewdly suspected, surprised at her being in possession of it. "What reason have you for thinking so?"

"I have the evidence of my ears and my eyes," said she in a tremulous voice, but with a certain doggedness, "that gambling has been carried on here, long after the guests were supposed to be gone. They went to the room which is absurdly—or artfully—called the billiard-room, and there they went on playing till four o'clock in the morning. And there have been quarrels, and another man has been—found out."

"Who?" asked Mr. Candover sternly.

"Madame de Vicenza's steward or secretary, I believe, the man called Johnson."

Audrey glanced up and down again quickly, and saw that Mr. Candover was really disturbed. She went on:—

"I needn't say that I don't intend to stay here another night. I only waited till this morning in the hope that Lord Clanfield would come and see me, as I wrote to him at once."

"Why?" asked Mr. Candover sharply.

"Because his sons are among the men who have been robbed here."

"Robbed!"

His tone was threatening, alarming. But Audrey, strung up to a high pitch of excitement, persisted steadily:—

"Yes. Robbed. So I informed him of what went on here."

"It was a mad thing to do," said Mr. Candover impatiently.

"It was the right thing."

"You have done yourself no good by it," retorted he angrily. "You see Lord Clanfield did not even answer your letter."

Audrey bit her lip.

"Well, I did my duty at any rate. Now I'm going away from this hateful place, and the men who come here will know, once for all, that I have nothing to do with keeping it up."

"You have kept it up for two months," said he drily.

The hot blood rushed into Audrey's face.

"I certainly did not keep up the billiard-room, or allow the play that went on there," she said sharply. "That can be proved. I had the keys yesterday for the first time."

"Well, it's easy to *say* that. Indeed, I should advise you to say it," said Mr. Candover, with a sudden change to provoking coolness. "But will you get people to believe it? I think the odds are against you."

A cold chill crept along Audrey's limbs. Was this true? It was, she felt, only too likely to prove so. If she were to assert that she knew nothing of the existence of the room where the late card-playing went on, the servants, who, as she guessed, were all engaged in the nefarious business carried on there, would be ready to swear that she did know.

She kept silence.

"Of course, in the circumstances, I applaud your resolution to leave the place," went on Mr. Candover; "though, as you have only ten days longer of your tenancy, to go now looks rather as though you were disgusted at being found out."

"Found out! I! Mr. Candover!"

"Of course, I'm putting the matter from the point of view of what people will say. Still, you're right to go. And now, may I ask where do you think of going to? I scarcely like to put the question, although once I flattered myself that I could have asked you any such thing freely. But lately—I don't know exactly how it is, for when I have offended you, I've always been very contrite and humble in asking forgiveness—but certainly there has been a change in your manner towards me, so that I scarcely like to say things now which I could have said freely when you were kinder."

Audrey felt the subtle influence of this man's insinuating manners, soft voice and deprecating attitude. But she steeled herself against him, and answered steadily:—

"I have not meant to be unkind. It is impossible that I should feel quite the same to you now that I know you do not think with me about—Gerard." She would not let him protest, but hurried on: "But, of course, I'll tell you where I'm going. It is to Mrs. Webster, who will put me up, I know, while I look about me."

"And may I ask what you have in your mind to do?"

"First, to sell the business, which I refuse to carry on any longer with all the unpleasant associations which seem to be attached to the name under which it is carried on."

"Rocada?"

"Yes. In the first place I shall offer it to Mademoiselle Laure, who is, after all, the real head of it. I am a mere puppet, and only for show."

"Without admitting that, I think your idea is a good one," said Mr. Candover. "Laure might take it, if you were not too hard in your terms. And I don't suppose you would be."

"Oh, no."

"Well then, you have taken a very sensible resolution, from your point of view. From mine, it seems a pity to give up a business which promised to work up into a first-rate one. In the meantime, I will see you safely as far as Mrs. Webster's flat—Oh, I insist upon it. Even if you are anxious to throw all the blame for what has gone wrong upon my poor shoulders, as I think you are, you must not cut me off altogether, when I am still only too anxious to be of use to you in any possible way."

Her protests were in vain. And poor Audrey began to feel, with a terrible sinking of the heart, that the words of the stranger were coming true, and that, try as she might to get out of range of Mr. Candover's uncanny and mysterious influence, she would be drawn back, invisibly but surely, every time.

This impression was increased when they reached Mrs. Webster's flat, for that good lady received them both with a broad smile of welcome, which was even more expansive for Mr. Candover than for his companion. Indeed it was evident that his gentle voice and insinuating manners had fascinated the widow, and Audrey soon perceived that it would be hopeless, as well as rash, to confide in her as to his suspected misdeeds.

And when she learned that Mr. Candover had called upon Mrs. Webster once or twice of late, Audrey felt another pang of the terrible fear that the net was tightly woven about her own feet. Every acquaintance, every friend she had seemed to have come, in one way or another, within his baleful influence.

She was, therefore, obliged to say nothing about the visit of the mysterious stranger, and she glossed over the treatment she had received from Lord Clanfield as much as she could. But again she noted uneasily that Mrs. Webster seemed to have been infected with the idea that Gerard had really been guilty of the forgery; and finding so little sympathy with her deepest feelings, Audrey toned down her discoveries at "The Briars" as much as she could, and dwelt more on the gambling than on the disputes which had resulted from it.

On the following morning Audrey went to the showrooms, with reluctance indeed but with a dogged resolution to go through the unpleasant business of bargaining with Mademoiselle Laure with spirit and keenness, not for her own sake only, but for that of Gerard.

If only this business had been unconnected with Mr. Candover and Marie Laure, and the adventure with the white lady, poor Audrey felt how gladly she would have had it to fall back upon, how proud she would have been to be able, by her own exertions and her own money, to do something towards making a home for Gerard and herself. As it was, she had sunk so much of her small capital in this business that, if she were to get nothing from it, she would have very little left, and no means of providing some sort of home in which to nurse her husband back to health and strength again.

So that it was with many a tremor that she re-entered the handsomely furnished rooms, where she found Marie Laure already returned from Paris, busily engaged in unpacking the new models which she had brought over, and affecting as much care and secrecy over them as if they had been royal robes.

Marie Laure received her effusively, though with the suspicious dryness under all her compliments which made Audrey mistrust them.

She refused to talk about business that morning, and insisted on enlisting Audrey's services in the matter of the rearrangement of the rooms, and in sundry other matters which occupied them both until well into the afternoon, when, to Audrey's annoyance, there streamed into the rooms, in twos and threes, but at very short intervals, quite a little crowd of the men who had been habitués at "The Briars" during her tenancy of the house.

The firstcomers made a pretence of making purchases of bonnets and laces, which Laure brought forward for Audrey to offer. But it was soon evident to the unlucky nominal head of the firm that her customers had other objects in view than these. There was a sort of freemasonry among them which irritated and alarmed her; and she caught an interchange of glances between them which sent the hot blood to her cheeks.

While preserving towards her that outward decorum which had always been carefully respected at "The Briars," Audrey felt certain that she was connected by them all with the scenes which had taken place there, and that they believed her to be fully cognisant of what went on in the billiard-room when the guests were supposed to have gone away.

She understood again that Mr. Candover's prediction had come true, and that they looked upon her departure from "The Briars" as caused by the disturbance of two nights before.

Probably, she thought fiercely, it was he himself who had put the idea into their heads.

She had answered a great many questions as to her hurried departure from Epsom, and requests that she would not be long in finding another house, when Mr. Candover himself, and a well-known baronet of sporting tastes, entered together.

Audrey's patience was at an end. Her spirit was roused to the point of recklessness, she felt that she hated Mr. Candover, and that she must, no matter what the risk, make one bold effort to defy and denounce him.

When, therefore, Sir Barnaby Joyce began to rally her on her sudden loss of "pluck," and to express the fear that it was the noise they had made two nights before which had frightened her away, Audrey, sombre, outwardly calm and dignified, but inwardly on fire with a sort of reckless indignation and despair, turned upon him fiercely.

"What noise do you mean, Sir Barnaby?" she asked, with subdued ferocity that made Mr. Candover move uneasily as he watched her.

"Oh, I think you know! There was some sort of disturbance, wasn't there? Some one accused somebody else of not playing fairly, I believe," said Sir Barnaby, evidently surprised by her fierce tone.

Audrey fixed upon him a pair of blazing eyes.

"Yes, somebody did," she replied firmly and steadily. "Somebody accused somebody else of cheating, and—in all probability he was right, quite right." There was a movement, a stir among the men, who were standing in idle attitudes about the room, and they turned to look and to listen as she went on in the same clear, resolute tones: "But I don't pity any of you; I feel no more sympathy for those who are cheated than for those who cheat." The sensation of amazement deepened among her hearers, and Mr. Candover grew deadly white. She went on, with rising warmth: "Ought you not all to expect underhand ways, when you meet to play in an underhand manner? Whom can you blame but yourselves when, meeting by stealth to play games which can only be played by stealth, you find yourselves the easy prey of——" And she stared defiantly at Mr. Candover—"a gang of swindlers!"

# CHAPTER XVII

THERE was a silence of amazement, of doubt, of consternation; and the men who thronged the showroom looked at each other, and then at the daring woman who had brought this accusation, as it seemed, against the well-known, the irreproachable, the wealthy Mr. Candover.

Perhaps the most shocked of all the listeners to this unexpected tirade was Sir Harry Archdale, who, himself a victim of the unfair play carried on at "The Briars," had been only too willing to look upon the intrusion of a black sheep there as an unhappy accident, and upon Audrey as a victim like himself of that intrusion.

But, wishing as he did to take her part, he had been considerably perturbed by the opposite views of her which were commonly held among the habitués of "The Briars," and now that she had the audacity and the bad taste to fling a direct accusation into the face of one of the most prominent men of his own set, Sir Harry at once took fire, and mindful of the fact that the man whom she accused was the father of the lovely Pamela, he stepped forward boldly, and was the very first to put a question to the angry lady.

"Madame Rocada," said he, deferentially as far as manner went, but in an offended tone, "you will, I'm sure, think it only right, when you say a thing which affects all, or almost all of us, to be more explicit. Whom do you accuse of cheating? Who are the members of the gang of swindlers you refer to?"

Audrey, already trembling from the effects of her own boldness, turned to him and answered in a broken but determined voice:—

"One of them you know. His name—or the name he goes by—is Durley Diggs. He was Mr. Candover's secretary."

"Was, not is," retorted Mr. Candover, speaking for the first time, and as coolly as if the accusation just brought were no concern of his, though his face was very pale and his eyes wore a strange and almost glassy look. "When I heard that complaints had been made about his play I discharged him at once from my employment—as you must remember, Madame Rocada."

"Yes, Madame, you told me so yourself," said Sir Harry.

But Audrey was not to be cowed, not to be forced into retracting a word, now that she had once strung herself up to the point of open accusation. Clasping her hands tightly together, and conscious, with a fierce feeling of resentment and despair, that all these men were as fools and children in the hands of this clever scoundrel who had made a tool of herself, she made no reply to this, but, after a moment's pause, went on doggedly:—

"Then there is a man who calls himself Johnson. There have been complaints of him."

"When?" asked Mr. Candover sharply.

"Only two nights ago."

"And will you tell us where these accusations were made, and by whom?" he went on with the same provocative calmness.

"They were made—the disturbance arose—about four o'clock in the morning, when cards were being played in the billiard-room at 'The Briars,' and they were made by more than one man."

"Were you present, Madame?"

"Not in the room. But I overheard the disturbance, and I challenge any of you who were there, you, Sir Barnaby, were one, and one of the young Angmerings was another—to deny that there was a disturbance, and that Johnson was accused of cheating."

There was a moment's silence. Then Sir Barnaby said, in a tone of veiled insolence that cut her to the quick:—

"I am greatly distressed at having to speak to a woman—a lady—upon such a matter. I had admired your tact, Madame Rocada, in keeping out of all discussions and scenes of this sort. We have all understood and admired the way in which you conducted the premises and managed the business, unseen, but making your presence felt, and keeping up a high standard of decorum. I cannot but think you are very unwise to have forced us, as you are doing, into speaking out upon a subject which could very well have been disposed of without the painful necessity of dragging a lady into it."

Every word burned into Audrey's brain. Careful as he was to speak with outward respect, Sir Barnaby was, as Audrey felt, absolutely convinced that she was the keeper of a gaming-house of a shady sort, and that she had known all about the play which was carried on in the billiard-room until the small hours of the morning. How, indeed, could she wonder at this being the case? Was not the strangest fact in connection with this business that she had been in ignorance of so much for so long? Even as she listened, she felt how impossible it would have been for her to believe in such a story as her own, in such a blind confidence as she had shown, in the possibility of a grown woman, perfectly innocent, allowing herself to be used as a puppet in such a scandalous affair.

This terrible consciousness began to oppress her, to paralyse her tongue, to blanch her cheeks, until she felt within her the dreadful certainty that not one of all the men who watched her, some furtively, some openly, doubted the truth of what Sir Barnaby was saying.

When he paused there was a sort of murmur, and some of the men moved towards the door, anxious to escape the rest of a painful scene.

But Mr. Candover, foreseeing their intention, quietly interposed his person between them and the door, anxious concerning the impression they might carry away with them.

"I—I have had nothing to do with it. I—I have always disapproved of the play—I have protested against it. And I—I knew nothing about the billiard-room until two nights ago."

These last words were too much for any one's credulity. There was again a sort of murmur, and Sir Harry Archdale openly smiled.

Audrey, conscious that the feeling was against her, turned her head away from them all without another word.

But the movement, her evident distress combined with her youth and beauty, turned the current of feeling suddenly in her favour again. Mr. Candover perceived this tendency, and spoke:—

"We are quite ready, Madame Rocada," said he, in a tone of exaggerated deference which hurt her more than open insolence would have done, "to believe what you say, that you disapprove of cards, that you have protested against play at 'The Briars,' and that you knew nothing whatever about the late hours in the billiard-room, although you knew all about the disturbance two nights ago."

Audrey turned fiercely towards him, but a certain consciousness that these last words had turned the tide of feeling once more against her, kept her dumb. He went on:—

"But you must understand that when you say you harboured a gang of swindlers under your roof——"

"I didn't say that!" cried she aghast.

Mr. Candover turned to the rest of the men with uplifted eyebrows.

"Then I'm afraid we've misunderstood you," he went on suavely. "Certainly I understood, for my part, that you said we were all either swindlers or swindled, and that you had no more sympathy for the one lot than for the other. Did we misunderstand you in thinking you said that?"

"I did say that," sobbed out Audrey, who was not crying, but who could not speak except in spasmodic jerks.

"I thought so. Well, then, is it too much to ask that you should be a little more explicit, that you should tell us, in short, who are the swindlers and who the swindled?"

There was another dead silence. Painful, pitiful as it was to see this young and lovely woman brought thus to bay, the matter was too exciting for any one to feel inclined to let the affair rest there. It almost seemed—Mr. Candover took care to let it seem—that they all rested under some sort of imputation until she could be made to speak out.

Audrey felt, however, that she would get no sympathy, no belief, if she were to tell the truth. And in despair she said so.

"What is the use of asking me," she said bitterly, "to say any more? Not one of you would believe me, if I did. No. All I say is this: the play at 'The Briars' was not fair play, at least it was not always fair. I have proved it to you in two instances. Well, that ought to be enough for you. For me to accuse anybody whose cheating has not been found out would be useless, even if it were possible. All I do, all I have done, is to warn you that the men who have done the unfair work were acting together, and, I believe, acting under orders. And as for the rest—as for discovering under whose orders they acted, they cheated, why, surely that is your business, the business of those who have lost money—not mine!"

"No, but it's not enough. You ought to tell us who it is. It's not fair to bring an accusation and then to draw back," protested Sir Harry, who felt all the more strongly because he had been inclined to look upon this lovely woman as a victim, and who now felt that he had been befooled.

Mr. Candover's voice broke in suavely after the young man's hot-tempered outburst.

"As far as one could judge," he said very calmly, but with an air which suggested a certain amused contempt under his quiet manner, "Madame Rocada appeared to accuse *me* of being the ringleader in the offences of which she spoke. Wasn't that your impression, Sir Barnaby?" he went on, turning to the baronet, who appeared disconcerted by the direct question, and who looked, as indeed he felt, reluctant to take further part in this unpleasant scene, in which a young, beautiful and unhappy woman was forced, as it were, to stand at bay against six or eight men.

"Oh, really I don't know. I heard nobody in particular accused, except Johnson and Diggs," answered Sir Barnaby. "Haven't we had enough of it? It's confoundedly awkward!" he added in a lower voice to Candover, trying to hook him by the arm and lead him away.

"I think," said Sir Harry, who felt the implied imputation upon Mr. Candover the more keenly that he was a great admirer of that gentleman's pretty daughter, "that Madame Rocada ought to do one thing or the other. Either to let us know who are the other members of what she calls the 'gang,' or else—to withdraw the imputations she has certainly made."

Sir Barnaby caught at the suggestion.

"Oh, certainly, certainly. I'm sure Madame will be ready to do that. We all allow—we can't deny that there were two black sheep, and that we were very dull not to have found them out before. I feel sure Madame said a little more than she meant to do, and that she is just as anxious to put an end to this as any of us. Aren't you, Madame Rocada?"

And he turned to Audrey, with real concern in his eyes, genuinely anxious to make it easy for her to retreat from the daring and dangerous position she had taken up.

But Audrey would not retract. On the other hand, as it was useless for her to try to maintain her position by words which, she felt, would only be looked upon as wild and malignant accusations, she merely said, looking at Sir Barnaby, and speaking in a low and unsteady voice:—

"I have nothing more to say—nothing."

"No, of course not. And you retract all accusations, or supposed accusations, don't you?" persisted the baronet, putting his good-natured red face persuasively near to hers, and smiling into her eyes in a coaxing manner which met with no response.

"I don't retract," she said simply. "There is nothing I can retract. And some day—sooner or later—you will all find out that what I've said is true."

Then she sailed away through the room to the door, and the men instinctively made way for her, while Sir Harry, who was the nearest to the door, opened it for her to pass out.

But before she could do so, while therefore she was still within hearing, there sounded suddenly through the room these words, spoken by Mr. Candover in a voice which was carefully subdued as if to escape her ears, but which was, in reality, so pitched that, while it was scarcely more than a whisper, every word reached her ears distinctly:—

"And that woman—who dares to talk to us all in that strain, to bring accusations, to talk of gangs of swindlers—is the wife of a convict!"

The words came like a bombshell into the group, and the very men who had felt compunction for their share in the scene, the very men who had been all but convinced by her spirit and her proud yet innocent bearing were on the instant filled with amazement and indignation, while the suspicions which had begun to melt away became at once as strong as ever.

For Audrey certainly heard the words uttered by Mr. Candover, since they caused a shiver to pass through her. Every eye was turned upon her as she wheeled round in the doorway, and said, in a low voice, with biting emphasis:—

"Gentlemen, I have done my best to protect you—from yourselves. I thank you—for your chivalrous return."

Then she tottered through the doorway, rejecting with a cold gesture Sir Barnaby's proffered help, and shutting herself into the little room at the back where she used to leave her walking dress when she came to and from the showrooms every day, she locked herself in, sat down on the nearest chair, and remained like a woman struck with paralysis, unable to think, unable to do anything but feel that last terrible wound inflicted by Mr. Candover.

The wife of a convict! The wife of a convict! This was the weapon he had held in reserve all this time, knowing that he could rely upon it to quench every feeling of pity or respect which might be felt towards the poor victim of his craft!

Audrey understood now better than ever how closely the net was drawn about her feet, how strong were the meshes which bound her.

The wife of a convict! And she had not been able to say one word in refutation of the taunt. She was the wife of a man who had been convicted, and that, in the eyes of the world, was enough to place both her and her husband beyond the pale of sympathy. Yet, why should it be so? Why should they take it for granted that she was worthless, just because they took it for granted that her husband, having been convicted, must be a criminal? Why were they so blind as to suppose that she, who denounced the cheating that had gone on at "The Briars," was in league with the cheats?

She could not understand it. She could not realise how subtilly Mr. Candover had been at work, representing her as a miracle of artful prudence, whose airs of innocence hid the most careful and cautious system of self-preservation.

While she wondered why they could not read guilt in his pale face, in his burning, angry eyes, the rest of the men were listening to Mr. Candover's comments on her behaviour, on her cleverness in being blind to everything until there was a "row," and in then running away and assuming airs of virtuous indignation over an occurrence which to her must have been an everyday affair.

For a long, long time Audrey remained in the little back-room, feeling so utterly miserable, so degraded in her own eyes by the ordeal through which she had passed and the malignant comments to which she knew she was being subjected, that she could not do anything but hold her aching head between her hands, and whisper in an agonised voice: "Oh, Gerard, Gerard!"

It was not until dusk had come, and she had long since heard the visitors go down the stairs and out by the side-door into the street, that at last she roused herself, bathed her red eyes, which, however, had shed but few tears, and summoning her spirit, made up her mind to go through the fateful interview with Mademoiselle Laure.

Her situation, poor creature, was so desperate, the humiliation to which she had been subjected was so great, that from very excess of misery there came a calmness over her spirits; a sort of desperate courage came to her aid, and told her that, as she had now experienced the worst, had defied Mr. Candover and made him her enemy, and had cut herself off, with his

118

assistance, from all these acquaintances for whom she did not greatly care, she was at least independent, and in a position to snap her fingers at fate.

There were only two things left to dread: the death of her darling Gerard, which Lord Clanfield had almost told her to expect, and which she told herself she would not long survive; or her husband's discovery of her desperate situation.

Deeply as he loved her, Audrey felt, with a sort of calm despair, that even his love would not be proof against the skill with which Mr. Candover would build up a case against her. And that this diabolically clever and cunning man, whom she had been simple enough to take for a friend, would add that last drop to the cup of her misery she felt convinced.

Gerard would learn enough of the truth about her and her life while he was away to believe what Lord Clanfield believed, what his cousins believed. And she remembered with a shudder that one of the Angmerings had been present on the night of the disturbance in the billiard-room, had been one of the loudest in denouncing Johnson as a cheat.

Well, there was no help for it. Life—such as it was—had still to be lived, and it was with a new doggedness, a determination that at any rate they should not rob her of the business she had bought with her own money, that Audrey came out of the room, and returned to the showrooms, where she found Mademoiselle Laure busy with a customer.

The Frenchwoman gave her a glance, enigmatic, unfathomable. And Audrey, who had not remembered until this moment how deftly Laure had closed the showroom doors and thus, as it were, kept Audrey and her visitors and their discussion confined within four walls and out of earshot of others, wondered how much the woman knew.

While she wondered, and put this question to herself, and glanced at the hard, dry, leathern face wreathed at the moment in perfunctory smiles, there came to Audrey suddenly a knowledge of the truth.

For in the Frenchwoman's cold eyes, straight mouth and well-shaped nose, and even more in the quick glance she threw, penetrating, intelligent, malignant, at her nominal chief, Audrey recognised that hitherto unsuspected likeness to Mr. Candover which confirmed part of the story told by her mysterious black-robed visitor.

And Audrey knew that in Mademoiselle Marie Laure, the Frenchwoman who "couldn't speak English," she had to deal with the half-sister of Mr. Candover, the woman of whom she had been told that "she was as wicked and heartless as he was himself."

# CHAPTER XVIII

Iᴛ was inevitable that such a scene as that which had passed in Madame Rocada's showrooms, should become matter of common gossip within a few hours.

The story reached the clubs before the afternoon was over, and on every hand it was discussed, with variations of all sorts, until poor Audrey herself would hardly have recognised either her own portrait or the details of the miserable affair.

Sir Harry Archdale, who had walked away with Mr. Candover, and who found an opportunity of expressing his admiration for Miss Pamela, even while he regretted having met her in the society of Madame Rocada, detailed his version of the occurrence to the young Angmerings, and they, after hearing various other accounts of it, went back next morning to their father's place in Hampshire, for the very purpose of enlightening both Lord Clanfield and their cousin concerning an event which touched the family honour nearly.

Both Edgar and his brother Geoffrey had shared the general suspicions of Madame Rocada's good faith, and had alternately chuckled and waxed indignant over the story that she was their cousin's wife, at one moment believing it and pitying Gerard, at another laughing at it as an invention, or growing angry at the notion.

Now, however, the aspect of affairs had changed. Sir Harry had told them of what Mr. Candover had said, that Madame Rocada, the artful keeper of a shady gambling-house, was the wife of a convict. And this statement, chiming in with Audrey's own confession that she was their cousin's wife, made them feel the necessity of communicating with their father, who would deal with the matter as he might think fit.

It was an awful scandal to have a cousin under their roof who, whether guilty or innocent, had undoubtedly been convicted of forgery; it was a worse thing for it to become known that this cousin's wife was a woman in whose house men were fleeced of their money.

It was luncheon-time when they arrived at the old red-brick mansion, where they found their cousin Gerard, as usual, in the garden, looking ill indeed, but a little less thin, a little less lifeless, than he had been a week before.

The sight of his wife, brief as it had been, the receipt of a letter from her, vague as were its contents, had undoubtedly done wonders towards restoring the unlucky man to that interest in life which had for the time been crushed out of him.

His cheeks were still hollow and pale; his eyes were still unnaturally large and filled with a mournful wistfulness. But in spite of his anxiety as to his wife's whereabouts, his irritation on account of his uncle's replies to questions about her, he had now begun to find his energy and spirits slowly returning, and it is possible that the very uncertainty and suspense he was in about Audrey rather helped than hindered his recovery, by stimulating his curiosity and increasing his desire to be able to go in search of her, as he meant to do as soon as he was able.

Edgar was the first to speak. Half shyly, looking askance at his cousin as he came up with his hands in his pockets, he asked how he was getting on. Gerard at once detected something unusual in his tone, and looked at him curiously as he answered.

"Got rid of the nurse, at all events," said Edgar.

"Oh, yes. I'm all right now."

"You only want a winter at Nice or Cannes to set you up again," suggested Geoffrey, who was close behind his brother.

Gerard was surprised at this solicitude, which was most unusual. Both his cousins, while not daring to be openly insolent to him in their father's presence, had taken no pains to hide their disgust at having to put up with the residence under the paternal roof of a man who had been in penal servitude.

"No," he answered, "I don't want to go abroad. I prefer to stay in England. I'm tired of doing nothing."

"Well, what can you do? You couldn't go back to the bank, you know!" said Geoffrey, with cruel bluntness.

Gerard's white face flushed, and he did not answer. The rather less boorish Edgar said quickly:—

"You couldn't work yet awhile, if you wanted to, could you? You will have to get strong first."

"Well, but I should get all right again faster if I had something to occupy myself with. I don't care for the life you fellows lead, loafing and getting into mischief," retorted Gerard.

"Well, you got into worse mischief than we," replied Geoffrey.

Gerard shook his head.

"I think you both know that isn't true," he said quietly. "My uncle believes me, I'm almost sure."

"But," urged Geoffrey, not without reason, "if you didn't do what they sent you to prison for, your story points a very bad moral. For, while you, who worked hard and did no harm got penal servitude as a reward, we, who've never done anything but enjoy ourselves and who never mean to do anything else, have managed to do it without interference from anybody!"

Gerard smiled grimly.

"Well, I don't envy your existence," said he. "On the contrary, my sympathy is with my wife, who has evidently deeply offended my uncle by doing what I admire her for doing, and setting up in business instead of starving on a wretchedly inadequate income."

As he uttered these words, Gerard could not help noticing that his cousins listened with a sort of demure grimness, and then that they exchanged furtive looks. Now he was himself suffering from an unsatisfied curiosity concerning his wife's whereabouts, and this attitude of the two young men increased his uneasiness about her.

He looked from the one to the other, but did not ask any questions; indeed, they gave him little time, for on catching sight of their father in the distance, on his way from the Home Farm, where he usually spent his mornings, they both nodded hastily to their cousin and made off to meet him.

Gerard's curiosity was roused by the unusual animation which both his cousins showed, as they caught their father before he reached the house, and both evidently began talking to him at once. Gerard was much too far off to know what they said, but it was clear that it was something of considerable importance, and after noting that they all cast more than one glance in his direction, he concluded that, since what they had to say could not concern himself, or they would have spoken openly to him, it must concern his wife.

At luncheon, a few minutes later, he noticed that a change had come over his uncle's manner to him, which had become uneasily kind. So, when they left the room, Gerard stopped his uncle on his way to the study, and asked if he might speak to him. Lord Clanfield, instead of answering, looked round anxiously for his sons.

His nephew looked round too.

"Let them come too," said Gerard shrewdly. "I know they have something to say which I ought to hear."

"Oh, no. At least I think—you'd better wait a little," said the viscount kindly. "What I have just heard from them is of such a nature that it would only give you needless pain to hear it. Wait——"

Gerard interrupted.

"Do you think I can wait," he asked earnestly, "when I know that what they have to say concerns my wife?"

The startled silence which followed showed him how good a guess he had made, and father and sons accompanied him without more words into the study, where Lord Clanfield took up his position on the hearthrug, with his back to the fire, Gerard was given an easy-chair, and the two other young men sat on the edge of the big writing-table, and waited for their father to speak first.

"Gerard," said the viscount, "I'm afraid, my poor boy, that your misfortunes are not over yet."

"Well, let me know the worst of them at once," said the young man, who was sitting upright in his chair, with a flush in his cheeks and very bright eyes.

"Really, I scarcely like—I don't think we had better enter upon this very painful subject until we have asked Dr. Graham's opinion as to whether——"

"Dr. Graham be hanged!" burst out Gerard, with a momentary return of his old boyish impetuosity and spirit. "I beg your pardon, uncle, but consider that this suspense is worse than almost any knowledge could be. Tell me at once what the news was that they brought you this morning."

"Well, to tell you the truth, it's only the confirmation of fears which I myself entertained. For I must tell you, Gerard, that I have had grave doubts as to your wife's prudence."

"Well. Go on."

"If I must speak, you must promise to listen quietly."

"I will—without a word," said Gerard hoarsely, clutching the sides of his chair, and keeping his head bent.

The viscount and his sons exchanged apprehensive looks; but they all felt that now there was nothing to be done but to go on with the story, and risk its effect upon the convalescent.

"Your wife, unfortunately, has got into the society of people who are undesirable in every way. She is passing under a name which is not her own. She calls herself Madame Rocada, a title which is, I regret to say, that formerly used by a well-known woman of foreign extraction, who used to keep a gaming-house in Paris."

The viscount paused, but Gerard said nothing, and remained in the same position as before. His uncle went on:—

"It was under the name of Madame Rocada that she became known to me, in the first place, before I had the least idea she was your wife."

Then Gerard looked up at last, eager, wondering.

"She was staying at a place at Epsom, a big place, called 'The Briars,' and receiving a great many visitors. In the evenings there was gambling carried on there—in fact it went on all night," said Lord Clanfield. "I went there to see her, and she professed not to know all that occurred there."

"She did know it though," put in Geoffrey. "For when there was a row one night she knew all about it, knew exactly what had happened, and then cleared out for fear of being called upon to give awkward explanations."

Gerard never said a word. He turned his head from the one speaker to the other, but forbore to interrupt by so much as an exclamation.

"Both Geoff and I got rooked there," put in Edgar. "The first time it was by a fellow named Diggs——"

Then for the first time Gerard spoke.

"Diggs!" exclaimed he, speaking in a hoarse, low voice. "What Diggs?"

"Fellow named Durley Diggs. A Yankee and secretary to Reginald Candover, the great connoisseur."

Gerard only nodded, and the viscount went on:—

"Now it appears she has run away to some showrooms she has near Bond Street, where there was a scene, a most unpleasant scene, as recently as yesterday afternoon. It appears she was followed there by a number of the men who had been robbed at her house at Epsom, and there was an explanation asked for. Your wife, still passing as Madame Rocada, a name one would have thought she would have dropped on hearing the associations connected with it, turned round upon them all, told them that they had only themselves to thank if they were cheated, and said that one-half of them were swindlers, and professed only to have discovered the fact a day or two ago."

"And may not that have been true?" asked Gerard, in the same low, hoarse voice.

Edgar answered for his father:—

"No. Impossible. I had it from Archdale, one of the best fellows going, that there was no one present but men of the highest standing—Sir Barnaby Joyce, Reginald Candover——"

Again Gerard looked up. But this time, though he frowned slightly, he said nothing.

Edgar went on: "And half a dozen other men equally well known. It seems your wife behaved like a fury, so that at last—to calm her, Candover was obliged to—to——"

"To do what?"

"To remind her that she herself was——"

"The wife of—of a convict, I suppose?" said Gerard steadily.

Lord Clanfield drew himself up indignantly.

"He had no right to say that!" he cried angrily.

"No. I don't say he had. But think of the provocation! She called them a gang of swindlers!"

"And didn't you say some of you had been swindled?"

"Yes. But she was talking to the victims."

Gerard bent his head again, and said nothing. He was taking the whole story with uncanny calmness, almost, thought the others, as if his brain had lost some of its reasoning power. Not a sign did he give of the burst of tempestuous indignation they had all expected. He merely let his head hang forward again, and listened, with clasped hands, while Geoffrey went on:—

"Of course, there's no end of a row and a scandal, and some take her part and think there's someone behind her, who does the work and makes her the figure-head. Sir Barnaby's one of those. You know what an eye he has for a pretty face."

Gerard moved uneasily, but said nothing.

"Well, he and one or two more are round again at her place to-day, and everybody's awaiting interesting developments. Nobody thinks *she* will come to any harm. In fact, the general opinion is that she's confoundedly artful, and that she got up this scene to attract attention, and—to nail Sir Barnaby."

Not even this insinuation had the effect of rousing Gerard to any open expression of indignation. He just sat as before, huddled up in his chair, staring at the fire, while the others offered different, more or less guarded, comments on the unpleasant news.

At last Edgar and Geoffrey went out and then Gerard seemed to wake up as if out of a dream, and to realise that he was alone with his uncle, who evidently wanted to get rid of him, for he fidgeted, and looked at his watch, not liking to leave the presumably disconsolate young husband by himself, yet anxious to take up the occupation upon which he was engaged.

Gerard rose quickly, stammered an incoherent apology, not with any appearance of dismay or despair, but quietly and conventionally, and then went out of the room.

The viscount was puzzled by his behaviour, but was, on the whole, thankful that these painful disclosures had passed off so quietly.

When the family reassembled at dinner, however, Gerard was absent, and inquiries elicited the fact that he had left the house almost immediately after coming out of the study.

Lord Clanfield looked uneasily at his sons.

Geoffrey nodded astutely.

"Gone to have it out with her, you bet!" he muttered to his brother.

Lord Clanfield caught the whisper.

"It's very unfortunate. We ought to have foreseen——" he muttered uneasily.

But Geoffrey shrugged his shoulders, and said in a low voice:—

"Better that he should know all, and have done with her, sir! After all, it had to come. And it's less disgrace to the family to break with her than for the present condition of things to become known and talked about."

"Perhaps, but it's confoundedly unpleasant!" said Lord Clanfield, with a frown.

# CHAPTER XIX

AUDREY, meanwhile, had been passing an uneasy time since the terrible scene at the showrooms.

When, later in the same day, she had made the important discovery that Mademoiselle Laure was really Mr. Candover's sister, her first impulse was to challenge the woman, and to accuse her of being a party to the plot which had been laid for herself.

But that day's experience had taught her wisdom, and she reflected in time that nothing was to be gained, while much might be risked, by a want of prudence and caution.

Had she not just found that out to her cost? For what was the result of her well-meant and bold attempt to open the eyes of the men who had been robbed of their money at "The Briars"? Mr. Candover had been artful enough to turn her accusation back upon herself, and all the men present had gone away, so she believed, thoroughly convinced that she was a particularly cunning adventuress, and that Mr. Candover was an honourable man whom she had insulted!

This latest discovery—for that Laure was the wicked sister of whom Mr. Candover's ill-treated wife had spoken she had no doubt—had frightened Audrey more than all the rest. There was something more uncanny about the near neighbourhood of an unprincipled and unscrupulous woman than that of a man of the same class; and Audrey shivered at the thought that Laure was her enemy too.

What should she do? Should she consult a solicitor? If so, to whom should she go? Not, certainly, to the cold, steely-eyed man who had persisted in believing Gerard guilty. Audrey knew of no other, and had a vague idea that lawyers were for the most part wicked people, whose one object was to get fees; besides which, she had a much better grounded feeling that her own tale was too incoherent, and her own history too chequered, for her to have a good chance of getting believed without stronger proof than she could at present bring of the doings of the gang.

She thought, however, that Mrs. Webster might be able to give her the name of a solicitor to whom she could apply, and in the meantime she decided that her best course was to behave as much as possible as if nothing had happened of an unusual nature, and to sound Mademoiselle about the purchase of her interest in the business.

When, therefore, Marie Laure had done with her customers, and had dropped the conventional smile of the tradeswoman for the severe expression she wore when there was nothing to be sold, Audrey approached the subject in her mind by saying that she was tired of the business, and wished that she could sell it.

Marie Laure listened in stony silence, with a quick little arrowlike glance at the younger woman's face which revealed a greater knowledge of the lady's reasons than she professed to have.

And she answered very drily that she supposed Madame would consult Mr. Candover about that.

"Oh, I have no need to consult anybody," replied Audrey quickly, speaking in French, the only language Mademoiselle Laure professed to know. "I have made up my mind."

"You have not been long enough at the head of the business to make it your own," answered Mademoiselle sharply. "What have you done as yet except drive away some of the customers other people have brought you?"

This, Audrey thought, argued a very close acquaintance with what had taken place that afternoon, and a better knowledge of the English language than Laure professed to possess.

"I've paid fifteen hundred pounds," answered Audrey, "for the lease and furniture, and I am entitled to get something for those."

Laure looked grim.

"When you have worked up the business," she said drily, "which you will do better when you have sacrificed some of your British primness and coldness, you will have a right to talk of your interest in it. At present what you have given is as nothing to what others have supplied."

"I don't pretend that I've given everything," answered Audrey gently but with firmness, "I only said that I have a right to expect to get something for my share. Would you be inclined to buy me out? You are a much cleverer saleswoman than I should ever make."

"Not at all. You want experience, not cleverness. We should do wonders by-and-by if you would lay aside your primness. Beauty like yours is an asset of great value in business as in everything else. If I had your face I would become a millionaire," added Marie Laure with conviction.

But flattery was wasted upon Audrey.

"You may become one as it is," she answered earnestly, "and without me. I want to know what you would give me for my share?"

The dry-faced woman looked at her steadily.

"I must first be convinced," she said drily, "that it is yours to sell."

Audrey almost gasped.

"What do you mean?" she said breathlessly. "You know it is mine; you know I bought it, paid for it, and that I am the head—not a very active or clever head, but still the head."

The cold eyes watched her intently as the reply came:—

"The business was bought and paid for by Madame Rocada. Now you say you are not Madame Rocada. You tell everybody so."

"Everybody has known that from the beginning," retorted Audrey. "It is true I signed the lease as Rocada—I'm sorry I did even that—but it was with no intention of deceiving any one. It was known that it was only a trade name, and it makes no difference."

"I'm not so sure of that," answered Laure. "I have an idea that it does make a difference, and that your having signed the lease in a name not your own may make it invalid."

"You think then that Mr. Candover would have allowed me to sign a contract which was no contract?" asked Audrey drily.

This was well put, and Laure's sallow face changed colour a little.

"Why don't you consult him about it?" she said quickly. "You have let yourself be guided by him throughout the business; you took the place on his advice; you furnished it at the shop he chose. He has all the documents concerning the sale, I believe?"

"Yes," admitted Audrey, recalling, with a heightened colour and a faster beating heart, that she had indeed, at the time of her great distress, left the whole affair in the hands of the man who had made such strong professions of friendship and kindness to her and her husband.

"Then why not ask him how you stand? Why not suggest the sale to him, and see what he says? It will be, I think, this: that the business was bought in the name of Rocada, and that it belongs to the trading firm of that name, and not to any individual person. Certainly not to the woman who persistently injures the business by declaring that she is *not* Madame Rocada!"

Audrey was puzzled. She remained a few minutes in deep thought, and it was Mademoiselle Laure who broke the silence.

"Think this over, take the night to consider it," she said, with a coaxing change of tone. "It would be a most unwise thing to give up in a hurry a business which you are certainly the head of at present. What do you want? You are making money, and you will presently make more. Don't be rash. Be advised, and remember that I am ready, in the future as in the past, to take the greater part of the hard work upon my own shoulders, and to leave the ornamental and easy and pleasant part to you!"

"But it's not pleasant," protested Audrey, "to be always at the beck and call of a class of people I don't like!"

"Bah! All the people are lovable when their purses are long!" retorted Laure. "Think it over; sleep upon it; and we will have another talk about this in the morning."

Audrey agreed to this, not that there was the least prospect of her changing her mind, but because she wanted time to consider the rather gruesome prospect opened by the woman's words.

Was she really to lose all the money she had invested? Was it possible that, by cunning devices of which she was ignorant, Mr. Candover had induced her to sign mock-agreements, and that she had left herself no alternative but to remain at the head of the shady and repellant business which was, she felt sure, only a blind to the more nefarious one which had been carried on at "The Briars," or to lose all her fifteen hundred pounds?

"Be here early in the morning," were Mademoiselle Laure's last words, "and I will tell you what conclusion I have arrived at, and you shall tell me if you agree with me."

So on the following morning Audrey, who had gone back to her old rooms and found them vacant, came to the showrooms at an early hour, and found Mademoiselle Laure gracious and unusually conciliatory.

"I have considered the matter we talked about last night," she said, as soon as they were alone together, "and I am sure that the business goes with the name. As long as you are Madame Rocada, therefore, the business is yours; but when you say you are no longer Rocada, then it is yours no longer."

Perhaps Mademoiselle Laure exaggerated the simplicity of the woman with whom she was dealing. At any rate Audrey looked at her in open-eyed surprise.

"I don't know much about these things," she said bluntly. "But I think that's very strange."

"It's true though. Ask Mr. Candover if it is not."

Audrey hung her head thoughtfully, and then looked up.

"No," she said at last, "I shall not ask him. I shall go straight to a solicitor, and see what he says."

Mademoiselle Laure's face changed and grew very repellent in its expression. She laughed harshly.

"What a little sceptic it is!" she said. "Look here, Madame. You will do as you please. You will see your solicitor, see a dozen solicitors. But first I will go myself to Mr. Candover, and see if he can help us out of this business. It may be he will say it is you who are right, and I who am wrong. At any rate, we will take his opinion first. And if you do not like it, you can then get another one."

This seemed reasonable, particularly as Audrey saw, by the Frenchwoman's excitement, that she was anxious and agitated. In all probability, Audrey thought, the two would think it wiser to come to a fair understanding with her, so that she could get out of the disagreeable business in which she found herself involved, at some loss indeed, but without the sacrifice of the whole of her fifteen hundred pounds.

Mademoiselle Laure was in earnest, for she started at once on her errand, after giving such recommendations to Audrey and the assistants as she thought might be useful; and the poor little head of the firm was left in sole command.

She would not, however, take any part in the day's work, but shut herself into her little back-room on the approach of a customer, determined to have nothing more to do with the business until one of two things should happen: either she would erase the name Rocada from the windows and the firm's stationery, and free the place from Laure; or she would retire altogether after receiving such compensation as she could get from that astute and unscrupulous pair, Mr. Candover and his half-sister.

But she tried in vain to escape the annoyances which her position entailed upon her.

Mademoiselle Laure was away a long time, and Audrey went out to luncheon and returned to find her still absent. It was late in the afternoon when she heard from her room, a voice she recognised asking for Madame Rocada.

And Audrey knew that the newcomer was Sir Barnaby Joyce.

She heard one of the saleswomen tell him that Madame was out, and the voice of the jovial baronet saying in reply that he would "wait till she was in then".

Hurriedly deciding that she had better see him, and find out if she could what opinion was held about this miserable affair, and whether it was her version or Mr. Candover's which was the most generally received, Audrey came out of her room, and following Sir Barnaby into the first of the showrooms, bowed to him with sedate dignity and stood waiting for him to speak, in a regal attitude which suited her tall figure, and the trained dress with its sparkling trimming of jet paillettes which set off so well her fair skin and golden hair.

The baronet turned quickly to meet her, bowed low in his turn, and greeted her with the most effusive courtesy. But Audrey was in no mood to meet his advances halfway, and she allowed him to stammer out a suggestion that he wished to make his wife a present "of—of—of—in point of fact of a—a—hat or bonnet or something of that sort," without any attempt to help him out.

She bowed again, and turning in the same queenly manner to an obsequious assistant who was waiting near at hand, told her to bring "some hats and bonnets, the prettiest you have," to show Sir Barnaby.

As the girl went swiftly away on her errand, the baronet, who saw that he was to be given no opportunities and that he must make them for himself, hastened to say, lowering his voice and gazing at the beautiful woman before him with what he considered a killing look:—

"I can't tell you, Madame, how deeply grieved I was to be present the other day when that young fool Archdale made himself so objectionable——"

Audrey cut him short. Raising her eyebrows haughtily, she asked:—

"Did Sir Harry make himself more objectionable than anybody else? I was not aware of it, I assure you."

Sir Barnaby was taken aback. He began to stammer and to twist the ends of his carefully dyed and waxed moustache.

"Did he? Oh, well—er—I'm very glad if you—you didn't think so. It seemed to me that he—he said things which I should have resented, which in fact I did resent, and which—which—In short, I was disgusted at the whole thing. Considering how charmingly we have all been entertained at your house, Madame Rocada——"

"Oh, pray don't call me that. It is not my name. My name is Angmering, Mrs. Angmering," interrupted Audrey. "I am the wife of an unfortunate man who was wrongfully convicted of forgery, but whose people are already hard at work to get the conviction quashed."

Her boldness, her frankness, the simplicity with which she spoke, surprised Sir Barnaby and extorted his admiration, even while it made his position difficult. For he wanted to take up a stand as her champion and defender, and her independence and resentment of the situation into which she had been forced made him uncertain how to address her.

"Indeed you have my best wishes that they may succeed," said he. "A woman so young and beautiful needs a protector, and I shall rejoice to hear that your husband is at your side once more. In the meantime, should you ever need a friend, a disinterested friend, I hope you will remember that I am always at your service."

"Thank you," said Audrey coolly, as she took from the hands of the attendant maiden a sweet thing in white felt and ostrich feathers, with engaging bunches of violets tucked in here and there about the brim: "Would this suit Lady Joyce, do you think?"

"I—I—I'm afraid it's a little—little young-looking," murmured Sir Barnaby, by no means pleased to find himself thus ruthlessly recalled from chivalrous sentiment to matters of sordid business.

And the "young ladies" around, who all knew that Lady Joyce, though her husband's contemporary, had allowed herself to age at a faster rate than he, exchanged stealthy looks, and wondered at Madame's want of tact.

"I think something in velvet with a tuft of feathers at the side and something stringy about the neck is what Lady Joyce generally wears," said Sir Barnaby at last, desperately, when picture-hats and dreams in ermine and ostrich feathers had been paraded before him in somewhat bewildering succession, and tried on the head of one of the pretty attendants with great gravity.

"Perhaps you had better bring Lady Joyce here to try on some bonnets and choose for herself," suggested Audrey gently.

At which there was a further exchange of demure looks, unseen, among the assistants. Sir Barnaby answered rather stiffly:—

"Lady Joyce is content to follow my taste. I'll take that one."

And he pounced upon an ermine toque with an osprey at the side, and pulled out a five-pound note to pay for it.

"How much is it?" asked Audrey of the assistant who held the toque in her hand.

There was a smile on the face of the girl as she answered that it was four guineas. And Audrey felt that she had betrayed unseemly ignorance as she blushed and carefully counted out her customer's change.

Sir Barnaby looked up plaintively into her face as she did so.

"I want to ask you," he said in a low voice, when the attendants had retreated a little way, and were busy packing up the bargain, "whether you won't have mercy upon your friends, and let us come and see you again sometimes. We had such a pleasant time at 'The Briars'——"

"*I* hadn't," interrupted Audrey in a high-pitched voice. "I was induced to take the place under the impression that I could spend a quiet summer there. But I had nothing but annoyance and worry the whole time. I disapproved of what went on there, and I would never allow the same thing to happen again in any house I lived in."

Sir Barnaby looked puzzled. Although he knew, as every one else did, that Audrey was only the figure-head of an organisation of which gambling was the object, he had not believed her to be so entirely a puppet in the hands of others as this speech and her passionate vindication of herself two days before would have seemed to suggest.

Even now he found a difficulty in believing that so much beauty was compatible with extreme innocence. Such a combination was contrary to his experience, which was large. He even felt nettled by these airs—as he considered them—of an irresponsibility which did not accord with the facts.

Audrey was moving towards the door, as an intimation to the baronet that his business was over. He had given the address to which his parcel was to be sent, and she had no wish to hear any more about the recent scene or about his disinterested devotion.

He lingered, however, when they had reached the outer doorway, and stood a moment holding up the portière, and turning to her with a sentimental expression on his rubicund, genial face.

"You are very severe, Madame. But indeed you are wrong if you think that the cards were the only or even the greatest attraction for us at 'The Briars'. We will consider that settled, if you like, that there is to be no more gambling—if that displeases you. But surely you will not let your quarrel with Candover and Archdale interfere with your arrangements. You——"

"My quarrel with them!" repeated Audrey in surprise. "I have no quarrel with Sir Harry. I am displeased with Mr. Candover, certainly, for inducing me to accept a false position."

"Candover! Was it Candover who——"

Audrey interrupted him. Speaking earnestly and distinctly she said:—

"Mr. Candover was my husband's most intimate friend, and it was he who induced me to take this business, to use the name of Rocada, and who introduced me to the people who had the letting of 'The Briars'. I have acted on his advice throughout, and I cannot but think the advice was very bad."

Sir Barnaby looked interested, incredulous.

"Candover was a friend of your husband's, you say?"

"Yes."

There was a moment's pause. Audrey wished to get rid of her visitor, but Sir Barnaby was anxious to say more. Neither noticed, as they stood in the doorway, that on the staircase, which was softly carpeted and illuminated only by one jet of electric light, a young man was standing, watching them.

Sir Barnaby suddenly seized her hand and pressed it to his lips.

"Never trust a husband's friend," said he. "Trust me. I'll be yours."

But Audrey scarcely even heard him. She had caught sight of the waiting figure beyond in the obscurity on the staircase, and her eyes were straining to pierce the gloom.

"Thank you," she said mechanically, as she drew her hand away, and Sir Barnaby, having nothing more to say, was forced to go out.

She followed him to the three or four stairs which led to the little second landing. And standing on the top, she looked down while her face quivered with excitement, Sir Barnaby ran downstairs as fast as his somewhat gouty feet allowed, and she waited until she heard him go out by the side-door.

Then, leaning forward, supporting herself on the banisters, she uttered, very faintly, almost in a wailing tone, the one word:—

"Gerard."

And when, shaking like a leaf, he came out of the angle of the wall where he had been standing, and ran up the stairs, she just held out her arms to him, and trying to whisper something incoherent, unintelligible, she fell, scarcely conscious, into his arms.

# CHAPTER XX

IN the first moment of this unexpected meeting, Audrey, still with nerves strung up by the recent interview with Sir Barnaby and the unpleasant associations called up by his words, could find nothing but relief and comfort and joy in her husband's presence.

He, on his side, kissed her tenderly, whispered to her to hold up her head and pull herself together, and tried to make her realise how inopportune this weakness was.

She struggled to regain the self-command she had lost, and looking eagerly, pitifully into his face, whispered:—

"You're not angry with me? I thought—I was afraid—you would be."

"I'm angry, very angry, at being kept out on the stairs," replied Gerard, with a touch of the old boyish humour which went to her heart like a stab.

She tried to smile, but her face quivered.

"I can't take you in there—among all those giggling, whispering girls," she said, under her breath. "Come in here."

And very quietly, almost on tiptoe, she led him down to the second landing and into her own room.

There she gave way again, and throwing herself face downwards on the sofa by the small fire, she burst into a passion of tears.

It was in vain he scolded her, tried to comfort her.

"Are you sorry I've come?" asked he at last, as, kneeling beside her, he put his head against her shoulder and tried to look into her tear-blurred face. "Don't you feel glad to think you've got me back again to take care of you, to save you from scenes like that, and from having to be civil to a lot of gouty old idiots like the one I saw hobbling downstairs?"

Audrey sprang up, and peered into his face. Then she drew a long, sobbing breath of relief.

"Oh," she cried, "thank Heaven, thank Heaven you take it like that! That you're not angry! I—I was so afraid you wouldn't understand!"

Gerard, whose own eyes were moist, looked into her face.

"My poor girl," he said, "I've never had a thought—since I first heard—three hours ago—of what you've gone through, but to thank Heaven that I can take care of you again!"

"What have you heard?" asked Audrey quickly.

"Everything, I fancy. Of the infamous way in which that rascal Candover——"

"Sh—sh!" Audrey put her hand on her husband's mouth. And she whispered in his ear: "If you know so much, you *do* know everything! Or everything that matters! But to find you taking my part—when I was afraid—when I was dreading what you'd say, what you'd think—oh, Gerard, Gerard, I can scarcely believe it!"

She was sobbing hysterically, feeling the relief of this great and unlooked-for comfort, this joy which she had not dared to hope for. Gerard, Gerard whose passionate anger she had been dreading, had only one thought, one idea, that he could take care of her again.

Presently she grew calmer, and nestling close to him on the sofa, whispered to him to tell her exactly what he knew, and how he had found her. He told her how his two cousins had arrived at Lord Clanfield's that morning and what they had said; how they had given their account of the scene in which she accused her gambling guests, and how Lord Clanfield had recorded his first interview with her, and how he, Gerard, had listened quietly, and simply made up his mind to go to her without delay.

"I found out this address from Geoffrey," he went on, "without telling him I meant to come to you. And then I set out at once, not saying a word to anybody, and I caught the first train I could and came straight here. And now you have to put me up, for I don't mean to leave you again. You dear little goose, you can't keep out of mischief without me!"

But though he spoke as lightly as possible, and tried in every way to soothe and calm her, she saw by the frown on his face, by his uneasy glances at the door, that all the while he was no more at ease than she was. And Audrey clasped his hand tightly in hers and whispered:—

"Did you ever have any doubts about him, about Mr. Candover, Gerard?"

"Yes," answered he in the same tone. "Often. When I was alone—such awful loneliness, Audrey, I can't talk about it yet!—I used to wonder whether this selfish man of pleasure would really be a safe, trustworthy friend. And I used to go very nearly mad with jealousy, wondering whether he would—would—Tell me, Audrey, did he make love to you?"

She nodded, shuddering.

"The scoundrel!" said Gerard between his clenched teeth.

She drew closer to him.

"There's something more to tell you about him than that!"

"I know! He encouraged you to take this house at Epsom and let people think that you kept a sort of gambling club."

"Oh, Gerard, there's worse to be told than that." His grasp tightened upon her hand, and a look so piteous came into his eyes that she hurried on: "They cheated there, they cheated at cards, Gerard, and—I'm sure—I *know*—that Mr. Candover was concerned in it."

This speech, in spite of all that he had feared, had guessed, came upon the young man with a great shock. That the rich, prosperous, easy-going, fascinating Mr. Candover should make love to his beautiful wife, was no surprise; it was what he had feared. But that he should be involved in such a nefarious business as card-sharping seemed too preposterous. He looked at Audrey as if he doubted her perfect sanity.

"Oh, I knew what you'd say, what you'd think," whispered she, putting one arm round his neck, and lowering her voice still more, as if the very walls might have ears. "And I knew you wouldn't believe. But when you hear all I have to tell you, I think you'll say I'm right."

Then, still in the same subdued tones, still clinging to him, she told—incoherently enough, but yet intelligibly to his sympathetic ears—the whole story of her being induced to take the business and to pay for it, and to assume the trade name of Rocada. She told the ghastly story of the lady in white, and of her mysterious disappearance without leaving even a trace for the doctor's eye to discover. She told of her being induced to take "The Briars," of her uneasiness there, of the episodes of Diggs and of Johnson, and then of her flight to town.

"Now," she said impressively, "they—he and the woman who I am sure is his sister—this Mademoiselle Laure—want to force me to give up this place without any compensation. She pretends that it is the property of Madame Rocada, and that, as I am not Madame Rocada, it is not mine. And when I told her I would go to a solicitor, she said she would consult Mr. Candover and see what he would say."

"That part of the business is soon disposed of," said Gerard, with decision. "They're acting 'on the bounce,' and we've only got to go to a lawyer for them to sing small directly."

He seemed quite confident, but Audrey, who had more recent and more alarming experiences of the precious pair than Gerard, was not so easy in her mind as he.

She shook her head warningly.

"If you begin by thinking it will be easy to show them up," she said solemnly, "you will do no good at all. What I'm quite sure of is that they are the cleverest and wickedest pair that ever lived. And that they have means to hand for working all kinds of villainy, means that we don't dream of. Oh, you can't understand the consciousness I've had lately, always—always—that there has been a net about my feet, drawing me tighter and tighter, so that I could not get away."

She was shivering, and Gerard tried to laugh, comforting her.

"You don't feel that now, surely, surely! Now you've got me back."

But she hung round his neck, and with wild eyes whispered:—

"Shall I tell you the truth? What I feel now is that they have got not me only but *you* in the net as well. I can't get rid of the feeling, I can't, I can't!"

He rallied her on her cowardice in vain. But presently she noticed that he looked deadly pale and tired, that his voice had become hoarse and his eyes dull. And she jumped up from the sofa, and taking out from a cupboard a little store of provisions, put her kettle on the fire, and prepared to make him some tea.

Then she looked at her watch and found that it was seven o'clock.

"I must leave you in here," she said, "and go and see whether Mademoiselle Laure has come back. If she has not, it is I who must dismiss the girls, and see that everything is safe for the night. One of us always does that. Stay here. I don't suppose anybody has seen you, and they never come into this room. I'll be back when they've all gone."

She made him lie down on the sofa, covered him with a rug, and returned to the showrooms, where the girls were waiting to be dismissed.

Mademoiselle Laure had not returned, and this made Audrey uneasy.

However, she attended to the duties of the evening, saw that the hats and dresses had been properly covered up and put away, and bidding the assistants good-night, waited till they had all gone down the stairs before returning to Gerard.

Then she made the usual final tour of the suite of rooms, and was about to turn down the electric light, when she heard the slight sound of heavy tread on the soft carpet outside, and looking round, saw that two men, respectably but not exactly well dressed, were standing in the room.

A foreboding of evil came upon her at once. One of the men, she thought, was a policeman in plain clothes. She looked at his boots, and was confirmed in this uncomfortable impression.

"Who are you? And what do you want?" she asked sharply.

And as she spoke she made a step in the direction of the door, feeling that Gerard ought to be present.

But the man with the policeman's boots stepped quietly in her way and said respectfully enough:—

"I beg pardon, ma'am. Madame Rocada, I believe?"

Audrey hesitated. What ought she to say?

"What do you want with Madame Rocada?" asked she.

There was a moment's hesitancy on the part of the man, and then his companion nodded to him to go on:—

"Well, ma'am, it appears that Madame Rocada was a lady that lived in Paris, and that came over here. And her friends have set to work to trace her."

Audrey's breath came fast. The lady in white! The White Countess!

"Well!" said she.

The man went on:—

"She has been traced, ma'am, to London, and to this house—this very floor—but no farther."

There was another ominous pause. Audrey merely bowed her head. She dared not speak.

Then the man went on:—

"So we've been sent—among other things—to make inquiries, ma'am."

"Yes. Well."

"We understand, ma'am, that you are now Madame Rocada? That you call yourself by that name?"

"It is a trade name only. I am not the woman of whom you are in search."

"So I understand, ma'am. But—h'm—we are led to believe that *you are the last person who saw her alive!*"

Audrey uttered a low cry.

"No, no," she cried hoarsely. "I saw her alive, it's true, but I was not the last person to see her."

The men looked at each other.

"You admit you did see her, ma'am."

"Yes, but oh—let me——"

She wanted to run to Gerard, to ask him to help her, to disentangle, if he could, the awful thoughts that crossed and recrossed each other in her poor distracted mind. But the men gravely, not rudely or aggressively, intervened.

"I'm sorry, ma'am. You will have proper advice presently, no doubt. But we must ask you to come with us now. We have a warrant."

"A warrant! What for?" gasped Audrey.

"For your arrest. On suspicion of causing the death of Madame Rocada."

# CHAPTER XXI

AUDREY, when the blow had fallen, neither screamed nor fainted, nor even moved. She heard the man's words with a dumb, awful consciousness that what she had dimly feared had happened, that the crime which had been committed within these rooms was now attributed to her.

Some vague foreshadowing of this had haunted her from time to time, long before she guessed that Mr. Candover was concerned in the death and disappearance of the White Countess. Mademoiselle Laure and the doctor—the one of them secretly inimical, the other probably suspicious—these were the witnesses who would both aver that she had confessed to seeing the White Countess in the rooms, and who would also be able to bear witness that her excitement and nervous distress were great, and her bearing inconsistent with the perfect innocence she professed in the matter.

The men waited respectfully enough for her to speak. At last she said:—

"I don't understand. Who is it that accuses me?"

"We can't answer that, ma'am," said the man. "We've got nothing to do but just execute orders. And to say that you'd better not say anything yet, as what you say may be used in evidence against you."

Audrey shook her head.

"Oh, no," she said with spirit. "This is all nonsense; there is no evidence, and there can be no evidence against me. For I can tell who it was that was last with the woman alive."

Both men, she thought, looked interested, though they said nothing. She went on:—

"It was a man whom she called Eugène. But the name by which he is known here is not Eugène Reynolds, but Reginald Candover."

"Well, ma'am, you needn't tell us all this," said the man who had stated that he had the warrant. "It won't do you any good now; but if you tell it all to your solicitor at the trial, or rather before then—he'll find out what he can for you, no doubt."

"In the meantime, ma'am, if you'll come along with us," said the other man, who now spoke for the first time, "we've got to take you before a magistrate. It will only be the affair of a moment, and then you can send for your solicitor to see and advise you."

"We've got a cab waiting, ma'am," said the policeman.

But Audrey shook her head.

"I won't go away with you," she said firmly, "until I've had an opportunity of consulting some one."

The men looked at each other.

"Can't be done, ma'am, at least not yet. You must go before the magistrate first," said the man with the warrant. "Afterwards, every facility will be given you."

The other man, more impatient, made a movement as if to hurry her towards the door. But she hung back, looking so determined, with her teeth tightly clenched and her breast heaving, and her eyes very bright, that they hesitated a little as to the best means of proceeding.

"I won't go. I simply refuse to go," she said firmly, "until I've had an opportunity of—of conferring with—with my friends."

She had at first intended to say that her husband was at hand, but on second thoughts she hesitated to let Gerard know the dreadful thing that had happened, without due preparation for the shock it would be to him. If only she could send word to his solicitor. Things were too desperate now for her to trouble her head about his former doubts of Gerard—she would take counsel with him as to the best means of breaking the news to her husband, and also as to what she ought to do for her own defence.

"We don't *want* to have to use force, ma'am," said the man with the warrant, warningly.

For answer Audrey rushed to the nearest window, and was with difficulty restrained from breaking it with her fists.

"Come, ma'am," said the second man persuasively, "I'm quite sure a lady like you don't want a disturbance. And we've done everything as quiet as possible on your account. We've waited about on purpose so as not to come in while your young ladies were here. And for your own sake you'd better be quiet. If, as you say, you can tell who did this, why you may be able to get it all hushed up so that nobody shall know anything about it. For the sake of your business, ma'am, you'd better not call a crowd about the place."

Audrey made them a commanding gesture to stand back. They obeyed, and stood, the one between her and the window, and the other between her and the door. She waited a moment, collecting her thoughts. Then she spoke steadily and quietly, though with quickly drawn breaths and many pauses:—

"All I want to do is to be allowed to consult some one before I go. I intend to do this, whatever you may choose to do to try to prevent me. As for your using force, you will do that at your peril. For I'm quite sure that what I ask is reasonable enough."

The man with the warrant nodded to the other.

"Very well, ma'am. If you'll write a note, I'll give it to some one to take for you, and we'll wait here till your friend, that you write to, comes back."

Audrey went into the inner showroom, closely followed by the two men, opened her writing-desk, and wrote a hurried note to the solicitor who had been employed by Gerard on his trial, telling him she was accused of connection with a murder, and asking him to come to her at once. When she had fastened the envelope, one of the men put out his hand offering to take it. But she refused, saying that she would send it by her own messenger.

As a matter of fact, she was wondering whom she was to employ, but happening to catch an odd look exchanged between the two men, her suspicions were aroused as to whether they meant the note to be sent at all.

Perhaps it was against the rules for any communication to be sent in such a case by a person newly arrested. Perhaps the men would merely retain the note and hand it over to the magistrate!

With these thoughts in her mind, Audrey hesitated to give up the note, and stood holding it tightly in her hands, while the men began to show unmistakable signs of impatience.

"Come, ma'am, we've given you a good deal of indulgence. If you're going to send the note give it to me, and if you think better of it please come down with us and let us get this business done with."

A voice from behind startled them all.

"What business?"

There was a cry from Audrey, an exclamation from the man with the warrant.

Standing between the heavy curtains that divided the one showroom from the other was Gerard, very pale, very quiet, grasping the hangings tightly, and gazing steadily at the group in front of him.

Brave as she had been, valiantly as she had resolved that she would not burst in upon him with the knowledge of the awful blow which had fallen upon her, Audrey was so overjoyed at the sight of her husband that, forgetting everything in the relief she felt, she dashed across the room and fell into his arms.

"Oh, Gerard, Gerard! thank God you've come," sobbed she.

Gerard looked down at her for one second, and then again at the two men.

"What is all this?" said he shortly.

"Very sorry, sir. We've got a warrant for the arrest of the lady," said the man who had taken the most prominent part in the affair, the man in the policeman's boots.

"Upon what charge?"

Audrey, even at that moment of intense excitement, was amazed at the perfect calmness which Gerard showed. She had expected an outburst of indignation on his part, an angry repudiation of the insult put upon her; but instead of that, it seemed to her that he took the matter as coolly as if he had expected this to happen and had been quite prepared for it.

"On the charge of being concerned in the disappearance of a woman known as Madame Rocada, otherwise the White Countess," said the man.

Gerard looked down at his wife, who was still clinging to him without uttering a word.

"This is serious," said he.

"Oh, Gerard, surely——" moaned Audrey in a husky whisper.

An unobtrusive but reassuring pressure of his fingers upon her arm checked her, and she, feeling the intense relief of having another arm, another brain at her service, remained silent, listening, wondering, while he went on:—

"Of course my wife—this lady is my wife—is entirely innocent of any hand in the disappearance of anybody. But, at the same time, I recognise that it is a serious matter. What is it she was asking you if she might do?"

"Oh, Gerard, it doesn't matter now," sobbed out Audrey. "I—I wanted some one to break it gently to *you*, that was all. But now that you know, nothing matters, nothing matters. I was afraid it would be a shock to you, that's all."

"Well, it is a shock, a great shock, naturally," admitted Gerard. "You can understand this when I tell you," and he turned to the two men, "that I am rejoining my wife to-day after a long absence."

Audrey was rather surprised at this unexpected and apparently uncalled-for confidence on her husband's part, and she was still more astonished when he went on:—

"But our domestic affairs are, of course, no concern of yours. At the same time I daresay, now that you know what I have just told you, you will make allowance for the irritation my poor wife has shown, and you will not suppose she had any wish to interfere with the course of justice!"

"Justice!" echoed Audrey faintly, more amazed than ever at the calmness with which her husband received the horrible news.

"I repeat—justice," said Gerard firmly. "If this unfortunate lady has disappeared, naturally she must be found, or traced. You can't expect her friends to take her disappearance calmly. And may I ask," and he turned from the one man to the other, "which of you has the warrant?"

The man in the policeman's boots nodded.

"I have it, sir," he said.

Gerard turned to the other man.

"Are you a policeman, too?" he asked.

The man answered in a voice which made Audrey look round. It was not that, she thought, in which she had previously heard him speak.

143

"I'm a detective, sir," he said.

"And was it necessary, do you think, to threaten a woman—a lady—with using force, when all she wanted was to write a letter to her solicitor?"

The man with the policeman's boots would have answered, but Gerard put up his hand, refusing to take his answer except from the person he had addressed. Again his calmness, and the impression his behaviour made on the policemen, surprised Audrey and excited her admiration.

"Well, sir, what we meant by force was not exactly that," said the man in a voice that was hardly audible.

Gerard looked at him intently.

"Well," he said, "it would have been better not to use the word at all, don't you think so?"

"Perhaps, sir, we did exceed our duty a little," said the detective hurriedly. "I'm sorry."

"So I think you ought to be," said Gerard, still fixing him with his keen blue eyes as he went on speaking, and disregarding every attempt made by the other man to distract his attention by casual comments. "You know very well that there was nothing surprising in the fact that a lady, brought face to face with such a charge, should wish to exchange a few words with her friends. I believe such a privilege is usually allowed, is it not?"

"I believe so, sir."

"Then why were you so strict?"

The man looked at his companion, but Gerard refused again to divert his gaze from the man he questioned, who fidgeted uneasily under this interrogatory.

"Ladies are difficult people to deal with, sir," he said, in the same hoarse whisper as before. "One doesn't want to be harsh, yet one is afraid of being talked round. Especially in such a case, sir."

He was conciliatory, almost apologetic. At last Gerard relaxed his look, and turned to the other man.

"What is it you want my wife to do?" he asked briefly.

There was a hesitating silence.

"Do I understand that she is to be taken before a magistrate to-night?"

No answer.

"Or would it be possible, say by your good offices, if I were to promise that she would still be here to-morrow morning, for you to go away now and return then?" went on Gerard, with an easy confidence which made Audrey look up at him askance in fresh astonishment at his self-possession.

There was another pause, and Gerard pressed his wife's arm with another reassuring touch.

"If you'll allow us, sir, to discuss this a moment," said the man with the warrant civilly.

"Oh, certainly, certainly. Shall we retire and leave you here? Or will you——"

Gerard drew apart the curtains that hung between the two showrooms; and the men, with another "Thank you, sir," passed through and conversed in a low voice in the outer room.

Once alone with her husband, Audrey wanted to speak. But he put his hand upon her mouth, and with a warning frown, kept her silent. Meanwhile he listened with keen ears to the whispering that was going on in the outer room.

In a few minutes the man in the policeman's boots reappeared, alone. Saluting Gerard, he said:—

"We think, sir, it might be managed as you suggest. If you, sir, will give an undertaking that the lady will be here to-morrow morning, when we shall have to come again, and when we hope she'll make no objection to coming quietly."

"I'll give the undertaking," said Gerard. "Would you like it in writing?" he added quickly, going towards the writing-desk, and gently disengaging himself from Audrey's arms.

"Oh, no sir. Not with a gentleman. I understand you are sure there is nothing in the charge, sir?"

"Nothing whatever. Indeed I think you'll find that on further consideration, this charge won't be pressed further against my wife."

"Oh, well, sir, in that case we'll take further orders, sir."

"Thank you," said Gerard, as he followed the man out through the second showroom, and found that the other man had already taken his departure.

"Can you see? Mind the corner stair. It's an awkward turn. That's right."

These words, in Gerard's voice, reached Audrey's ears as she stood trembling in the inner showroom, listening and waiting.

Then there was a pause, and she presently heard the door at the bottom shut sharply.

A moment later Gerard came back into the room. His eyes were very bright; all his calmness had disappeared, and he was shaking from head to foot with violent excitement.

"Gerard, Gerard, how did you manage it? What did you do? How is it that they went away so quietly? I thought the police had to execute a warrant, and that they couldn't go away like that without orders!"

Gerard had by this time come close to her, and the brilliancy of his eyes, the heaving of his breast, frightened her.

"Of course they can't, of course *real* policemen can't," he answered promptly.

"Real policemen! Oh, Gerard, who—who were they? Who were they?"

"They were members of the gang you told me about, the gang that's controlled by that rascal Candover, I've no doubt," said Gerard in her ear. "They thought you were all alone here, and that they could frighten you away, frighten you into giving up possession of this place which is yours."

"Oh, Gerard, do you really think that?"

"I do indeed. They never meant to take you away—at least, if they had, they would have taken care to drop you at the first convenient halting-place. Probably they would have left you at some door which they would have represented to you was the door of your solicitor's. And then they would have driven off. That they merely meant to work upon your woman's fears to make you give up these premises I feel certain."

"But how do you *know* all this? Surely you're only guessing!" objected Audrey, who could not understand her husband's confident yet excited manner.

He looked earnestly into her face.

"Can you keep a secret, a dead secret?" he whispered into her ear.

"*Your* secret! Yes, oh, yes!" panted she.

He put his lips close to her ear once more.

"The second man—the one who disguised his voice—who didn't want to speak—was——"

"Go on, go on. Who was he?"

"Tom Gossett, the man whose false evidence secured my conviction. Hush!"

And even as the little cry rose to her lips, Gerard silenced it by pressing his own mouth long and tenderly against hers.

# CHAPTER XXII

BOTH husband and wife were in a whirl of excitement so intense that for a little while they could do nothing, say nothing, but look at each other and exchange muttered and incoherent thanksgivings.

Then Gerard said:—

"Look here. We're in a tight place still, though I think we shall get out of it. But we must be careful, very careful. And we must keep our mouths shut. Do you think you are clever enough to keep a straight face while I fall on the neck of Candover, and receive him as if he were a long-lost brother?"

"Oh, Gerard, could you?"

"Yes," snarled Gerard. "I could do anything to bring to book the scoundrel who has pretty well wrecked my life and who tried his hardest to wreck yours!"

They had exchanged these words in whispers, and now they remained silent, keeping close together, and instinctively looking round them as if in fear of being overheard.

"What are we going to do?" said Audrey helplessly.

Gerard hesitated.

"In the first place," he said at last, "we must not leave this place, either of us, just yet. They want to get rid of you, Audrey, and I've not the slightest doubt that they would like to get rid of me, but they can't do it as long as we're both together. But on the other hand, we must have advice. This is too big a business for us to tackle without help. This Candover seems to be about as artful a rascal as they make 'em. For remember, so far, though we've found out a good deal about different members of the gang, we've got nothing whatever to convict *him* by."

"There's what his wife said!"

"That doesn't count—as evidence. Don't you know that a wife can't give evidence against her husband?"

"Well, I heard the poor woman—the White Countess, call out 'Eugène'!"

"But you didn't see him?"

"No."

"Then I'm afraid that wouldn't count for much—unless you could prove that you told the story to other people as soon as it happened."

"I—I think I may have told the doctor!"

"What, the doctor who was so like Johnson, the card-sharper!"

Audrey uttered a low cry.

"Why! Do you think he too was one of the gang?" she asked, almost giddy with these revelations, following so swiftly the one upon the heels of the other.

"I think it most likely. However, we'll have a hunt in the directory in the morning. In the meantime I'm going to write to my cousins. They're a rackety pair, and will welcome the chance of being in any shindy. And I'll get them to come here and help us through with this business."

"Oh, Gerard, what are you going to do? I feel so frightened! I feel as if we—you and I—were standing together on the edge of a precipice."

"And I," whispered Gerard back, with his face aglow, "feel as if I had escaped from the edge of the precipice and as if I had my hand on the rascal who drove me there!"

There was silence for a few minutes. Neither had even dared to mention yet the thought that was uppermost in the minds of both—that the crime of which Gerard had been accused and convicted, was the work of the man, whom they had known as Reginald Candover, and whom Audrey had heard of also under the name of Eugène Reynolds.

The possibility of tracing the crime to its author, of clearing Gerard from the stain upon his own honour, was so bewildering, so overwhelming, that both the young husband and his wife felt almost crazy at the exciting prospect.

But Gerard felt so strongly that the man in whose hands they had both been as clay in the potter's fingers was an adversary of consummate strength and craft, that he was anxious not to discuss the glorious prospect which he began dimly to see glimmering in the distance, lest some chance word should be overheard and carried to the ears of the arch-conspirator himself.

Even if they were really alone now, it was better by over-reticence to school themselves to a prudence that should leave no loophole of danger, and even, if possible, to behave as if they did not believe in the momentous discovery which both were sure they had made.

So Gerard sat down to write a short note to his cousin Edgar, and, as he could not feel sure whether the young men had stayed the night at their father's place or whether they had returned to their chambers in town, he duplicated the note, and directed the one copy to their own address and the other to the Hampshire house. The question then was how to get these letters posted. They could neither leave the premises nor leave each other; so at last they went down the stairs together, and waited at the door on the chance of lighting upon a trustworthy messenger.

They were lucky in the passing of a tradesman's boy known to Audrey; he not only took the letters to the post for them, but fulfilled for them certain small commissions which resulted in their being able to enjoy, in the little back-room to which they retreated after they had made all secure for the night, a somewhat casual but none the less welcome meal of slices of boiled ham, penny rolls, cream tarts, baked potatoes and bottled stout these being the various viands selected by the boy on being told to bring back "anything he could get" in the way of food and drink.

So uneasy and suspicious were the two young people, that they took it in turns to rest on the sofa, while the other sat up in a chair by the fire.

No amount of prowling about the first floor, of peering into corners and listening at doors, sufficed to render them perfectly at ease in their minds while on the premises where things so uncanny had already happened.

When morning came it was resolved that the presence of Gerard should, if possible, be kept a secret from every one but the woman who swept out the rooms and lit the fires: she was old, deaf and uncommunicative, and could be trusted not to chatter.

Within an hour of the beginning of work for the day, Audrey, who was on the watch, heard a hansom dash up to the door, and met the two young Angmerings at the head of the staircase.

Both were surprised to find themselves welcomed with effusion by Audrey, who forgot all possible causes of disagreement in the joy of finding that they had responded so quickly to Gerard's appeal.

"I—I thought—Is Gerard here?" asked Edgar, as he shook hands.

Audrey put her finger on her lip.

"Yes, but we are keeping the fact as quiet as we can. He wants to see you both. Come in here."

She glanced as she spoke at the door of the little room. It was ajar; a hand pulled it gently open and Gerard peeped out.

In another moment the young Angmerings were shut in the room with their cousin, and his wife, who kept watch near the door while the story was rapidly and succinctly unfolded to the astonished young men.

Whatever they might think, whether they believed in Audrey's complete innocence and in Candover's guilt or not, they both took the affair as a huge "lark," and entered with zest into the part which they were required to play.

"In the first place," explained Gerard, "we want advice. Now we don't dare leave these premises together, or we should never be allowed to get in again; and we daren't let one of us go without the other, as we don't feel ourselves to be in particularly safe quarters."

"What are you afraid of?" said Geoffrey.

"I'm afraid," said Gerard, "that some further attempt will be made by Candover and his gang to get rid of us. The more so that I think it very possible Gossett knew that I recognised him. Now if we could once prove that the man who swore I gave him the cheque to cash is the same man that came here last night masquerading as a detective, and pretending to have a warrant for the arrest of my wife, we are in a fair way to lay some of these rascals by the heels. But from what we know of Candover, he won't allow himself to be unmasked without a struggle. So we can't be too careful, we can't have too many to help us, and we can't have too much pluck."

"Right you are. Tell us what we're to do," said Geoffrey.

"Well, I want you, Edgar, to take my wife to my solicitor's, and to wait there till he's heard everything, and to take his advice as to what we are to do. Perhaps he'll come here at once and see me. Or perhaps he'll go to the police, and get Audrey to make a statement about last night's affair. I don't think Gossett knew I recognised him, but I can't be sure. If he did, I'm afraid he may have got out of the way. At any rate, we mustn't lose any time."

"All right," said Edgar, as Audrey seized her hat and fur stole and prepared to go with him.

"And what am I to do?" asked Geoffrey in a disappointed tone.

"I want you to stay with me in case I have to receive any more dubious visitors."

"All right," said Geoffrey eagerly. "Have you got anything for me to knock 'em on the head with?"

A burst of subdued laughter met this speech, in spite of the tension of feeling from which his hearers were suffering. Geoffrey put his hands in his pockets and tilted back his head.

"Oh, you may sneer and you may laugh," said he. "But it'll be odd if we get off without a bit of a shindy. Disappointing too," he added reflectively. "I must say I should like to crack a skull or two, if these fellows are really all members of a gang and partners of those rascals Johnson and Diggs!"

Gerard took him good-humouredly by the shoulder.

"It's not likely to be a question of blows, Geoff," said he. "On the contrary, if only I can get hold of Candover, I want to persuade him that I'm deeply indebted to him for his constant kindness to my wife, and to apologise to him for her rudeness to him the other day."

Geoffrey opened wide eyes and whistled softly.

"If you were to talk like that to him before me," said he, "I should give you away. I couldn't stand still and smile at the man whom I knew to be a scoundrel."

"Then you'll have to keep away," said Gerard. "For our only chance of running him to earth is to make him think we have no suspicion of *him*, at any rate."

Geoffrey looked bewildered.

"Remember," said Gerard, "we have no proof against him yet—of actual crime on his part. We only suspect. Now that's not enough."

"I don't think myself," said Edgar, who was less impetuous than his brother, "that you ever will get any proof. To me it seems absurd to think that a man in Candover's position would be concerned with cheats and card-sharpers."

"Well, then," said Gerard, "that's a very good reason why we should treat him civilly to begin with."

"What makes you think he'll come here at all?" asked Geoffrey, who could ask pertinent questions when he was in the mood.

"Well, if we're wrong in believing that he's the head of this gang, he won't come," said Gerard concisely. "There will be nothing to come about. But if, as I think, he *is* the head of it, he'll be bound to turn up, to find out what we think about last night's affair."

"Then he won't come," said Edgar with decision.

"Now, I think he will," said Geoffrey.

Gerard and Audrey remained silent on the point, and, with many injunctions to Gerard to take care of himself and to Geoffrey to take care of him, Audrey accompanied Edgar downstairs and out of the house.

Then Gerard and his cousin had a long conversation. Geoffrey, who was by far the more intelligent, if he was also the wilder, of Lord Clanfield's two sons, was more and more inclined to share his cousin's views as they discussed the whole matter from various points of view.

But he was also inclined to think that the man who had been concerned in the disappearance of the white lady might use other means than strategy, and again he deplored the absence of a revolver or other weapon in case Candover should show fight.

Gerard laughed at him, and was secretly glad that no such dangerous means of offence or defence were at hand.

Both the young men kept their voices low, and their ears on the alert, and presently both raised their heads at the same moment when, hearing a footfall on the stairs, they caught the sound of Mr. Candover's voice and that of one of the assistants in the showroom answering him.

Gerard, with a sign to his cousin to remain where he was and to be quiet, went out of the room and met the visitor at the top of the short flight of half a dozen stairs, which lay between the little back room and the showrooms.

Nothing could have been heartier than the greetings on both sides. Each held out a hand, each uttered the usual commonplaces, and Mr. Candover overwhelmed the younger man with congratulations on his freedom. He did not, however, take the precaution to lower his voice as he said this, so that the curious young women in the showroom a few paces

151

away were all made aware in the course of his remarks that the pale young gentleman with the curly fair hair had been only recently undergoing a term of penal servitude.

Whereat there was a little alarmed rush towards the inner recesses of the premises, and much excited comment.

Gerard, who was quite aware of this manœuvre, which was calculated to confirm his suspicions, invited his too effusive acquaintance into the little back-room, where he expected to find his cousin. He was annoyed to discover that Geoffrey had disappeared, and he conjectured that, with his usual impetuosity, Geoffrey had gone off to invest in a revolver or a thick stick.

He was angry with his cousin for this unexpected defection, but there was no help for it, and he asked his suspicious guest to take a chair by the fire, while he himself took one on the opposite side of the hearth.

"I didn't expect to find you here," said Mr. Candover, when they had exchanged comments upon the weather, which was cold and wet. "I understood that you were staying at your uncle's place."

"So I was till yesterday, when I found out my wife's address, and came here at once to see her."

"By-the-bye, what have you done with her? It was to see her I came. I'm in sad disgrace with her, for having introduced some people to her, some of whom turned out to be rather less strait-laced than she cared for her friends to be. I suppose she told you about it?"

And Mr. Candover threw at the young man a piercing look.

"Yes. I told her she was silly and ungrateful."

"Where is she?"

"I've sent her to see my solicitor. A most unpleasant thing happened here last night. Two sham detectives came with a pretended warrant for her arrest."

"You don't say so!"

Gerard was sitting with his face to the light, while Mr. Candover was in shadow. The elder man, therefore, had the advantage, in that he read the face of the younger like a book, while Gerard was not even aware of the curious and furtive movements by which his visitor had taken something out of one of his pockets and was holding it against his breast, just covered by his overcoat.

But Gerard, feeling uneasy that his own expression had betrayed him, and that the red blood was rushing into his face, looked down at the fender, and as he did so, perceived that the poker was missing.

At once suspecting something, he looked up and round the room, believing that his cousin Geoffrey was in hiding somewhere.

As he turned his head, he saw a sudden movement on the part of Mr. Candover, and then, almost at the same moment, there was a crash, a thud, and some one burst out of the cupboard close to the visitor's chair; the next moment Mr. Candover was lying on the floor, stunned and motionless, with a great wound in his head, from which the blood was flowing, while Geoffrey, flushed and excited, was standing over him with his own weapon, the poker, bent and stained, in his right hand, and in his left the revolver which he had wrenched from Mr. Candover's hand.

"I've settled him, I think!" said Geoffrey hoarsely, as he bent over the motionless body of the adventurer.

"I'm afraid you have, by Jove!" said Gerard, in an awestruck whisper.

# CHAPTER XXIII

BOTH the young men stood still for a moment, shocked beyond the power of speech at what Geoffrey had done.

But it was only for a moment. Then Gerard knelt down beside the huddled-up form of Reginald Candover, and laying a hand on his heart said:—

"I don't think he is dead, after all. Look here! There's a doctor who lives quite close—a Dr. Fendall. Go and fetch him. And mind you come back, there's a good chap. We may want more help, and there's nobody here but a parcel of silly, giggling girls."

But Geoffrey was watching the face of the man whom for the first moment he thought he had killed, and he said:—

"It's my belief that he's not only alive, but that he's shamming. He hears what we're saying, I'll swear."

Gerard, however, was not so sanguine.

"Go and fetch the doctor, there's a good chap," said he. "And I'll find some one to give me a hand, and we'll get him on the sofa."

Geoffrey went away, not quite happy, but putting on an air of bravado.

"If he is dead, mind you," said he to his cousin at the door, as he went out, "it serves him jolly well right. For he was going to shoot you when I, watching him through the crack of the cupboard door, sprang out just in time to stop him."

Gerard expressed his thanks for the service by an emphatic nod and ran up the short flight of stairs to the showrooms.

Here he found little promise of competent assistance. The girls in the showroom, who were all young, had been thrown off their balance in the first place by the absence of Mademoiselle Laure and Audrey; and when they heard the unusual sounds of men meeting and conversing on the staircase, and peeping out saw them disappear into the little back-room, and then reappear and go out again, they were all seized, naturally enough, with the idea that something was wrong, and that the business had come to an abrupt standstill.

Whereupon they took, some to their hats, and some to hysterical tears; when, listening intently for any indication of what might be going on in the back room, they heard the heavy fall of Mr. Candover's body on the floor, followed by the exclamations and muffled ejaculations of Gerard and his cousin, a panic seized upon them all; and when Gerard came out in search of help, he found the last of the girls taking flight, with her jacket on her arm and her hands in the act of ramming long hatpins into her big picture hat as she followed the others to the door.

"Tell me where I can get some water, and—and come and give me a hand, there's a good girl," said he persuasively. "Mr. Candover's fallen down and—er—and hurt himself."

But the girl, seeing blood upon his cuff, answered with an hysterical scream:—

"Oh, I couldn't, I really couldn't, sir! The sight of—of anything dreadful would upset me, I know. But there's water in the jug in Mademoiselle's room, through there, sir—and I believe she keeps a drop of brandy in the cupboard. I'll send some one up to help, if you like, sir."

He shrugged his shoulders.

"Thanks. If it's anybody as useful as yourself, you needn't take the trouble," said Gerard sarcastically, as he passed the young lady and went in search of the restoratives of which she had spoken.

But Mademoiselle Laure kept the door of her room locked when she was away; and angry and impatient, Gerard dashed back through the rooms and ran downstairs into the shop below in search of more intelligent assistance.

By the time he got back to the little room where he had left the body of Reginald Candover stretched upon the floor, however, a strange thing had happened, a thing which reminded him of a certain mysterious occurrence related to him by his wife.

For the door of the little room was open, and there was no one in it but Mademoiselle Laure, sallow, forbidding, with stealthy eyes, and a district messenger boy to whom she was giving money and a telegram to be dispatched.

Mademoiselle looked at him steadily and he returned the look. Though they had not met before, each guessed who the other was, and mutual antagonism was apparent in their stiff greeting.

"Mr. Candover is gone then?" said Gerard, raising his hat and holding out the brandy he had brought.

She merely shrugged her shoulders coldly, pretending not to understand, and walked up to the showrooms, leaving him to enter the little room where the unlucky incident had occurred, and to await, in much perplexity, the return of his own emissaries.

In the meantime he remarked that the rug on which Mr. Candover had fallen, and which had been stained with his blood, had been taken away.

It seemed a long time before Geoffrey came back, and when he did so, he was alone. He came slowly and as it were reluctantly up the stairs, and opening the door of the room very slowly, put his head inside, and asked in a fearful whisper:—

"Has he come round yet?"

"He's come round and gone off," replied Gerard rather gruffly. "So if you've brought a doctor——"

"But I haven't," retorted Geoffrey briskly, as he swung himself into the room with a look of great relief, and stared in some bewilderment at his cousin. "What have you done with the fellow?" said he.

"I? Nothing. I went to get brandy, and when I came up he was gone, and there was a horrible old Frenchwoman here."

"Old Laure, I suppose. I know her."

"And she pretended not to understand my questions. So we bowed to each other, and separated. But what has become of the man I haven't the least idea."

Geoffrey looked round him apprehensively, and thrust his hand through his cousin's arm.

"Look here," said he, "I've had enough of this den. And so have you, I should think. You look awful, white as a sheet and with eyes like two holes burnt in a blanket. Come along and let's have some luncheon and a bottle of champagne."

Gerard freed himself.

"No," said he. "I've got to stay here, where there's something to be found out. I couldn't go away, if I would, till Audrey comes back. You forget that. You needn't stay unless you like."

Geoffrey gave a grotesque and uneasy sigh.

"No. I must stand by you, now we're in for it," he said. "After all, I'm nearly as much interested in the business as you are, and if we're really going to find out that this Candover was at the bottom of the forgery business——"

"Sh—sh," said Gerard, who knew how very necessary it was to be cautious in such a shady neighbourhood.

So they dropped into a long silence, broken only by occasional whispered remarks, until, as minutes grew into hours, both men grew restless, anxious and suspicious that something untoward had happened.

Neither cared to leave the other to go to the lawyer's in search of Audrey; but when she had been away nearly four hours, the anxiety felt by Gerard grew so keen that he was about to send his cousin on a mission of inquiry, when, to the intense relief of both the young men, they heard the voices of Edgar and Audrey upon the staircase.

A moment later the door was thrown open, and the four met, all haggard, pale, excited, and worn out with suspense.

"What news?" asked Gerard, as soon as they were all shut in the room, after making a careful survey of the big cupboard in which Geoffrey had concealed himself and of the staircase outside.

"Nothing good," said poor Audrey tearfully, as she let him take her limp, nerveless hand.

"You saw Mr. Masson?"

"Yes. And told him everything. He listened, asked questions, made notes. But I don't think he believed one word in ten!"

And the poor overwrought woman burst into a flood of tears.

"Oh, come, he must have thought something of what you said. He kept you a very long time!" said Gerard.

She shook her head.

"A good deal of that time," she said, "I was simply waiting, waiting. For when I had told him everything, he went out of the room, and was away nearly an hour. And when he came back he seemed to have forgotten everything, for he made me go all over it again. Every word. It was heartbreaking. And after all he could give me no hope, no help, no encouragement. He simply got up, wished me good-bye, and said he would write to you."

But Gerard saw that this was much better than it seemed to the unsophisticated woman.

"It's all right," said he. "Masson never wastes time. If he made you repeat it all it was with an object. Perhaps to see whether you would tell the same story twice."

"But why should he think I wasn't telling the truth? Why——"

"Listen," said Gerard quietly. "It's all right. He would never have kept you so long if he hadn't considered your statement important. Wait patiently now till you get his letter."

"And you, what has happened to you?" asked Audrey curiously. "Something, I'm sure. You both——" and she looked from him to Geoffrey—"have a curious look, as if—as if——"

"Does he look," said Geoffrey in a deep-voiced whisper, leaning across to Audrey, and pointing dramatically at Gerard, "as if he'd been within an ace of being murdered?" She uttered a low cry. He went on: "And do I look"—and Geoffrey thumped his own chest with an air of triumph—"as if I'd saved his life?"

"What?" said Edgar, who had returned in a depressed and nervous condition, fully convinced that his cousin and Audrey were in league with each other for the concoction of a monstrous string of fables.

Geoffrey insisted upon telling his tale himself, which he did in the same loud whisper, illustrating his points with expressive gestures:—

"Gerard heard Candover's voice, and went out to speak to him," said he. "And I, thinking it as well he should have a witness, got into the cupboard here, and took the poker with me."

"Poker! What on earth for?" said Edgar.

"You shall hear. Candover smelt a rat directly, though Gerard smiled and tried to look pleasant. And as the two came in, I, peeping out through the crack of the cupboard door, saw that Candover meant mischief. They sat down together here," and he pointed to the hearth, "and began to talk. And though Gerard betrayed nothing in his words, he did by his face. And presently I saw Candover fumbling with—a revolver."

"Oh, nonsense!" said Edgar.

Audrey only clasped her hands, but said nothing.

"He was getting up from his chair, with the revolver hidden under the front of his overcoat, when I dashed out and knocked him over. And, by Jove, we thought I'd killed him!"

"You'll get yourself into a nice mess if you've hurt him!" said Edgar uneasily.

"I'll risk that," said Geoffrey recklessly. "At any rate I can prove why I did it, for I've got his revolver."

And as he spoke he took out of his pocket and flourished before his brother's eyes the weapon he had taken from the hand of Mr. Candover as the latter lay on the floor.

It was loaded in all the five chambers.

A silence fell upon the group as they looked at it, and the sense grew strong upon them all that they were involved in an affair more desperate than they had guessed. Edgar, perhaps for the first time in his life, showed the spirit of a man, and spoke in words befitting the future head of a noble house.

"By Jove!" said he, "this is serious! Gerard, we'll see you through this. But we must first put your wife in a place of safety. She ought not to stay here!"

But Audrey refused to go away.

"I must stay with Gerard," she said. "And for that matter, what have we got to be afraid of now that Mr. Candover's gone away?"

"Well, we can't feel sure about that," said Gerard dubiously. "I'm more inclined to think that he is on the premises still. Mademoiselle Laure may be keeping him close, at any rate, till she's patched him up a bit. He was scarcely in a fit state to go out when we last saw him, was he, Geoff?"

"Hardly! However, whether he's here or not, it's not likely he will dare to make another attack on anybody just yet."

"Hadn't we better go again to the solicitor's," suggested Edgar, "and tell him of this fresh outrage? If he didn't think the case strong enough before, he will now, I should think!"

"I think the best place to go to would be the police-station," said Geoffrey.

"Not yet," said Gerard. "I should like this gang to think we're shy of calling in the police, so that we may have the chance of running up against some more of them."

"Well, while waiting," said Geoffrey, "we'll have something to eat and drink. I'll go and order some luncheon to be sent in from the restaurant up the street. But first, let me tell you of an odd thing that went out of my head when I came back and found the bird flown. You know you sent me for a doctor, a Dr. Fendall. You said he lived near here?"

"Yes."

"Well, there's no such person. I asked everywhere, and at last I found a good-natured chap who looked the name up in the directory. There's no doctor of that name about here."

Audrey listened with keen ears.

"I was sure of it!" she said. "Dr. Fendall was the man Johnson. And being one of the gang, of course he saw nothing, or said he saw nothing, no trace of the woman in the white dress!"

The number of uncanny revelations which were forced upon them made them all feel sick and shivery. They made no further objection therefore to Geoffrey's proposition, and he had left them on his errand when, on reaching the bottom of the stairs, he suddenly ran up again to report the surprising intelligence that there were "two awfully pretty girls outside, in a hansom, asking for Madame Rocada".

Audrey uttered a little cry.

"It must be Pamela and her sister—his daughters!" cried she in consternation. "Oh, what shall we do?"

There was upon them all a terrible sense of the difficulty of the position in which they were being placed. But Gerard whispered:—

"There's nothing to be done now but for you to see them and see what they want. They are coming upstairs now. Go and meet them."

Audrey, trembling from head to foot, obeyed, and going out of the room, saw that Pamela and Barbara, smiling but shy, were standing at the top of the stairs, looking about them.

They uttered little cries of delight when they saw Audrey, who ran up to them and kissed them both, scarcely able to speak in consequence of the vivid emotion caused by their arrival at such a moment.

"We're in a terrible difficulty, Madame," said Pamela, "and we want your advice and help."

"Yes," said Babs, "we want you, please, to speak for us to papa!"

Audrey shuddered as the innocent girls poured these words into her ears.

They wanted her to "speak for them to papa!" To the very man, who, unless Geoffrey had made the most grievous of mistakes, had tried, not two hours ago, to murder her husband! And who was, in all probability, at that very moment lying unconscious from the effects of a blow administered by the avenging arm of Gerard's cousin!

"Come in here," said Audrey, mechanically, in a low voice, as she led the girls into the deserted showroom.

# CHAPTER XXIV

"You know, Madame, we consider that you've treated us very badly," began Pamela, as soon as they were inside the room.

"Have I, dear? How?" asked Audrey, trying to smile, and meanwhile wondering who were in the rooms at the back, the shut-up rooms which Mademoiselle Laure kept to herself. Was Mr. Candover there? And Laure? And was it safe to converse within these walls at all?

She looked into the inner showroom, and, finding nobody there, drew open the curtains, and placed herself in such a position that she could see, by the big mirrors against the wall, any one who might enter from the back part of the premises. Then she beckoned the girls to come close to her, and sitting down on a big Chesterfield settee, she placed herself between them and took a hand of each.

"On second thoughts," said Pamela, "I think I won't scold you after all, as I meant to do, because you look worried. Aren't you happy, dear? What's the matter? Is it anything you can tell us?"

And Babs, from the other side, echoed the question, as they hung round her, and looked with their innocent young eyes into her harassed face.

"Well, yes, dears, I am a good deal worried just now. But—no, it's nothing I can tell you about," said she. "Now for my crimes. Pamela, what have I done to displease you?"

"Well, you know you promised to see——"

"Hush. Speak lower."

"You promised to see the woman who said she was our mother, and to write to us afterwards."

"Yes. And I did see her."

"But you didn't write to us afterwards!"

There was a pause. Audrey felt the tears coming into her eyes.

"Why didn't you?"

"I—I was very busy. You know I—I left 'The Briars,' and—then I met my husband again unexpectedly—I suppose you haven't heard of that?"

The girls clung to her, all excitement and interest.

"Oh, how beautiful for you! Tell us about it! Is he——"

They did not like to finish the question, but Audrey, holding their fingers tightly in hers, said:—

"Yes, yes, he's not many yards away from us at this moment."

"Oh, how glad you must be!" They kissed her, congratulating her, rejoicing with her, till poor Audrey, knowing the awful burden of a secret concerning their own father which she had to bear and to keep from them if she could, could scarcely refrain from a burst of tears. "But you don't look as happy as you ought!"

"He's been ill—he's not strong yet."

"Never mind. He'll be all right soon, now he's got *you*! Will you tell us all about it, or would you rather not just yet?"

"Hush, Pamela, don't chatter so much. You're making her cry," said Babs.

"Am I? Oh, dear, I didn't mean to do that."

Audrey, who did not know which was the more painful of the two, listening to their pretty congratulations on her happiness, or to their questions about their unknown mother, tried to control her emotion, and said:—

"No, no, I've been through an exciting time this morning, seeing a lawyer, and—and other things. Now go on, dears, tell me what you've come to see me about."

"Well, then, I must go back to the beginning," said Pamela. "We waited and waited to hear from you after you'd seen this lady, and then Miss Willett heard from her, I think, for she seemed much disturbed, and she wrote to papa. And she wouldn't tell us what he answered, but yesterday a lady came to Miss Willett's and said that she was our aunt——"

"Your aunt!" interrupted Audrey sharply.

"Yes. She said she was sent by papa to take us away to live with her at 'The Briars'——"

"The Briars!"

Audrey forgot her prudence, and uttered the word in a high key.

"Yes, yes, the house where you were staying."

"Go on, go on."

"She wanted us to go with her at once, but Miss Willett, though, as she told us afterwards, she had heard from papa that our aunt was to fetch us away from school, didn't like to let us go."

"The truth was," put in Babs bluntly, "that Miss Willett didn't like the look of this aunt of ours any more than we did."

"What was she like then?" asked Audrey quickly.

"Oh, I can't tell you exactly what it was about her that we didn't like, but she was hard and cold and repellant, even though she pretended to be delighted with us."

"Who is this aunt? I didn't know you had one!"

"Well, we did know just that, but we hadn't seen her for so many years that we'd forgotten her. She's papa's sister."

"Did she speak French or English?" asked Audrey.

The girls looked surprised.

"Oh, English, of course," said Pamela.

Who then was this fresh personage, thought Audrey?

"So Miss Willett refused to let us go, saying we were not ready at such short notice, and our aunt went away. Then this morning Miss Willett brought us up to town and took us to papa's flat in Victoria Street, but he wasn't there. Three or four friends of his were waiting for him, and when we had been there a little while, Babs and I asked Miss Willett if we might get in a hansom and come here to see you. And at last she said yes, and so we came."

"But my dear girls, what do you want me to do?"

"Well, first we want you to tell us what you thought of the—the lady who came to see you. Did you think"—and Pamela put her lips close to Audrey's ear—"she was really our mother?"

Audrey's fingers quivered in those of the two girls.

They must know the truth sooner or later, even if, as she began to suspect, they had not some notion of it already.

"What did Miss Willett think?" she asked evasively.

Pamela whispered again:—

"She thinks she *is*. But oh, Madame, she—she told us—that if what the lady says is true—then—then papa has not treated her well!"

Audrey gave a sigh of relief. Gently as the words were put, there was a suggestion in Pamela's intelligent eyes that she knew or guessed more than she liked to say. Audrey took the girl's hand and pressed it to her breast, and said in a low voice:—

"My dear, I'm afraid—very much afraid, you may find that's true."

Then Pamela said:—

"It's awkward for us, isn't it? Papa has been kind to us, but—we want to see our mother. And—neither Miss Willett nor we like Miss Candover. Now what are we to do? What can you do to help us? Do you think papa would listen to you?"

"I'm *sure* he wouldn't," answered Audrey with decision. "But we must find out something about this aunt before we let her have the care of you two girls."

There was a pause and they all three sat, with anxiety on their faces, while Audrey debated with herself as to the steps she ought to take.

Should she send the girls back to Miss Willett at the flat in Victoria Street, with a note advising her to take the girls at once to Windsor with her, and a warning not to let them go out of her custody on any account?

Against this plan there was the fear that the "three or four friends" spoken of by Pamela as waiting for Mr. Candover at the flat might really be persons whom it was better that the girls should not meet. Mr. Candover was evidently desperate, to have conceived the idea of shooting Gerard. Might it not be that the "friends" were really detectives waiting for an opportunity to arrest him?

The possibility was not lightly to be dismissed. And Audrey was on the point of suggesting that she should telegraph to Miss Willett or dispatch a messenger to ask her to meet them at Paddington station, when her attention was attracted by the sound of a key grating in the lock of a door, and a rapid step across the floor of the inner showroom.

"Hush! It's Mademoiselle Laure!" she said, having already caught sight of the reflection of the Frenchwoman in the long mirror against the wall.

The next moment Mademoiselle Laure appeared in the doorway between the two rooms.

The two young girls turned towards her, and both uttered an exclamation, while Pamela started to her feet.

"Aunt!" she cried.

Audrey turned pale, and Mademoiselle Laure, after making a feeble attempt to retreat, remained standing without a word, with an angry flush in her face, and her lips tightly pressed together.

Audrey had risen also.

"Mademoiselle Laure," she said, "or Miss Candover, which am I to call you?"

The woman came forward into the room, recovering herself and trying to smile at the girls.

"Oh, Madame," she said, as she advanced her face to kiss Babs, who stood up straight and stiff, resenting the embrace, "you may call me whichever you please. I answer to both names: to that of Laure, the Frenchwoman, when you are Madame Rocada, the countess. To that of Candover when you are—Mrs. Angmering."

It was the first time that Audrey had ever heard her speak any language but French, but after the revelations she had heard, she was surprised at nothing.

The girls, meanwhile, were evidently uneasy and disturbed. They remained close to Audrey, Babs in particular showing open dislike of her aunt, who turned to the elder girl and said:—

"I'm very glad you've come. But how did you know I was here?"

"We didn't know it," answered both girls together. "We came to see Mrs. Angmering," added Pamela.

Mademoiselle Laure raised her eyebrows.

"Well," she said, "it's of no consequence, since you are here. I've changed my plans since I saw you yesterday, and now I'm going to take you to Paris with me, instead of settling down here. You will like that, won't you?"

But the girls instinctively drew closer together, and Pamela said:—

"We would rather not go away, out of England. All our friends are here, you know."

Audrey gave them a look which encouraged the girls, while it evidently angered Mademoiselle Laure. She laughed harshly.

"What friends have you? None. You can't count your school-friends. You want to go into the world, to make new friends, new acquaintances. And in Paris, with me, you will enjoy yourselves. You will have what you call 'a good time'. Don't look at Madame Rocada. Answer me."

Pamela did answer, very boldly.

"We don't want to go away. We won't go away. We want to see our mother first."

At these words their aunt, intensely astonished, seemed to lose all self-control, and breaking out into a tempest of passion, cried:—

"Your mother! What do you know about your mother? Your mother is mad, has been shut up in a lunatic asylum for years. She is no fit companion for you. Your father would never allow you to see her. If Madame Rocada has been encouraging you to ask to see her, she has done wrong, very wrong."

And Mademoiselle Laure turned angrily to Audrey.

"You are always making mischief, always," she said.

But the girls took the part of their friend.

"No, she hasn't made mischief," cried Babs. "She's quite right, and whatever she says we'll listen to. Mrs. Angmering, do you think we ought to go away to Paris with our aunt, without knowing where she is going to take us to?"

But at these words the storm of Mademoiselle's rage grew so violent that, whatever they might have thought of her as a guardian of youth before, all doubts on the subject melted away as she clenched her fists, and gnashed her teeth, and stamping her foot declared that they must and should go away with her, that their father wished it, and that they had no choice.

"You are under age, both of you," she said, "and until you are twenty-one, you are not able to choose for yourself. It is for your father to choose what is best for you."

"Well, then, let us see papa, and ask him to say whether we are unreasonable," said Pamela, who was as daring as she was pretty. "He knows that it's natural we should want to see our own mother, and even if he and she didn't get on well together——"

"Who has been telling you that?" snapped their aunt. "Madame Rocada, I suppose!"

Pamela went on:—

"Even if, as I say, they quarrelled, and haven't seen each other for years, that's no reason why we shouldn't see her, now we know she's alive, and know too that she is as sane as we are!"

"Oh, that is saying very little!" sneered Mademoiselle Laure, who seemed to have lost all sense of self-control, and to be crazy with rage at the girls' opposition to her wishes.

Audrey grew anxious to put an end to the painful scene.

"Well," she said, "you can't start off for Paris without any preparation, that's certain. Let these girls go back to Windsor with Miss Willett——"

"They shall not go back. They have been long enough with Miss Willett, and they are too old for school. They shall go to an hotel with me——"

But Audrey, remembering the suggestion that the girls should go to "The Briars" with their aunt, would not suffer this.

"No," she said firmly, "they shall not go away from here with you, Mademoiselle Laure, they shall not go without me; since they have come to me I mean to take care of them."

"You! You! What are you? A convict's wife! A wretched tool, a keeper of a gaming-house!" shrieked Mademoiselle Laure, beside herself with impotent rage, as she saw the girls shrinking back from her and clinging to Audrey.

Pamela protested indignantly.

"Don't listen to her, Mrs. Angmering, don't listen," she said passionately. "The woman is mad, and wicked too. I wouldn't go with her or let Babs go if she were the only person belonging to us in all the world!"

Suddenly Mademoiselle Laure changed her tone. She seemed to realise that she was harming her own cause by every word she spoke, and that she must use very different methods if she wished to attain her ends.

Subsiding into outward calmness with great abruptness, she turned away for a moment as if to consider some point, and then, addressing Pamela, said:—

"You will have to go with me, if your father tells you to!"

Pamela turned pale, and hesitated.

"I don't want to——" she began.

But Mademoiselle Laure cut her short.

"It is not a question of what you want, but of what you must do," she said sharply. "You admit your father is your proper guardian, and that you are bound to go where he chooses?"

"Ye-es, but——"

The woman turned haughtily to Audrey.

"You can retire, Madame," she said; "hide yourself in any corner you please, with your husband and your friends. I am going to take these dear girls to their father."

Babs clung to Audrey.

"She shall go with us then," cried she.

For one moment Mademoiselle Laure, her face dark with suppressed rage, hesitated. Then, saying sharply:—

"Wait here then, for me—and for him," she disappeared into the room at the back which was called hers, and reappeared in a few seconds, with Mr. Candover himself leaning on her arm.

All were shocked at his appearance. His head was bound up, and his dull eyes seemed to show that he had scarcely yet fully recovered consciousness after the blow he had received from Geoffrey's poker and the fall which had resulted from the blow.

As if still more than half-dazed, he tottered forward, leaning on his sister's arm, and stared about him and at the three ladies as if unaware who they were.

Pamela cried out, in an awestruck voice:—

"Papa, papa! Don't you know us, papa?"

And Babs ran forward to kiss him.

The touch of the warm young lips made him look round and say almost mechanically:—

"Babs! Hallo, Babs!"

Then his sister spoke.

"The girls don't want to go away with me. Will you tell them what is your wish?"

"My wish is that you should come away with her—with us," said he, after a moment's pause, as if to collect his thoughts. And then he seemed to recover himself a little, and went on: "Yes, and we must make haste. There is no time to be lost. We will all go together and at once."

"But, papa, we're not ready. We didn't come prepared for a journey!" protested Pamela in great distress and alarm.

His sister whispered to him, and Mr. Candover said quickly:—

"No matter. Paris is not at the other end of the earth. Your things can be sent on after you. Call a hansom—No, a hansom won't hold us. Go to the window and hail a four-wheeler, or get the porter to whistle for one, and let us start at once. Pamela, you go with your aunt. Babs, come with me."

And before the frightened and almost weeping Audrey could do more than try to intervene with faint words of entreaty, of protest, Mr. Candover and his sister had carried the girls off before her very eyes, and led them downstairs and out of her sight.

Audrey made a rapid step towards the door, when a loud and piercing cry reached her ears.

# CHAPTER XXV

Now there was upon the face of Mademoiselle Laure, as she followed Mr. Candover and Babs downstairs, with Pamela struggling to get free from the firm grasp of her lean fingers, an expression which betrayed the fact that she feared mischief.

And her alarm was well founded.

Scarcely had Mr. Candover reached the last stair, when a man rushed out from behind the door, where he had evidently been waiting, and barred his passage.

Babs uttered a shrill scream, and her father told her fiercely to hold her tongue.

"Where are you off to, Mr. Candover?" asked the man roughly.

Shaken as he was by the fall from the effects of which he was still suffering, Mr. Candover had been considerably startled by the unexpected appearance of this man; but after a pause of a few seconds he recovered himself, laughed, and leaning back against the wall, said:—

"Gossett! What are you doing here?"

The young man, frowning sullenly, looked for a moment somewhat confused by the question, which was put quite quietly and without apparent discomposure.

"Well, I—I want to have a talk with you. We all do," he said sullenly, as Pamela, who had pressed forward behind her sister, recognised the man as one of the "friends" who had been waiting at her father's flat in Victoria Street that morning.

"Certainly. But not here. Didn't I tell you to be at my flat this morning?"

"Yes. You said twelve o'clock, and we've been waiting there ever so long, all of us," returned Gossett, who appeared to have been drinking. "And then these young ladies came, and they waited. And when they came off after you, we thought we might as well follow them and see where they were coming to. And we've run you to earth right enough!"

"Run me to earth!" repeated Mr. Candover, in a tone of extreme astonishment. "What do you mean?"

"Well, we mean we want to speak to you—all by ourselves. We will come up."

"No, you won't," answered Mr. Candover quietly, "You'll meet me at my flat in an hour. I'm going to take these ladies to Charing Cross station to see them off first."

At that moment Mademoiselle Laure, who had run past them into the street, reappeared, panting, and pointed to a four-wheeled cab which she had brought from the cab-rank which was not many yards away.

"Come, my dears," said Mr. Candover to his daughters, who were hanging back, and looking up at Audrey, who, with her husband and the young Angmerings, all of whom had run out on hearing the girl's cry, stood in a group at the head of the staircase, not liking to interfere, but uneasy and anxious.

"Hadn't we better wait, papa, and come afterwards?" said Pamela. "We're not ready to go yet."

But for answer he seized his daughters, one with each hand, and forced them to accompany him as far as the door, where they suddenly found themselves free, and glancing round, saw that that was the result of the appearance, just outside, of two more men, one of whom was Johnson, while the other they recognised as their father's secretary, Durley Diggs.

Both men looked angry and threatening, and it was undoubtedly the sight of them that made Mr. Candover relax his grasp of his daughters' arms, and make a dash for the cab-door, which Mademoiselle Laure was holding open.

But just as he reached the step, Gossett, rushing out from the doorway where he had been lingering, caught Mr. Candover's up-raised foot with his own, and tripping him up, flung him heavily backwards on the pavement.

Even before the usual crowd had gathered round the scene of this outrage, Mademoiselle Laure, with real alarm and concern in her face, was on her knees on the pavement beside her brother, while the two poor girls, shocked and distressed by this attack on their father, hung about him, and did their best to help their aunt to raise him from the ground, which was wet and slippery from recent rain.

While this was taking place, a cab which had been waiting a little way up the street came quickly up, and two gentlemen stepped out of it; while at the same moment three or four policemen in plain clothes ran out of the nearest shops, and arrested not only Gossett but Johnson and Diggs, all of whom appeared more indignant than surprised by this occurrence.

Gossett, indeed, was the only man who made any observation above his breath.

"Game's up, eh?" he said, with an air of recklessness as the man who had him in charge ended his struggles by clapping a pair of handcuffs on his wrists.

The other two men suffered themselves to be arrested quietly, Diggs in particular laughing, and telling his captor that he had got the wrong man.

"That's the fellow you should be looking after!" he added, pointing to Mr. Candover who, rendered completely unconscious by this second fall coming so soon after the first, was being placed inside the cab which he had been attempting to enter.

Mademoiselle Laure, speaking English as fluently as any of them, laid a strong hand upon the policeman who was peering into her brother's face:—

"What are you doing? You can't touch him," she said fiercely. "If he's not dead, he is dying, as you must see."

"We'll take him to the hospital, ma'am," said the policeman. "You can come too."

A cry from Pamela, faint, miserable, made them both look round:—

"Papa!"

It revealed a world of shocked discovery, an agony of distress, and every man who heard it felt a lump in his throat.

As for Babs, the younger girl, she stood clinging to her sister, white, trembling, without even uttering a cry. But in her eyes there was a look which showed that, if anything, she understood the situation even better than did her elder sister.

Mademoiselle Laure waved her hand rapidly to the girls, and forcing a smile, told them he would be well soon, and that they must go back to Miss Willett and wait for her to write to them. But they did not answer. They stood close together, half inside the doorway they had just left, and looked disconsolately at the cab as it drove away to the hospital, while the policemen made the three men whom they had arrested enter the cab which had just been left vacant by the two strange gentlemen.

These two gentlemen now came across the road, looking sympathetically at the two forlorn young girls.

"Come in, Pamela," whispered Babs, "come up to Mrs. Angmering. She'll be kind to us."

And they withdrew hurriedly through the doorway, and hurrying upstairs, fell upon Audrey, who was holding out her arms to them, and who led them with her, whispering soothing words of comfort, into the deserted showroom.

It was Babs who spoke first of the dreadful thing they had seen.

"Why did they want to kill papa, Mrs. Angmering?" she said in a low voice, nestling close to her, and looking up through her tears. "What has he done?"

"Oh, hush," said Pamela, the elder and wiser. "Don't let us ask. I don't want to know."

But the younger girl was more inquisitive.

"Do you think," she said, "that the police only took up the other men for attacking papa?"

"I don't know anything about it, dear," said Audrey, "except what you've told me, that your father was knocked down and taken to the hospital, and that the other men, the three who wanted to speak to him, including the one who struck him, have been taken into custody."

But Pamela looked intently into her face.

"Yes, you do know more than that. You know a great deal more," she said, with depressed conviction. "I noticed the way you looked at him when he came in to take us away. Oh, Mrs. Angmering, what are we going to do? We seem to have neither father nor mother now!"

"We shall have to go back to Miss Willett's," sobbed Babs.

Audrey drew both the girls close to her.

"You shall be well taken care of, and you shall not have to go away with your aunt, at any rate," said she.

And in the shuddering silence with which the girls received this assurance there was evidence enough that they understood vaguely that they had escaped some great danger.

In the meantime the two gentlemen who had got out of the waiting cab in time to witness the arrest of Mr. Candover's three friends, had followed the two girls into the house and up the stairs, and had been received by Gerard and his cousins, who, standing back for the young girls to go up with Audrey, came forward again, to greet the gentlemen with intense astonishment.

"My father! By Jove!" cried Geoffrey, as Lord Clanfield came up, looking about him uneasily, as if he expected trap-doors to fly open under his feet and secret panels to slide back on each side of him.

"And Mr. Masson!" exclaimed Gerard, as he recognised, in the gentleman who was following close at his uncle's heels, the solicitor whom Audrey had reported as having received her narrative so coldly.

The two gentlemen had by this time reached the little landing upon which opened the small room where so many exciting interviews had taken place that morning.

Lord Clanfield looked from his nephew to his sons.

"So you've been mixing yourselves up in this business! What mischief will you be up to next?" he asked, addressing Edgar, and speaking in a voice which betrayed the agitation which he felt at the unpleasant affair in which he was being forced to take part.

"Well, it's more surprising still to find *you* mixed up in it!" retorted Geoffrey from behind his brother. "When there's a scrape to be got into, you expect to see us on in that scene. And for once we've not been so much getting into a scrape ourselves as helping Gerard out of one."

"Indeed! And what has been your share?" asked his father incredulously.

"Well, I knocked that Candover down when he was going to shoot Gerard," replied Geoffrey coolly.

And he related the story of that event, while Gerard himself, having heard the news of the arrest of the confederates, stood silently by, waiting for Mr. Masson to speak.

The solicitor's keen face wore a look which told him that he knew a good deal more than Gerard himself did about the confederacy which had just been broken up.

"I'm afraid your wife thought me very unsympathetic this morning," said he. "But I had to guard against the chance of any betrayal of my plans. As a matter of fact, I had no sooner heard her story of last night's pretended arrest of herself than I telephoned to Scotland Yard, and when I made her repeat the tale, she did so in the hearing of one of our cleverest detectives, whose near neighbourhood she never suspected."

"I suppose you had known something before?" suggested Gerard.

Mr. Masson smiled.

"There's no harm in letting you know now that a note which was part of the cash given in exchange for one of the forged cheques was traced to—Mr. Candover."

"Then why was I not told? Or at least my wife?" asked Gerard indignantly.

"I'll tell you. Certain facts were discovered which seemed to point to the existence of a strong criminal confederacy, and it was thought wiser to wait and mature plans for seizing the whole of the participators, than, by hastening matters, to run the risk of losing some of our birds. Do you see?"

"But it was hard upon me, upon us! You must have found out that I was innocent."

"Well, your uncle was consulted, and the authorities decided to make your illness a pretext for giving you your liberty, reserving the whole truth till a convenient season. In the meantime the police were hard at work in various ways, but it was not till this morning that they were able to get hold of the four principals at once."

"Who are they?"

"The chief of the gang, Reynolds or Candover, and the three men who call themselves Diggs, Johnson and Gossett. It was your recognition of Gossett last night, when he came here disguised, not expecting to meet you, and knew that you suspected him, which upset all their plans, I think. At any rate, Candover, who was of course informed of the fact, seems to have made up his mind that the case was desperate, or he would never have attempted to shoot you. And his three accomplices must have made up their minds that the game was up, for they waited for him at his flat, and then came on here, evidently with the idea that he was going to leave them in the lurch."

Gerard was silent for a few moments. Then he said suddenly, in a hoarse voice:—

"My wife! I must tell my wife!"

And he was running up the short flight of stairs towards the showroom, when he caught sight of the three pathetic figures, Audrey sitting on a large settee, with one of the girls on each side of her.

He stopped short, and turned hesitatingly to his uncle.

"Those two poor girls!" whispered he.

"Who are they?" asked Lord Clanfield, who had seen the two pretty young creatures, but in the excitement had failed to find out who they were.

"His daughters, Candover's daughters!"

The viscount's kind face softened sympathetically.

"Dear, dear! Poor things, poor things!" he muttered in reply. "Something must be done for them! Something must be done!"

Gerard went up to the showroom shyly, with a subdued manner, and his uncle followed. The girls looked down and reddened uncomfortably, feeling, poor lassies, all the awkwardness of their position, and unable to keep back their tears.

"Mrs. Angmering," said Lord Clanfield, taking her hand, as she rose to greet him, and looking kindly into her face, "I'm afraid you've had a very hard time of trouble and distress of mind to go through, and I'm heartily sorry I didn't know earlier what I feel sure of now. You must come back with me at once, with me and Gerard."

Audrey, grateful, tearful, pressed his hand warmly, but shook her head:—

"You're very, very kind. But I think I'd rather—now—take these girls with me somewhere, and arrange for their seeing their mother, who's longing to have them with her again," said she.

Lord Clanfield beamed upon the two poor lassies, and held out his hand to Pamela.

"Let them come with us too," he said. "And write to their mother and tell them where they are. We shall be delighted to see her whenever she can come."

"And we'll come down with you too, to help to entertain the ladies," suddenly cried Geoffrey from the rear.

The violently startled manner in which Lord Clanfield turned on hearing his son's voice behind him made them all smile, and afforded a welcome relief to the tension of feeling from which they were suffering.

Five minutes later they were all trooping downstairs and out of the house on their way to the station; and at the same time a couple of police-officers came quietly up to take possession of the premises.

# CHAPTER XXVI

Before the day was over, Gerard and Audrey learned fuller details of the confederacy into whose net both of them had so cleverly been drawn.

From the first moment when, a month previously, the police had got upon the traces of Mr. Candover as the actual forger of the cheques by means of which Sir Richmond Hornthwaite had been robbed, they had been working silently, and with the knowledge of Lord Clanfield and Mr. Masson, to bring the arch-scoundrel to justice.

The irony of fate, however, prevented his being made to suffer the legal penalty for the crime which he had contrived to lay upon the shoulders of the unfortunate Gerard Angmering.

His artfulness was so well known, that at first there was a strong suspicion that his illness was in part at least assumed. But on examination at the hospital, he was found to be dying, and, although he lingered through the night and part of the following day, he died within forty-eight hours from the moment of his attempted arrest, from extensive injuries to the brain and spine, the result of the two attacks which had been made upon him, the first by Geoffrey Angmering, and the second by his own associate, Tom Gossett.

So carefully had the police gone about their work, that not an inkling of the truth that they were on his track had reached Mr. Candover's ears when, his daring and audacious plan for turning Audrey out of the premises for which she had paid having failed owing to Gerard's unexpected intervention, he had been brought suddenly face to face with the fact that Gerard had recognised in one of the sham detectives the man who had procured his conviction for forgery by means of false witness against him.

Tom Gossett was so certain that Gerard had recognised him that he caused a panic amongst the confederates, and the failure of the device for frightening Audrey having struck terror among them all, Mr. Candover found himself in a dilemma, and for once lost his self-possession.

On no other grounds could his mad attempt to shoot Gerard be accounted for. It could only be surmised that he intended to let it be supposed either that Gerard had committed suicide or that he had shot him by accident in self-defence.

In the meantime the three subordinates who had had the principal share in carrying out the various swindles of which Candover had been the promoter, had conceived the idea that he meant to give them the slip and to prepare his own escape in case of a crash. When, therefore, he failed to appear at the flat at Victoria Street at the hour he had appointed for the meeting at which they were to discuss the situation, they had all decided to follow his daughters, in the well-grounded belief that by so doing they would reach him.

And when they discovered him in the act of flight, Tom Gossett's impulse for revenge brought about the act which caused the arch-conspirator's death.

At the trial of the three remaining prisoners, which came off within a few weeks, an astounding career of crime and fraud was disclosed, by means of which Reginald Candover, alias Eugène Reynolds, had lived in princely style upon the earnings of his subordinates in crime.

Forgery was almost the only share of the rascally business which he undertook in person. He left to lesser lights cheating at cards, perjury, and the hundred and one various forms of crime of which he had been the instigator, and the perpetrators of which he took under his august protection, passing them off, now in one capacity and now in another, as his servants, his dependants or his friends.

Wherever he went, he always took care to have one or more of these precious assistants near him; and Jim Johnson, who was one of the three, confessed to the whole story of the disappearance of the unfortunate woman who called herself Madame Rocada, and to the share he had had in that mysterious occurrence.

This woman, who had formerly been a great beauty, had fallen into a rapid consumption, so that she could no longer carry on the gaming-house in Paris, which had been one of Mr. Candover's most prosperous speculations.

Left in Paris to die, the unfortunate creature had learnt, by some means, that it was Mr. Candover's intention to make capital out of her reputation by starting a similar establishment in England under the old title which was to be used by another and a younger woman.

Filled with rage and the wish for revenge, the unfortunate White Countess had struggled with the disease which had laid its cruel hand upon her, and managed to reach London, fired with the intention of disturbing the new régime.

Mr. Candover had obtained intelligence of her movements, and had been on the alert, he and one or other of his confederates having been constantly about the premises held under the name "Rocada," in the expectation of her arrival.

On the evening when her sudden appearance startled Audrey, both Mr. Candover and Johnson were on the watch, and though they had been unable to prevent her entering, they had prevented her doing more than that.

Johnson's story was that she died a natural death from the bursting of a blood-vessel, caused by intense excitement on meeting the man who had ill-used and betrayed her, after having exploited her beauty on behalf of his gambling-house.

Johnson it was who had disguised himself as the "Dr. Fendall" whose address could not subsequently be ascertained; and he said that, immediately after Audrey had left the showrooms in search of help, he and Mr. Candover had brought a cab, had covered the dead woman with a long cloak belonging to Mademoiselle Laure, led her out between them as if she had been still alive, and carried her, under cover of the darkness, a gruesome companion, out to Willesden, where, in an empty house in a half-built street, where building was at a standstill for lack of funds, they had buried the body of the wretched woman under the flooring.

Having taken the precaution to make the driver of the cab too tipsy to take much notice of what was going on, they returned to the West End, Johnson sitting by the cabman and giving sufficient assistance with the reins for his condition to pass unnoticed by the authorities.

A search of the premises he indicated having been made, the truth of this part of Johnson's story was established, and an inquest was held, which resulted in an open verdict, the condition of the body warranting the belief that the man's story was substantially true.

This was not the only information which Johnson, now convinced that the truth was his best refuge, gave to the prosecution.

He confessed that, as far as he knew, no one of the name of Madame de Vicenza ever existed. The "Duchess" was a figment of Mr. Candover's brain, and "The Briars" had been rented by him. It was also discovered that the premises which poor Audrey had believed to be rented in her name, and which had actually been paid for with her money, were really taken by Mr. Candover in the name of his sister, Mademoiselle Laure. The various documents which she had been made to sign were concoctions of his own, and the "solicitor" to whom he had introduced her had been one of his own creatures.

As for Tom Gossett, he had been chiefly employed as a tout, to discover likely victims for his employer. In his employment as a solicitor's clerk in the city he had unhappily been able to find out all the details about Gerard Angmering's habits and ways, which had been necessary to involve him in Candover's net.

Durley Diggs had been chiefly employed as a card-sharper, in which capacity he had used his misdirected abilities to bad purpose both in Paris and in England.

Mademoiselle Laure had been clever enough to keep out of the confederacy, as far as could be proved. But although she now posed as the victim of her half-brother's deception, and professed to have known nothing whatever about the various crimes in which he and his subordinates had been involved, it was strongly suspected, not only that she had given him all the assistance in her power, but that the comparatively small value of the property left by him, and her speedy disappearance to the Continent as soon as the trial was over, were facts not unconnected with each other, and of an extremely suspicious nature.

All three confederates got terms of penal servitude, and though it was believed that there were other members of the gang who had not been brought to justice, there was reason for thinking that not only was the gang completely broken up, but that all the chief offenders had been dealt with.

The effect of the revelations made at the trial was enormous.

Mr. Candover's social position had been so well established, his friends and acquaintances had been so uniformly in the best set, his fame as a connoisseur and collector had been so widespread, that the whole story of his delinquencies came as a bombshell upon society.

The result was fortunate for Gerard and his wife. For while no one could boast that he had detected the cloven hoof, no one could cast much blame upon Audrey and her husband for the ease with which they had been deceived. They became, indeed, a sort of hero and heroine in the public eye, not a little to their discomfiture.

Very gladly would they and Reginald Candover's two daughters have hidden themselves away until the excitement of the trial had subsided. But Gerard and his wife had to give evidence against the prisoners, and they were, therefore, compelled to remain in England. And Pamela and Babs, after the first painful sting of mortification and distress was over, found some comfort in the society of Audrey, who loved them both, and in the kindness of Lord Clanfield, who insisted on keeping the whole party at his place in Hampshire until the public excitement had subsided, and they could all make up their minds as to their future.

The two girls were heartily glad of this arrangement; for although they frequently saw their mother, by the viscount's express desire, that unfortunate lady had lived so long shut up from the world, that she was wholly unfitted for the society of young people, and even in the presence of her own daughters she was reserved and eccentric to the point of making them wonder whether long confinement had not indeed injured her brain.

It was evident that the best plan both for her and for the girls would be for her to remain with her sister, and for the young people to find some other home.

It was while this matter was still under discussion among the various persons concerned, that an unexpected visitor arrived one day at Lord Clanfield's place, driving swiftly through the park in a smart dark green motor-car.

Pamela was walking in the park, with a couple of collies at her heels. The February air was keen and cold, and she was running, with her white muff held up to her pretty pink cheeks, while the dogs, both young things, full of life and of play, leapt and bounded round her.

One of them, however, attracted dangerously by the motor-car, ran barking towards it, and was only saved from annihilation by a dexterous movement on the part of the driver.

Pamela ran forward, calling the dog and scolding him, and the motor-car stopped.

"How-do-you-do, Miss Pamela?"

"Oh, Sir Harry!"

"Drive on," said Sir Harry Archdale to the chauffeur, as he got out, and shook hands with the girl, whose sudden loss of colour betrayed the mingled feelings of shame and shy pleasure with which the meeting inspired her.

They had not met since the terrible discoveries of the trial, and tears of mortification sprang to Pamela's eyes when she remembered the difference there was between her position when they had last met and her position now.

Then she had been one of the daughters of the rich, well-known, highly-respected Mr. Candover, well off, happy in some vague but yet dazzling future, full of hope and happiness.

Now she and Babs were outcasts, none the less that they had found kind friends; they were the daughters of a man whose name could not be uttered in their presence, they were poor, they were overwhelmed with doubt as to the future.

The young man seemed conscious of all this too, though the knowledge only served to deepen the kindly feeling with which he spoke, to fill his eyes with sympathy which he did not dare to express in words.

Instead of speaking on any subject of interest to either, he rambled into a confused account of his adventures with various dogs and other animals during his first attempts at driving his own car. It was disconnected enough, but Pamela laughed politely and made no attempt at conversational efforts on her own account.

And then presently he came to a dead stop. His stock of vapid anecdote had run dry, and she showed signs of being about to call her dogs and continue her walk.

Something must be done, something bold, something daring, desperate.

"I—I knew you were staying here," stammered he at last, suddenly losing control of the muscles of his face, and growing red and white and all sorts of colours. "But—I—I—I didn't like to come before.

Only—when somebody said you—you were g-g-going abroad, I—I—I felt I must come."

"To say good-bye. It's very kind of you," panted Pamela quickly.

"No, no, no. You know I didn't mean that. Look here. I—I want to ask you something. Isn't it—a little awkward—to be here—even if they're nice, and of course they are nice?" said Sir Harry, speaking more and more quickly, and wholly unable to choose appropriate and inoffensive expressions.

Pamela raised her pretty head proudly.

"Oh, of course it's awkward, dreadfully, dreadfully awkward. But what of that? It must always be awkward—for us—everywhere—*now*."

"I don't see why it should."

She turned upon him fiercely.

"Oh, yes, you do, you must. Everybody knows who we are, and all about us. And kind as everybody is, it's dreadful all the same. Of course we shall get over it some day, but now—oh, don't talk about it, don't, don't."

"Young Angmering looks much better!" said Sir Harry by way of a diversion, glancing towards the garden, where Gerard was walking briskly, whip in hand, from the stables towards his wife, who was leaning out of one of the lower windows and smiling at him.

"Oh, yes. It's hardly possible to believe that he was threatened with consumption only a few months ago. I'm so glad, for poor Audrey's sake. After all she went through, it's lovely to see her so happy at last!"

"Yes. I don't quite like, myself, to approach her. I—I feel most awfully uncomfortable after—after—er—er—er."

The unfortunate young man stopped short, remembering that it was through the misunderstanding created by Pamela's father that he had misjudged poor Audrey.

Pamela laughed sadly.

"Oh, you can speak out," she said. "It's of no use for me—for Babs and me, to pretend not to know the mischief *he* caused. But I am thankful to say the last traces of it are passing away now."

The young man twirled his moustache fiercely.

"I'm so sorry——" said he. "I—I don't know how I could be such a donkey as to—as to——"

"Don't call yourself names," said she with a sort of forlorn resignation. "It can't be helped. Every one knows it. Every one will always know, and look round at the name of Candover."

Sir Harry was seized with an inspiration.

"Why don't you change it?" he said abruptly. Then, before she could answer, he saw his opportunity, and hurried on: "They look round at the name Candover, you say. They wouldn't if you were called—Archdale."

Pamela tried to pretend she took this as a joke.

"Why do you laugh?" said he. "You'll have to marry some day, you know! Why shouldn't you be happy? Oh, you don't know how soon you'd be able to forget, if you were!"

Pamela listened with her head bent, a feeling of deep gratitude and happiness stealing into her heart at the thought that this man, whom she had secretly liked so much, should come to her and generously offer to lift the great shadow off her life.

She shook her head, slowly, gently.

"There's poor Babs!" she said softly.

"Oh, we'll find a husband for Babs too! Babs is a dear girl!"

Pamela laughed, happily, tenderly this time.

"You seem to think," she said meditatively, as she let him take up the end of the long white fox boa that encircled her throat, and wind it round his own hand caressingly, coming nearer as he did so, "that marriage is a panacea for all evils!"

Sir Harry glanced at Gerard and Audrey, whose figures could be seen, framed in the long bare strings of Virginia creeper and the green glossy ivy, at the mullioned window of the old redbrick mansion.

"Well, it looks like it, doesn't it?" he said, as he got near enough to kiss her.

www.ingramcontent.com/pod-product-compliance
Lightning Source LLC
Chambersburg PA
CBHW011445170626
46816CB00008B/2526